Project Chartreuse

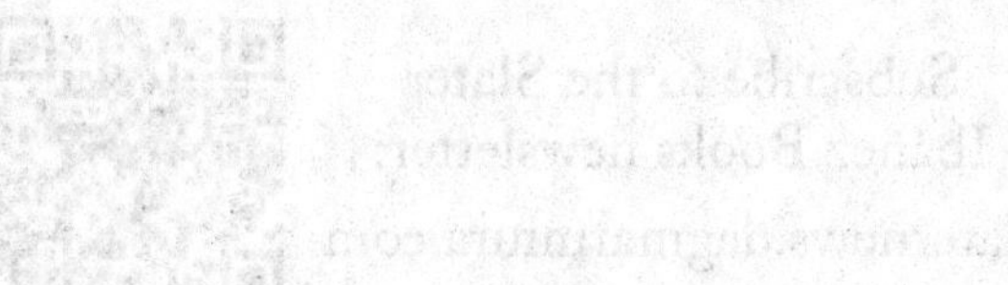

Also in This Series

That First Heady Burn

True Vermilion

The Dark Shill

A Stack of Sawbucks

The Hillside Roble

The Peroxide Pomp

The Incidental Twin

Brawl in Bardo

The Window-Shade Job

The Convenient Patsy

The Artisanal Grifter

Shrink in the Shadows

Project Chartreuse

From a Desert Playa

The Tired Canary

A Desperate Frame-up

Trail of the Blue Agave

The Saucer-Heads

The Satin Squeeze Play

Chiseler in Jade

Subscribe to the Slater
Ibáñez Books newsletter:
slaternews.dagmarmiura.com

Project Chartreuse

Project Chartreuse

George Bixley

DAGMAR
MIURA
LOS ANGELES

Published by Dagmar Miura
Los Angeles
www.dagmarmiura.com

Project Chartreuse

First published 2021

ISBN: 978-1-951130-79-4

ONE

S LATER WAS GOING TO have to deal with that nut job Crystal on the front desk, he knew, as he stepped off the elevator on 34. As he walked into the office, he saw that she was wearing a bright red jacket, her peroxided hair swept into an updo.

Slater paused in front of her desk. "She's expecting me."

"Can I help you?" Crystal said, her eyes vacant and icy, as if she didn't remember him.

"I'm here to see Della," he said, struggling to suppress his ire.

She gave him a pointed once-over. "Can I ask your name?"

"Fuck you, you washed-out freak," Slater snapped, and walked through into the hallway.

Down the hall, Della's office door was ajar, and he rapped on it as he stepped inside. Her window had an expansive view over the LA Basin, right now looking a little parched in the summer heat. The haze that lingered near the horizon was tinted brown. That meant it was smog, not mist like it was in the cooler months.

Pushing sixty, Della kept her hair sprayed in a tidy do, and her low-cut blouse showed some cleavage, even though it still looked like somber office drag.

"You're lucky I'm free," Della said, leaning back in her chair. "You weren't announced."

"That guard dog on the front desk has the heart of a berserker. If she had her way, I wouldn't even get into the building."

"I think she pisses you off because you can't intimidate her."

"Is that why you hired her?" Slater dropped into the chair in front of her desk. "That quality would make for a good front woman. Although, for the record, I've been unfailingly polite and professional with her."

Della's brow furrowed. "You might want to check a dictionary for what some of those words actually mean."

"So what have you got for me?"

"A life insurance claim." She sat up, and grabbed her mouse, and peered at her computer screen. "It's an old one. We can't make a payout until we can confirm there's only one living beneficiary."

"There's more than one named?"

"It's a fifty-fifty split between the policyholder's daughter, Raquel—we're already in contact with her—and the policyholder's estranged husband. The story is that the guy upped and disappeared years ago. A cursory check couldn't determine whether he's alive or not. Normally we just hand the funds over to the state and let them worry about it, but the way it's written means Raquel is eligible for the whole payout."

"If he wasn't around, it doesn't seem right that he picks up half the dough."

"Those are the rules," Della said. "She should have changed it, but she never did."

"So you want me to find the guy."

"Or at least find out whether he's alive. It's not a lot of money. I just want it off my desk, and you're my due diligence. I'll pay you for a week regardless of what you find."

"Even if I can't find anything?"

"Like I said, it's not a big payout. I'll email you the paperwork."

"I'm sure I can come up with something in seven days," he said.

"Five days." She met his gaze.

"Seven would give me more room to be thorough."

"I've already requested the funds."

"Della, you're breaking my heart."

She raised her eyebrows. "I'd love the opportunity to do that, if you were ever inclined to put out. I can't help but notice the way you fill out that denim."

"That's never going to happen."

"There's more to this world than dick, Slater."

He chuckled. "You make it sound like I'm narrow-minded."

"I guess it's part of your special charm."

"To start, I'll want to talk to Raquel."

Della nodded. "Her contact details are on the claim she filed. She owns a trendy little boutique on Cahuenga in Hollywood."

"Isn't that neighborhood all corporate retailers by now?"

"Not all of them. Not yet, anyway. The place is called Feel the Trend."

"I can feel it already," Slater said, and rose. "I'll be in touch."

As he walked out through the front office, he eyed the receptionist.

"Ciao, Crystal. Thanks so much for all your help."

"Keep walking," she said flatly.

Waiting for the elevator, he had to smile. Della was right—Crystal wasn't easily cowed.

He stepped off in the parking garage under the building and walked over to his wheels, a classic Thunderbird, black and sleek with a cherry interior. It was so old that it needed regular bespoke maintenance, and it wasn't the best ride when he wanted to go incognito, but it was worth it—he loved driving it.

Nosing the car up out of the garage, he drove east, out of the shadows of the office towers to the Fashion District, and pulled into the surface lot across the street from his building. A century ago it had been built as offices, but now it was almost completely small clothing factories, except the office he shared with his business partner, Max.

Slater hustled across the street in a break in the traffic and stepped into the lobby. Even though it was already late morning, a few day laborers were hanging around, waiting for gigs cutting or sewing or carting garments. The elevator lumbered up to the ninth floor, and he walked around behind the shaft to the door with their names on it:

SLATER IBÁÑEZ
MAXIMILLIAN CONROY
INVESTIGATIONS

When he stepped in, Etta was sitting behind the front desk. A curvy woman with butched black hair, she'd been hanging around the office all summer. Recently she'd done some redecorating for them, hiring a crew to paint the walls and bring in some deco-era furniture.

Etta had come into their lives as a witness in a case, and since then she'd started working as an operative for him and Max, mostly because she was curious about the business. She'd proved herself to be skilled at the work—she had the right amount of sangfroid without being cocky. Nobody else used the front desk anyway, and Slater didn't mind having her around. But he also wouldn't mind when she went back to her day job, when school started up again in a month or so.

Etta greeted him, then leaned back in her chair, lacing her fingers behind her head. "So what's a paperhanger?"

Slater paused in front of her desk. "In this business it means someone who's passing counterfeit cash."

"Not printing it?"

"That's the butterfly man, or the scratch man."

"Does a paperhanger write bad checks?"

"Yeah, that too. Does Max have you working a counterfeiting job?"

"It came up elsewhere. This week I've been helping him on a window-shade job."

"I freaking hate those," Slater said. "But they pay the rent. I hope he's paying you."

She frowned. "I'm not a patsy. Of course he's paying me. So what are you working on?"

"An insurance gig."

"Somebody's running bunco on you?"

Slater had to grin. She really was learning the lingo. "I'm trying to track down a beneficiary."

"Do you think you might need an operative? I've got the time."

"I'm not sure yet. I'm going to dig through the paperwork now."

His small office was positioned opposite Max's, and he stepped behind Etta and went in to sit at his desk. He heaved his boots up onto the blotter and pulled his keyboard into his lap.

The files that Della had sent showed that the outstanding beneficiary was named Daniel Martínez. It made sense that he wasn't easy to find—it was a common surname, so there'd be a few of them around. The only indication of his identity, apart from the original policy, was a joint bank account held by him and Carlota, the decedent.

In the notes it said that someone in Della's office had found the bank account. It had been abandoned years ago with a balance of thirty-six bucks. The slimeball bankers had claimed the money as a penalty for ignoring the account, but the record of it remained.

Slater scanned the original policy application, scrolling through it on his computer screen. Daniel's relationship to the policyholder was listed as "husband," which meant there'd be a marriage certificate somewhere.

A while later he got up and waved good-bye to Etta on his way out. Down in the parking lot, he climbed into the Thunderbird and started the engine, then got the air going full blast. Pulling into the street, he navigated to the freeway and headed toward Hollywood.

This stretch of Cahuenga was changing, he saw, once he'd exited onto surface streets and cruised past Feel the Trend. It was on the cusp of arty and trendy, and if it followed the path of other hip neighborhoods, it would soon shift from trendy to wealthy. At that point, it was over—money sterilized these places, filling them with bland corporate chain stores. It would look like any other high-end dead zone in the country.

A block farther along, Slater nosed into an open street space and climbed out to feed the meter. There were a few people plying the sidewalk on a weekday afternoon, but not so many that he'd call it bustling.

As he walked back toward the shop, a guy on a skateboard appeared, wearing board shorts and moving fast. He wasn't very skilled at the slalom, and careened into Slater as he tried to arc around him, knocking his shoulder and spinning him sideways. The guy hopped off his ride and trotted a few steps as the board clattered into the wall.

"You need to step out of the way, *cholo*," the guy said, glancing at Slater as he walked toward his board.

Rapidly striding after him, Slater grabbed his upper arm and spun him around, then slapped him hard, left and then right, a rapid kovac. He planted a hand on his chest and shoved him away.

"You fucking psycho," the guy spat, red-faced now.

Slater stepped over to the wall and scooped up the skateboard. "I am not a *cholo*."

The guy was bigger than he'd thought, a few inches taller than him even off the board. As he took a step toward Slater, with his face contorted in fury, Slater raised the board to one side, like a baseball bat. Unsure now, the guy stopped.

"Give it back."

"Say it," Slater demanded.

He stood taller. "Say what?"

"I'm not a *cholo*."

"Fine. You're not a *cholo*. Give me my damn board."

Slater stepped toward the curb and paused, eyeing the guy and waiting for the delivery truck that was moving toward them to get a little closer. As it rumbled by he stepped into the gutter and tossed the board toward the middle of the truck. It landed on its wheels and rolled underneath.

"You fucking prick," the guy roared.

Resuming his path on the sidewalk, Slater listened for the crunch of the big tires demolishing the board, but it never came. The truck didn't brake either. Maybe the thing had survived. He didn't bother to look back. The skateboarder wasn't going to come after him—he'd be more concerned about retrieving his prized toy.

When he came up to the awning marked FEEL THE TREND, Slater ducked inside. The shop looked like it was mostly women's clothes, along with some jewelry and tchotchkes. The fabrics were in tans and browns and earthy greens and blues.

A guy with his hair in knobby twists was standing at a rack of jackets, doing something to them with a little yellow gun. Slater paused and admired the pleasing curves of his pants. Sensing his presence, the guy turned around, revealing a T-shirt that said VEGAN, and below that, EAT THE RICH. The message didn't quite make sense, but he had great pecs.

"Can I help you?"

"You're in good shape," Slater said. "Do you work out?"

"Are you flirting with me right now?" he demanded, and waved the yellow tool.

"That depends on whether you're into it or not."

"I'm straight."

"So spare me the chin music."

"Dude," he said intently.

"Settle down," Slater said. "I'm looking for Raquel."

"She's in the back."

"How difficult was that?" Slater threw up his hands and walked farther into the store. "Idiot," he muttered.

The place was roomy, with a section of tie-dyed shirts and dresses, and another with canvas sandals and shoes. As he got toward the back, a woman stepped out of a doorway, pushing apart a beaded curtain. Around thirty, maybe, she had her dark hair pulled back and wore a green batik-print dress like the ones he'd just walked past. Her breasts were out of proportion with her slender frame, but then being augmented was pretty standard in LA.

She smiled and greeted him in Spanish. It happened a lot in this vast Latin American city, as Slater had his father's black hair and dark Latin coloring, but he didn't have much of the culture.

"I only speak English," he said.

"Just let me know if you need a hand." She spoke with the authority of ownership. "I'm Rocky."

"Rocky as in Raquel?"

"Very good." She cocked her head. "Have we met?"

"I'm looking into a claim you made with Cudahy Mutual Insurance."

"You don't look like an insurance adjuster."

"I'm not. I'm an investigator." Slater dug in his hip pocket and handed over his business card.

"Are you investigating me?" she said, studying it for a moment.

"Have you done something that needs investigating?"

Rocky laughed. "I hope not."

"I'm looking for the other potential beneficiary. I wanted to interview you about that."

Her brow furrowed. "Can we go up the block?

There's a coffeehouse. It'll be easier to talk at a table. Let me get my bag."

Slater waited as Rocky stepped into the back room, emerging a moment later with a small handbag slung over her shoulder. She led him through the store, and near the entrance paused to talk to the staffer.

"I'm going out for a few minutes. Keep an eye peeled for that delivery."

Once they were outside, it was just a few paces to the coffee place. It occupied a corner and had tables on the sidewalk, with the windows wide open for the warm weather. Rocky stepped through the front door, but Slater stopped to look at the planter boxes flanking it.

"Is that the stuff they plant along the freeway?" Rocky said, turning back. "Ice plant, I think it's called. Supposedly it doesn't burn."

"This is different. It's called green Dudley." He pinched off a dead leaf. "They're from Catalina, but that's close enough that it qualifies as a native here. That's why it's thriving."

As he followed her in, she eyed him sidelong. "You're a gardener in your spare time?"

"I studied horticulture, and I worked in it for a hot minute. It's good to see natives. Usually in a spot like that they plant some invasive."

Rocky stepped up to the counter, and ordered a chamomile tea from the clerk, and waited as Slater ordered an oat-milk latte.

"I'll get it," he said, digging his wad of cash out of the pocket of his jeans.

There were a few people at the tables, some clearly here on vacation, and a few locals staring at laptops, bathed in the blue glow of their screens. Rocky sat at a table near an open window, and Slater joined her a minute later, drinks in hand. He sat opposite and slid her tea across.

"Tell me about Daniel."

"That's his legal name," Rocky said. "My mother called him Danilo."

"Did he always use that nickname?"

"I guess." She wrapped her hands around her cup. "I don't remember him. Carla never bad-mouthed him, but then she didn't talk about him much at all."

"The paperwork says your mother's name was Carlota."

"Right. Shortened to Carla."

"You must have been curious about Danilo," Slater said, and sipped at his coffee.

"Of course. At a certain age I wanted to know who my father was. I remember Carla said he was trying to get his college degree."

"Do you know where, or in what field?"

"I have no idea."

"Did he grow up around here?"

Rocky pursed her lips and gazed out the window. "That seems likely," she said finally. "I remember once asking her if he might have emigrated back to the *patria*. She said his *patria* was Boyle Heights."

"That might be useful too. Are there any photos of him?"

"I didn't find anything like that in Carla's stuff."

"Do you think you look like him?"

She smiled. "Who knows? My boyfriend says I look like my mother. I know he's my biological father, though. Once I got angry with Carla and said something like, 'My father could have been anybody.' It was like I was calling her a slut. She explained to me at high volume that Danilo was the man on my birth certificate, and he was the only possibility."

"Does your birth certificate include his signature?"

"I don't think so."

"What about a middle name or an initial?"

"I'm not sure." Rocky lifted her bag and pulled out a cell phone. "I have a scanned copy of it." She spent a moment tapping at the screen, then handed it to him.

As he swiped around the document, Slater saw that the box for parent 2 said "Daniel Martínez," with no initial, and no signature. The address listed for the parents was familiar too—it was the same as on the report about the abandoned bank account.

Farther down, Daniel's occupation was listed as "student." That fit with the story Carla had told Rocky. The document didn't list the parents' birth dates, but the father's age was given as twenty-seven. He scrolled back to the top to check Rocky's date of birth.

"You're the same age now as Danilo was when you were born," Slater said.

"Seriously? I wonder if that's a meaningful coincidence." Her brow furrowed. "That also means Danilo is in his mid-fifties."

If he was alive, Slater thought. Either way, knowing his age would significantly narrow the pool of potential candidates.

"Can you send me a copy of that?" he said, handing the phone back.

"If you promise not to identity-theft me."

"Insurance people take confidentiality pretty seriously."

"You don't seem like a typical insurance guy," she said, eyeing him briefly as she pulled out the business card he'd given her. Setting it on the table, she thumb-typed on her phone.

"The policy was drawn up around the time you were born," Slater said. "Danilo is a beneficiary, so obviously he was still in the picture. How long after that did he walk out?"

"My earliest memories don't include him, so I'd say it must have been before I turned five."

"Where were they living when you were born?" Slater said.

"South Gate. Their address is on my birth certificate too. By the time I was in school, we lived in East Hollywood."

"Is there anything else you can tell me about Danilo?"

She slowly shook her head and set her phone aside.

"Tell me about Carla, then. What kind of person was she? What kind of work did she do?"

"She was in the clothing industry. When I was young she worked as a seamstress in the factories downtown. Later she worked as a floor manager, even a bookkeeper, but always in that business." Rocky tucked a wisp of stray hair behind her ear. "There weren't a lot of guys around. Over the years she'd take an interest in a man once in a while, but I think she was content being single."

"Not a party person?"

She chuckled. "More like a church person. That's where her friends were. The Sunday mass crowd."

"The file says she was living in East Hollywood when she died."

"For a while she was in a hospice," Rocky said. "We moved a few times over the years, but always in that neighborhood." She looked away, her hands absently massaging the teacup. "I can't even imagine having a kid right now. I don't even feel like an adult half the time. But Danilo was my age when he had me." She met his gaze. "I'd really like to know more about my father."

"I can pass on whatever I find."

"Now that my mother is gone, I don't really have any family."

Slater shifted in his seat. "To level with you, the insurance company isn't all that motivated to find him. They just want to make sure they're not missing something obvious that would come back to bite them. Like if they issued you the full payout and then Danilo turned out to be living nearby. I'm only getting paid to work on this for a week."

"If you get any information that might take more than a week to follow up, maybe you could keep working on it. For me." She smiled. "I have an insurance payout coming."

"I'd be willing to do that," Slater said, and swirled the contents of his cup. "But let's see how far I get."

She looked down. "You don't want to get my hopes up."

"I haven't even started yet."

"I had a lawyer handle Carla's estate. She filed the life insurance claim. I didn't even know Carla had a policy. I still don't know how much money is involved."

"It's thirty grand total," Slater said. "Half for you and half for Danilo, unless he's dead or I can't find him, in which case you'll get the whole payout."

"So it's not a life-changing amount of money," she said. "But it'll be nice to have it. I'll probably redo my kitchen cabinets, or just stash it in a retirement account."

"Would you rather have Danilo or his fifteen grand?"

Her eyebrows shot up. "The man, of course. No question."

"That tells me you're serious about this. We should do a DNA comparison. If you know he's your biological father, it's the only way to be completely certain I've found the right man."

"You want my DNA?"

"I'd run it through a private lab. Just to compare it to any potential father I scrape up. The information won't go into any database. I won't share it with the insurance company either."

She shrugged. "Fine by me."

"I'll come back in the next day or so with a collection kit." He pulled out his phone. "Can I get your cell number?"

Rocky recited it, and he typed it into his contact list, then tucked the phone away.

"Thanks for the tea," she said. "I should go—I have a business to run." She rose, but then hesitated for a moment. "I'm really happy that you're willing to do this."

"No promises," Slater said, holding her gaze.

She flashed a sad smile, then turned to leave. Slater drained his cup, and went out to the street, and walked back to his car. The next step was either Norwalk or Andy. He climbed in behind the wheel, and started the engine, and got the air blowing. Norwalk, he decided. That trip had to be during office hours, and if he went to Andy's late in the day, he might be able to segue into a hookup.

Once he was on the freeway, he headed south, through downtown, and onto the 5. The county records office was in Norwalk, and soon he pulled into the surface lot, and climbed out, and walked toward the sprawling redbrick building. He hated this place, the convoluted atmosphere, the bureaucracy, the indifferent staffers.

It took a minute to find the right door, and inside he went to the counter and found the relevant forms in the rack. One was to request Daniel Martínez's death certificate, if that existed, and another was for his marriage certificate. Once he'd filled out everything he knew, he rang the little bell and slid them across the counter. The clerk who rose from his desk and stepped over was a man in his twenties, with slicked-back black hair and vague sweat stains in his armpits. The county must not spring for air-conditioning in here.

Slater joined a couple of other people who were waiting, absorbed in their phone screens, on the row of plastic chairs along the wall. Eventually it was his turn.

"Mr. Ibáñez?" the clerk said, and Slater rose and approached the counter. "You didn't provide enough information to pull the death certificate."

"Can you just print a list of everyone with that name who's died?"

"We don't entertain fishing expeditions," he said flatly. "The fee for a copy of the marriage document is twenty-five dollars."

"Interesting that you were able to find that one without going fishing," he said, digging out his wad of cash.

The clerk frowned. "You must have known we had it. You wrote down the pertinent details."

Slater peeled off a twenty and a fin and slid them across to him. "I wasn't sure they got married here or not. Your little fiefdom isn't the only jurisdiction on the planet."

The clerk stepped back to his desk to retrieve a manila envelope. "Do you need a receipt?"

Ignoring him, Slater scooped up the envelope and walked out into the heat of the day, pulling out the lone sheet that was inside. The document showed only Daniel's first and last names, without an initial or a middle name. But it did have his scrawled signature, and the same home address in South Gate. The box for his date of birth bore only the year.

Turning on his heel, Slater went back in to the counter and rang the little bell. The clerk looked up, and scowled at the sight of him, but got up and came over.

"This doesn't have the guy's birth date. Just the year."

He spun the sheet toward himself and studied it for a moment. "We see that sometimes. Especially with events that were recorded before electronic filing. In those days it was the officiant's responsibility to obtain all the information. If the spouse was born abroad, it's possible they didn't know their actual birth date. Or the officiant forgot to ask and just estimated it later when they filled out the paperwork."

"That seems a little sloppy for the recorder of the biggest county in the country."

He shrugged. "I wasn't here thirty years ago."

"So the full date of birth isn't buried in one of your byzantine archives somewhere?"

He slid the document back. "What you see is what we've got."

TWO

DRIVING TOWARD DOWNTOWN, THE late-afternoon traffic was slowing the freeway, and Slater crawled along in the sea of brake lights. By the time he got to his office, the day laborers had cleared out of the lobby for the day. Upstairs, Etta was gone, but the lights were on, and Max was in his office, parked behind his desk.

Max was a beefy guy, in his forties, and even though they worked together, Slater regularly had to resist the urge to punch him in the face. He looked the part of the heavy, with his sidearm bulging under his jacket, but at least his girlfriend made sure he kept his mousy brown hair in a natty style. Today he was wearing his dark-red suit, a dramatic contrast to the paint Etta had picked for his office walls, a kind of warm yellow. He only wore that suit when he wanted to be taken seriously, when he needed to take up space.

Slater stood in his doorway. "You're delivering bad news?"

Max sat back in his chair. "I'm presenting a client with my bill this evening."

"You think you'll get paid?"

He chuckled. "She'll pay up. I found out who her husband was sleeping with."

"A window-shade job. Etta told me. Is anyone going to get greased?"

"I don't think so. My report will give her leverage in the divorce, though."

"Have you got a minute?"

"Always," Max said, and gestured to the chair in front of his desk.

He liked that about Max, his willingness to collaborate, to talk whenever Slater needed to.

"Who do you use for paternity tests?" Slater said as he sat down.

"I'll send you the contact. Her name is Lenore. She runs a company called Zippy DNA." He fished his phone out of the inside pocket of his jacket and peered at the screen, then jabbed at it with his meaty fingers.

"Is she around here?"

"In Hyde Park, in the Forties. She's very discreet, and works fast, but she's not cheap."

"My client will pay for it."

"I'll tell her I'm referring you, so she'll know you're coming." He thumb-typed for a moment, then tucked the phone away. "You're on a new case?"

"It's an insurance job," Slater said, and told him about Rocky and the missing beneficiary.

"Why do you need a paternity test?" Max said. "Wouldn't this guy know that he has a daughter?"

"He may or may not cop to it, for whatever reason. Plus there's a payout—I suspect some of the possible matches will try to get their hands on that."

"Everybody's going to lie to you," Max said.

"Everybody," Slater said emphatically, and got up.

At his own desk, he woke his computer, then fed the marriage certificate into the document scanner, and added it to the folder in his cloud storage with the files Della had sent him. Pulling out his phone, he sent a text to the number Max had sent for Lenore:

> This is Slater, Max Conroy's business partner. Do you have time to meet with me tomorrow?

Her reply came a moment later:

> I'll be in the lab all day. Swing by anytime.

A second message contained her street address, and he checked to make sure it matched the one Max had sent.

With a keystroke he locked his computer, then got up and went downstairs to the Thunderbird. The traffic was heavy, and it took way longer than it should have to drive the few blocks to Broadway, where he parked in the surface lot behind Andy's building. He paid the attendant the flat evening rate, then walked around to the street, and into Andy's building, and up to his loft.

Andy didn't move very fast, and sometimes it took a minute for him to get to the door to answer his knock. Slater started to wonder if maybe he wasn't in, that he'd gone out for drinks with some sweaty twinkie, but then he heard movement inside. When he finally appeared, Andy was wearing his usual boxer shorts and tank top, and flashed a wry smile. He had a few days' stubble on his chin, and his hair was a perfect tousled mess.

"Are you here for work?" he said, waving him in.

"I need to track someone down."

Slater followed him inside. The building had

been a textile warehouse in its original incarnation, now reworked as lofts. This one was mostly one big room, with the original multipane windows looking over Pershing Square.

Andy dropped into his gaming chair, in front of the desk with its array of monitors, and swiveled to face him.

"Who are you ... looking for?"

Standing adjacent, Slater pulled out his phone. "I'll send you a scan of a marriage certificate. It has all the details I've found on him. His name is Daniel Martínez. The document shows the year he was born and where he was living twenty-seven years ago."

"Are you sure he's ... still alive?"

"Maybe you can find out. If he's alive, I want to talk to him."

"You need to give him a tune-up?"

Slater chuckled. "Probably not. Cudahy Mutual hired me to track him down. They have money for him."

"So he's not a lowlife."

Slater waved a hand. "He may or may not be."

"If he's not, he'll be easier to find. I'll get into it tomorrow."

Slater wanted to ask what it was going to cost him, but he didn't bother. He'd just have to pay what he wanted. Andy's rates always felt extortionate, but he got results, and he seemed to make a living doing what he called "deep research." From what Slater had seen, his tactics were indistinguishable from hacking.

Andy leaned back in his chair. "While you're here, do you have ... time to ride on this?" He pointed to his crotch with both index fingers.

Slater had to grin. "Why not?"

He sat on the edge of the bed to untie his boots, and pulled them off, and then slid his jeans off, and his shirt. Andy got up and tossed his shirt aside before he reached the bed. As he ditched his shorts, Slater saw that he was already hard.

Pushing him back, Andy climbed up and straddled him, lowering his weight onto him. His random muscle movements telegraphed into Slater's thighs.

"You're so warm," Slater said, and grabbed his cock, and stroked them together.

Andy held his gaze. "I'm going to fuck you until … you scream."

"Bring it on."

Despite the big talk, sex with Andy took careful orchestration. He lacked fine motor control because of his CP, and it was easy to get bruised if he got in the way of an unexpected muscle spasm.

Andy leaned down and scrabbled on the floor, producing a bottle of lube, and squeezed it into his hand, then rubbed it on his cock, and Slater's. Stretching out on top of him, Andy pressed between his thighs, and leaned in to meet his lips.

Running his hands into Andy's hair, Slater focused on his mouth, so warm and taut. Andy's rhythmic thrusting was getting him turned on too. It felt like he was flailing, but Slater knew by now that there was usually a pattern amid the chaos, and eventually Andy strained into him as he climaxed. Slater grabbed his waist with both hands, and pressed into him, rhythmically thrusting against his body. With his nose in Andy's hair, breathing in his sweat, he came too.

Andy slid off, and sprawled out beside him, working to catch his breath. As his own breathing slowed,

Slater folded an arm over his eyes. He started awake when Andy spoke.

"Have you seen Doris?"

"That's exactly what I want to talk about right after sex," Slater said flatly. "My mother."

"She has a book for me. She said she'd send it with you."

"Why are you hanging out with her?" Slater demanded.

He scowled. "We don't hang out. We talk once … in a while. She's so much less stress-inducing than my mother."

"Not for me."

Andy got up and went into the bathroom. The sound of the shower came as Slater drifted off. Sometime later, when he woke, Andy was beside him again, and the sky outside the windows was dark. He climbed out of bed and went into the bathroom to wash up. When he came back, he found his shirt on the floor and pulled it on.

"You can stay," Andy said softly, watching him from the bed.

"I know." Once he was dressed, and he'd crouched to tie his boots, he leaned in and briefly met Andy's mouth. "Bye, beautiful."

Slater's apartment was in gritty Westlake, a few blocks across the 110 freeway. When he got to the alley behind his building, there were folding traffic barriers blocking its breadth. He'd forgotten about that—the city was patching the concrete tomorrow. His landlord had warned him that it was going to happen, but that had been weeks ago. The upshot was that he couldn't park in his own garage.

It was always hard to find a place to park at night

in this dense neighborhood, and he drove around the block, and then the next one, trolling for a spot. He should have just stayed at Andy's. It was starting to get frustrating, but then he turned onto the boulevard and saw a van pulling out from a metered space. Gunning it up the block, he backed in, and killed the engine, then climbed out to check the sign. The meter went live at 8 a.m. That wasn't too unreasonable. Hopefully the Thunderbird would be safe here overnight.

It was a few blocks' walk back to his building, and he went in the front way from the street, past the shuttered cell-phone store on the ground floor and up two flights to his dingy apartment. It had a kitchen counter at one end of the room, and his thrift-store sofa and recliner at the other, and a bedroom off the side. The paint job was ancient, and the carpets were stained, but he stayed here because it had a private garage.

Once he'd pulled his boots off, he set the alarm on his phone for 7:40. If it was just about getting a ticket for an expired meter, he'd probably risk leaving his car there, but the boulevard was a tow-away zone in the morning.

When he pulled open the kitchen cupboard, he found the fifth of bourbon, the beautiful amber liquid stoic and patient as it waited for him. He poured some into a tumbler, eyeballing it so as not to exceed his ration. It ticked him off that he had to do this, but these were the new booze rules, an attempt to regulate his intake and keep himself out of recovery. No way was he going to be railroaded into a stretch at some beachside nuthouse where the wardens wore caftans and hemp sandals.

His paltry ration looked like next to nothing. He smelled the heady aroma, and took a sip, resisting the urge to slam it and pour more. Tucking the bottle away so that he wouldn't see it, he killed the lights and went to his recliner, where he stretched out, and sipped from the glass, gazing at the dark sky beyond the hazy window.

Of course he was tempted to go back for more booze, another delicious warm embrace, but then his mind was already slowing down. Inertia was easy too.

THREE

S LATER WOKE TO HIS alarm, and scrabbled for his phone on the bedside table to turn it off. For some reason he was in his own bed. His head didn't hurt, he decided, and that meant he must have managed to stick close to his ration.

There was a text from Andy, he saw, that had come just a few minutes ago:

Found something. Call me.

Either that guy got up very early, or it hadn't taken very long to find whatever he had. He'd remember that when it came to negotiating payment. Slater tapped the screen to call him.

"Did you know that … half the people in Latin America are named Martínez?" Andy said when he picked up.

"I figured it was a pretty common handle."

"There are so many men with your guy's exact name. I'm still … digging, but I found one that seems pretty likely."

"Is he in town?"

"Totally in town, but he might be hard to talk to."

"He's in the boneyard?"

"In prison," Andy said. "The federal one that's in the Civic Center."

"Damn it."

"Is it hard to get in there?"

"It's not that." Slater rubbed his eyes. "I don't really want to tell his moon-eyed daughter that her long-lost daddy is a lowlife."

"I'll text you his inmate number."

"Do you know what he's in for?"

"It just says fraud."

Slater ended the call and then checked for outgoing drunk-dials, relieved to find that he hadn't called anyone overnight. Forcing himself out of bed, he pulled on yesterday's jeans and found a shirt on a hanger in the closet. Black might get hot in the summer sun, but at least it was clean.

Hustling down the stairs, he tucked his shirttails in as he walked past the cell-phone place, its steel shutters up now and its interior bathed in brilliant white light.

It was a few minutes before eight when he got to the Thunderbird, glad to see it looked unmolested. There was a slip of paper tucked under the windshield wiper, he saw as he approached, but he knew it wasn't a citation. Those were red and white, and this was lemony green. Pulling it out, he saw that it was advertising, a flyer emblazoned in big letters with WE BUY JUNKERS.

"Idiots," he muttered, and looked around the street, but the leafleter was nowhere in sight. Even so, he said loudly, "This is not a junker."

Folding the flyer in half, he tucked it into his shirt pocket as he climbed in behind the wheel.

Even with the morning traffic, when seemingly

every parent in the city chauffeured their offspring to school, Hyde Park wasn't that far, and soon he was pulling up on the address for Zippy DNA. The building was ancient, with a low pitched roof and tiny barred-over windows, more like a prewar house than a commercial space. It had a sign on the front that said FLOWERS.

Looking around, there weren't any commercial storefronts nearby. This wasn't a boulevard, but it was an unusually wide street, and most of the buildings lining it were multistory apartments. The combination of width and density meant this had once been a streetcar line. The railroad right-of-way was still in the middle of the street. Even though the tracks had been pulled up a lifetime ago, the right-of-way was legally hard to erase.

Slater grabbed his phone and double-checked the address. The little house with the old sign was definitely the one Lenore had texted him. Killing the engine, he got out and walked up to the front door. It had heavy bars and a metal screen, grimy with decades of air pollution, but at the side was a modern video doorbell. He pressed it and stepped in front of it so that he'd be in full view of the camera.

A woman's voice came through the little speaker: "Come around to the side door."

The side street was narrower, and lined with pre-war bungalows and towering *washingtonia* palms. Most of the yards had grassy lawns and no front fences, stretching down the block like a golf course. The sight of it made him scowl. Planting a single species of grass like that effectively sterilized the local ecosystem, and it was such a waste of water to keep it all so verdant. In wealthier neighborhoods more people had put in drought-tolerant plantings, but this wasn't a wealthy neighborhood, and he knew that doing the right thing wasn't cheap.

The side door swung open, and a woman with her black hair in neatly piled braids stepped out. She had a smattering of freckles and wore a pristine white lab coat over a dark blouse.

"Slater?" she said, eyeing him.

"Lenore."

She smiled and beckoned him to follow her inside. It was a cramped little office with a small desk cluttered with two oversize computer screens. Through an archway Slater could see into the front room, where there were workbenches lined with modern-looking lab gear—machines with grids of buttons and LCD readouts. It looked like medical equipment. A faint humming came from that direction. Despite the close quarters, the place smelled clean. It wasn't soap or cleaning products. More like well filtered air.

"Is this your lab?"

"That's right. I do all the DNA analysis in-house." She gestured to a folding chair that sat against the wall. "Have a seat."

As Slater sat down, Lenore dropped into her desk chair and swiveled around to face him.

"During the peak of the pandemic a lot of the testing for the virus was done with these machines. Once the focus shifted to vaccination, I was able to buy the gear at a steep discount."

"I guess you'd call that part of the silver lining to a global health crisis."

Lenore chuckled. "Max has been good to me, so his referral carries a lot of weight. If he says you're

OK, I know you're OK. Tell me what you need."

"A paternity test, or maybe a few of them. I'll get a DNA sample from my client, and then I'll try to get a sample from her potential fathers."

"Great. I assume your client is cooperating? You're not going to bring me her hairbrush or her retainer, are you?"

"She'll provide whatever you need. How do I collect a DNA sample?"

"A cheek swab." Lenore swiveled to the shelves against the wall and grabbed a clear tube with a white stick inside it. She pulled a tab on one end, revealing the stick to be a cotton swab. "Just wipe this inside her cheek, and seal it in the tube, and bring it to me."

"That's easy." Slater took the tube and studied it for a moment. It was made of clear plastic, and it sealed with pressure, like a cork in a bottle. He handed it back. "What kind of sample can I bring from someone who might not be cooperating?"

"A can or bottle that they drank from, or a straw, or a cigarette butt. Half-eaten food doesn't work very well, but a napkin might. Just zip it into a freezer bag. If they spit, a saliva sample is ideal—just swirl the swab in it."

"What kind of cost is involved?"

"Four hundred per sample," she said, meeting his gaze. "That includes the comparisons. There's a surcharge if you want written reports about the results."

"I don't need paperwork," Slater said, and waved a hand.

Lenore nodded. "Most of my work is under the radar. You can get a formal lab report cheaper elsewhere, but not nearly as fast."

"How precise are the results? Could the test

mistake a brother for a father, for example, or a grand-father?"

"I extract enough data points that I can tell you exactly what the relationship is," she said. "Sibling, parent, grandparent, even how close two cousins are. There's no ambiguity."

"About the comparisons—can you look for my client's blood relatives online? I've heard about those consumer DNA databases."

"That's included in my rates if you request it. I'm not a genetic detective, but we can check whether there's anyone out there with a familial connection."

"It might save me some legwork," Slater said. "So how long does it take?"

"The better the sample, the faster it goes. To compare two clean cheek swabs, a few hours."

"That's fast. I bring the samples here? Should I call first?"

"I have a night deposit. Just write your code word on the sample and I'll know what it's about." She rose and pulled open the back door, pointing out a little metal flap. "Right in here."

It looked like a mail slot, but it was mounted higher in the door, at eye level. There was a slender box attached to the inside, Slater saw.

"Why do you use a code word?"

Lenore closed the door and sat down again. "I suppose I could use numbers, but words are easier to remember. You could write your name on it too, but I'm thinking you chose me because you value your anonymity, and your client's. If there's ever any police interference, or questions about the legality of my work, you probably don't want your client's name caught up in that."

"That's exactly the way I do things."

"If someone raids this place for some reason, god forbid, they won't know what samples and what data are connected to who." She smiled and tapped her temple with a finger. "That's all kept in here."

"What's my code word?" Slater said.

"Something that you and I both understand, but that no one else would."

"Do you have a suggestion?"

"How about chartreuse?"

"That's a kind of booze."

"And a color," she said, and pointed to his shirt. "Like your pocket square."

Slater pulled out the flyer. He'd forgotten about it. "I actually found this tucked under my wiper."

Reaching for it, Lenore folded it open and looked it over. "It's just advertising. And here I thought you were working a look."

"That color is called chartreuse, I take it."

"Easy enough to remember, isn't it? Just write 'chartreuse' on the sample tubes. You can put them through the slot anytime."

"Chartreuse it is." Slater took the flyer back and folded it, tucking it in his shirt pocket. "Are the swab kits expensive? I'm not sure how many people I'll have to test."

"They're included in the cost of running the analysis." Lenore rose and stood at the shelves, where she flapped open a brown paper bag, the kind that lunches came in, and grabbed a handful of the plastic tubes, dumping them inside.

Slater rose as she handed him the bag. "I'm thinking payment is in cash?"

"That's always best. You can put it through the

slot too. Just write 'chartreuse' on it."

"No one will intercept it?"

"I mostly work alone," she said. "Even if I get busy and get a lab tech in to help, I'm still the only one with a key to the box."

Slater glanced at it, and saw that it did have a decent lock on it. "I'll have something for you later today."

Out in the warm sunshine, he could hear the distinctive dull roar of the breeze in the tall palms, louder even than the traffic. He climbed into his car, setting the paper bag on the passenger seat, then started the engine and got the air blowing.

Pulling the flyer out of his shirt, he looked at it again in the daylight. He would have called that color green. On his phone he searched for "chartreuse." The first image that came up was the liqueur bottle. To his eye it looked yellow. There were photos of tennis balls, which he would have called green, but admittedly they were a pretty unique color. Next was a Miami fire truck. That seemed yellow to him. He swiped it away. Regardless of his own leanings, this was clear evidence—the consensus was that chartreuse was a thing, a kind of bright yellow-green.

FOUR

NEXT SLATER CHECKED ON the visitation rules for the prison downtown. It wasn't necessary to apply in advance, the website said, and the visiting hours fell within office hours. That seemed pretty lax—it must be a facility for low-risk offenders, the white-collar bankers and lawyers rather than the murderers and sex offenders.

Shifting into gear, Slater nosed the Thunderbird into the street and headed downtown. There was no street parking in the Civic Center, so he pulled into an underground garage. Before he climbed out, he took one of the sample kits and tucked it into his shirt pocket. It was small enough that it didn't protrude—it wouldn't be visible, and so it wouldn't evoke any awkward questions.

He'd seen the prison before, usually from the 101, but walking up on it now, he realized it was actually a massive high-rise. With slitty four-inch windows its purpose was unmistakable. In a way it was an odd place to put a prison, in a tower in the center of a metropolis. It would be depressing to be locked in there and look out at the freeway and the train station and all the running around that was going on.

Inside the lobby the countertop was high up, like in a police station, and he slid his business card across to the uniformed guard.

"I'm investigating an insurance claim," Slater said. "I want to talk to an inmate named Daniel Martínez."

"Fill this out," the guy said, boredom in his voice, and slid a sheet of paper toward him, along with the business card, not even bothering to glance at it. "You'll need a federally compliant photo ID."

Slater spent a minute writing down the details. The form was mostly about him, with just a few boxes for info on the person he wanted to talk to. He copied the guy's inmate number from the text Andy had sent him, then signed the sheet, and slid it toward the guard.

"ID?" the guy said.

Slater dug out his driver's license and slid it across.

With great effort the guard pushed himself out of his chair, and stepped over to a doorway behind him, and handed the sheet and the license to someone inside.

A minute later a guy with graying hair and a tight little mustache stepped out and eyed Slater. Clad in the same uniform, his name tag read WILSON.

"We'll see if he wants to talk to you," he said. "Have a seat."

"Can I get my ID back?"

"When you leave."

Scowling at that, Slater went over to sit on the wooden bench that faced the counter. If the wait grew too long, he couldn't even leave without dealing with Wilson again.

He got as comfortable as he could with his back against the hard tiles and surveyed the lobby space.

He was the only person here besides the guards. The one behind the counter seemed to be doing absolutely nothing. Not even staring at a screen. He was just sitting there. His eyes blinked occasionally, so he hadn't had an aneurysm and died, but he looked like he'd been switched off.

A while later Wilson reappeared at the counter and pointed down the hall. "Meet me at the metal detector."

When Slater got there, Wilson handed him a clear plastic bag.

"Empty your pockets. You'll get it all back when you leave."

Digging in his pants, he dumped his keys and his phone and his cards, but left the sample kit in his shirt pocket. When he stepped through the metal detector's frame, it emitted a shrill insistent beep.

Wilson heaved a sigh, and picked up a hand wand, and stepped toward him. With his arms outstretched, Slater stood as the guy waved it over him. It squealed angrily at his crotch.

"It's your belt buckle," Wilson said. "You'll have to leave your belt."

"Seriously?" Slater said, and unbuckled it, then pulled it off.

"Those pants look like they'll stay up just fine without it."

Slater eyed him as he handed it over. "You like what you see?"

He scoffed and waved for Slater to step out through the detector frame. When he walked back in, it didn't beep.

Wilson walked away, but there was another guard here now, a woman in her twenties with her black hair tightly bound behind her head. She led him to a set of elevators, and once they were inside, twisted a key in a socket next to the floor number to get it moving.

Upstairs she led him into a room with a few small utilitarian tables and stools bolted to the floor. There was already an inmate here, a guy in an orange jumpsuit, his thinning gray hair buzzed short. Surprisingly he wasn't cuffed or restrained, but there was another guard standing a few feet behind him. The one who'd brought Slater up here stood near the entrance behind him—clearly this wasn't going to be a private conversation.

"Daniel Martínez?" Slater said.

"You have to sit down," the guard behind the inmate said, waving to the table. "No physical contact."

"I usually pronounce it '*mar*-tin-ez,'" he said, using the loose English vowels. "Are you working for my lawyer?"

"I'm working for an insurance company," Slater said, as he dropped onto the stool across from him. "Do you use the nickname Danilo?"

"I've gone by Danny."

"Did you live in South Gate twenty-seven years ago?"

"More like fifty years ago. My parents were from South Gate. Twenty-seven years ago I would have been in Florida. What is this about?"

"Were you ever married to a woman named Carla?" Slater said. "She worked in the clothing industry."

The light in his eyes faded, and he shook his head. "You've got the wrong guy."

"I think you're probably right about that." Slater watched him for a moment. He didn't really look like

Rocky, but they could be related. "Have you got a college degree?"

"I barely got out of high school."

"I'm looking to find Carla's former husband. Would you be willing to take a DNA test?"

"The feds have already got that on file."

"The insurance company doesn't. It would save me a lot of paperwork."

"Maybe if you do something for me in exchange. Take a message to my gal."

"What's her name?"

"Gloria. She's a dancer at that place by the airport."

Slater took the test kit out of his shirt, and pulled out the swab, and handed it over. "What's her last name?"

This guy didn't need instruction, and briefly rubbed the cotton tip inside his cheek, then handed it back.

"I don't know her last name. It's just Gloria."

"Wait a minute," the guard behind him said. "You can't do that."

Slater half-turned to her. He already had the tube sealed. "The DNA swab? I cleared it with Wilson downstairs. He made me fill out a damn form and everything."

"Really?" she said, her brow furrowing, unsure now.

The other guard gave her a subtle shrug.

Slater tucked the tube in his shirt pocket and looked at Martínez. "What place by the airport?"

"It's on Century. Or maybe it's Aviation." He waved a hand. "You can't miss it. It's right there."

Slater stood up, and the guard behind Martínez stepped toward the table.

"On your feet, Martínez."

"Tell Gloria that I love her," he said, pushing himself up. "I didn't say it before, but I love her. Tell her I'll be back soon."

The guard opened the door behind them and led him out. Slater's guard gestured for him to walk out ahead of her, and he led the way to the elevators.

"So you struck out?" she said, twisting her key in the lock next to the call button.

"I'm thinking he's not the right Daniel Martínez."

"I wouldn't go looking for his girlfriend."

The elevator door rumbled open, and Slater stepped on. "Yeah, I wasn't going to do that."

"It would be a snipe hunt," she said, using her key again on the panel. "He doesn't even know her name. There must be a dozen strip clubs around the airport. If she doesn't come here to visit him, it means she's moved on."

"That sounds logical," Slater said.

"He says he'll go back to her, but Martínez is doing seven to ten. He's not going to be tucking singles into G-strings anytime soon."

The door rolled open, and Slater walked around to the counter, and eyed the clerk. He stood up and stepped into the office behind him, returning a moment later with the plastic bag full of his stuff, and slid it across to him.

The cash wad looked intact, Slater decided. That was the only thing he'd been concerned about, along with his driver's license, but that was in the bag too. He quickly loaded his pockets, and draped his belt around his neck, then turned and strode toward the door to the street. He wanted to be out of here before the guard from upstairs could confirm that he hadn't actually arranged to acquire a DNA sample. They might still come after him later, but it was usually easier to deal with the consequences than to try to get permission up front.

Out of view of the entrance, half a block up the street, he paused to thread his belt back into his pants, then trotted down the stairwell into the dimness of the parking garage. Once he was behind the wheel of the Thunderbird, he texted Andy:

The jailbird isn't the guy. Keep looking.

That's what his instincts told him, but he'd run the sample anyway, just to be sure. Digging in the glove box, he found a Sharpie, then fished the tube out of his shirt and wrote on it: "chartreuse—possible father no. 1."

Once he'd driven out into the daylight again, he navigated to the freeway ramp, gunning it and merging left. Traffic wasn't heavy yet, and a few minutes later he was in Hollywood, and parked up the block from Rocky's shop. He took one of the test kits from the paper bag on the seat and tucked it into his shirt pocket.

When he walked into the shop, he paused to let his eyes adjust to the light. The clerk with the knobby hair and the great body was standing nearby.

"Weren't you in here yesterday?" he said.

"What's it to you, toots?"

"You didn't buy anything. Am I going to have to follow you around the store?"

Stepping closer, Slater slapped him, right and then left, a rapid kovac. The clerk stumbled back.

"You goddamn bully," he growled. "I'm calling the cops."

Rocky appeared, wearing another batik dress, her

brow furrowed. "You're not going to call anyone. Don't be disrespecting the clientele."

"He's not a client," the guy snapped. "He's a damn hothead."

"Just chill," she said, and to Slater, "You know he was just messing with you, don't you?"

"That's what the kovac was for."

Rocky sighed. "You shouldn't take the bait." She nodded for him to follow and walked toward the back of the shop.

Slater jutted his chin at the clerk, a tacit challenge, then turned to follow her. Once they were out of earshot, she stopped.

"What's going on?"

"I came to get a DNA sample."

"Have you found anyone to compare it to yet?"

"I talked to a guy today who's the right age and has the right name, but I don't think he's the one. He doesn't remember Carla."

"You'll test his DNA?"

"He gave me a sample," Slater said. "I can also upload it anonymously to one of those genealogy sites. There's a chance we might find Danilo that way."

"That's a great idea."

"Here's the thing," Slater said, and held her gaze. "The insurance company is paying my salary this week, but they're not covering the DNA tests."

"I'll pay for those, of course." Rocky waved dismissively. "Your lab does PCR on the samples?"

"I don't know what the process is called, but it can compare DNA to assess familial relationships, and how close a relative the match is." He folded his arms. "I saw the machines. They look like overly complicated cash registers."

"That's probably PCR."

"How do you know the lingo?"

"Early in the pandemic they were using PCR to test for the virus. The shop was closed for a while. I had lots of time on my hands to read."

Slater fished the sample kit out of his pocket and popped it open. "Just run this over the inside of your cheek."

She dabbed it in her mouth, then handed it back.

"Oh—I got some lipstick on the stem."

Slater sealed it into the tube and peered at it. A little dab of dark red appeared on the stick, but it wasn't near the cotton swab.

"I'm sure it's fine."

"Thank you for helping me with this," Rocky said.

"I haven't achieved anything yet."

"Still." She held his gaze for a moment, and squeezed his forearm, then turned away.

As he walked out, the mouthy clerk was standing at the register. Slater glared at him, but the guy didn't even look up.

Once he was back in the Thunderbird, he got on the freeway. It was getting congested closer to down-town. When he got into the office, he flipped on the lights and eyed the small statue of Rey Pascual that sat on the front desk. He was glad Etta hadn't eighty-sixed him during her renovations. Rey was a skeleton who wore a crown and held a scythe in one bony hand. He was supposed to bring them luck, and Slater had grown used to having him around.

"Just you and me, Rey," he said, and went into his office. He sat and rolled his chair to the corner, where their squat black safe was bolted to the floor. It dated from another era, with faded gold-leaf lettering and a mechanical dial, but having a bona fide safe was useful in this business, as they often dealt with cash.

Once he'd twisted the combination into the dial, he pulled the heavy door open and grabbed a rack from among the stacks of cash on the bottom shelf. He broke the currency band and split the bundle in two, tossing half back inside. The cash was starting to accumulate in there, and he and Max had been trying to decide what to do with it. They couldn't really bank much of it without outing their clients to the tax people, and their clients paid them for their discretion.

The accounting envelope had a new page on it, he saw, neatly taped to the end of the envelope so that he could flip it up and see the older entries. That was probably Etta's handiwork. Grabbing a pen, he added today's date to the bottom of the list, along with the details:

Slater, expenses, -5G

Once he'd locked the safe again, he got up and went to Etta's desk, where he found a blank business envelope. Counting out eight C-notes from the stack on his desk, he tucked them inside, then wrote "chartreuse" and "800" on the front.

Digging in Etta's pen collection, he found a Sharpie, and sat at his desk, and fished out the sample tubes. On the one with Rocky's lipstick smudge, he wrote "chartreuse—client."

He tucked them back in his shirt, and added the rest of the cash to the wad in his pocket. Just as he was getting up to leave, he heard keys rattle in the front door, and he went out to the front office. Max and Etta were stepping in.

"What up, pup?" Etta said, flashing a smile.

"I'm on my way out," Slater said. "You look happy."

"Max showed me how to shoot a nine-mil. It was a lot of fun."

"She's not a bad shot," Max said. He was wearing his brown suit today, the one that Slater hated.

"Is that really necessary?" Slater demanded.

"Don't look at him," Etta said. "Look at me. I'm a grown woman. I don't need to be protected by you two yahoos."

Slater threw up his hands. "And I don't want to turn you into a lowlife."

"I'm just learning about weapons at the gun range. It's not like I'm going to start robbing pot dispensaries."

He gave her a pointed once-over. "If you say so."

"It's better that I show her the ropes than some gun nut," Max said.

"Why don't you ever pack heat, anyway?" Etta said.

Slater took a breath. "When you get into certain kinds of trouble, you can't."

"Does that mean you're a convicted felon or something?"

"It's not polite to ask," Max said.

"It's not that bad." Slater frowned and waved his arm. "It's nothing worse than what Max has done to me when he's ticked off."

"Seriously?" she demanded, eyeing Max. "You went for him?"

"He tried to decapitate me with a shovel," Slater said.

Max gestured dismissively. "That was one time. Before we got to know each other. Slater went pretty hard on me too—he cracked my rib, and threw my weapon into a swimming pool."

Etta's brow furrowed. "So how did you go from trying to kill each other to becoming business partners?"

"That's about trust," Max said. "It's built through experience. This guy has saved my butt on several occasions."

"And vice versa," Slater said.

"I'll need to hear those stories eventually."

"I have to go," Slater said, "but whatever he tells you happened, double-check the details with me."

FIVE

T HE LATE AFTERNOON TRAFFIC was sluggish on the way to Zippy DNA, and Slater parked a few doors down, then walked back to the side street. A guy walking a dog was approaching, so he slowed to a stroll, waiting for them to pass. The guy nodded hello, and once he'd rounded the corner and disappeared from view, Slater pushed the sample tubes through the slot in Lenore's side door, followed by the envelope with the cash. Inside the building he heard a faint chime, like an electronic doorbell.

As he turned to walk away, the door swung open, and Lenore poked her head out. She looked furtively up and down the street, then gestured for Slater to step in.

"I heard a chime," Slater said, following her inside. "You have a sensor inside the drop box?"

"It notifies me on my cell phone. In case I'm sleeping or out somewhere."

"I have to say, I admire your work ethic. You've got a nice little operation going here."

"Thanks," Lenore said, and beamed as she pulled out a ring of keys and used one of them to open the drop box. "What did you bring me?"

"Two cheek swabs and some cash."

"You know what I like." She tucked the envelope into the pocket of her lab coat, not bothering to open it.

"I'm pretty sure this guy isn't a match. But I have to be sure. You use PCR for your analysis?"

"That's exactly what I do. Have you been reading up on DNA testing?"

"I heard that was the tech they were using at the start of the pandemic," Slater said. "I hope to have a few more samples for you in the next few days."

"Whatever you need, I got you." Lenore read what he'd written on the containers. "So 'client' is the one I'm going to compare everything else to, correct? I'll get on it today."

Slater stepped out to the street, and heard her pull the door closed behind him. Climbing into the Thunderbird, he saw that he had a text from Andy:

Results. Drop by.

It took a while in the stop-and-go traffic on the 110, but eventually he pulled into the lot behind Andy's building, and went up to his loft. Andy pulled the door open for him, and he followed him in to his desk.

"Grab a seat," Andy said, "and I'll talk you through what I found."

Pulling a kitchen chair out from the little table, Slater sat at his elbow, facing his computer. He could smell his warm clean sweat.

"You smell amazing."

"Good to know." Andy rolled closer to his monitors.

"Like the first warm day of summer. It's totally

distracting."

"Focus," Andy said, eyeing him. "So you've already … eliminated the one who's a guest of your Uncle Sam?"

"He wasn't in South Gate at the right time, but I'm doing a DNA test on him today."

"I thought he … fit pretty well. But there are others."

Andy pulled up a photo on the screen. It was a gray-haired woman with big glasses and heavy eye makeup.

"This Daniel Martínez is in … the right age window," Andy said, "and lived in South Gate at the right time."

Slater frowned. "That's a woman."

"Now, sure, but she was born Daniel … Martínez."

"When did she transition?"

"I think there was a record of when she … legally changed her name. Let me check when that was." He clicked around on the screen and peered at it. "Almost thirty years ago."

"That's before my client was born. What's her new name?"

"She still uses Martínez, but her first name is Bambi."

"She totally looks like a Bambi." Slater studied the image. That washed-out color, and the blue background. "Is that a DMV photo?"

"Don't ask."

"I'm going to say this probably isn't our man, because she's not even a man."

"So that's in the 'no' pile," Andy said. "I'll keep the details in case … you want to circle back."

"Who else have you got?"

Andy pulled up a head shot of a dark-haired Latin guy with sunken cheeks.

"That's totally a DMV photo," Slater said.

"This Daniel lived in South Gate a little … after your target dates. He's in the Bay Area now."

"Was there an address for him twenty-seven years ago?"

"It just says he was posted abroad then. He was in the military."

"That's not going to be him," Slater said. "His daughter would have known if he was in the service."

Andy walked him through several more, offering details and answering his questions. They managed to weed out a few, and when they got to the end of the list, Andy took a deep breath.

"So that leaves three strong … candidates. The lawyer, the security guard, and the vagrant."

"We don't know for certain that he's homeless," Slater said. "He has an address."

"Sure, on Skid Row."

"My office is practically on Skid Row."

He raised his eyebrows and looked Slater up and down.

"Don't even say it. Let's just call him the local."

"I'll send you what I've got on these three. If you strike out, we can work farther down the list."

"Send the photos too," Slater said.

Andy leaned over the keyboard with his plastic gauntlets. They were some kind of input device to compensate for his tremors, and watching the chaotic movement, it was hard to believe he was accomplishing anything coherent. A moment later he sat back.

"Done."

"What do I owe you?" Slater said.

Andy swiveled his chair to face him. "Don't get angry with me."

"When you say things like that, it induces anger."

"I suspect that anger is … your resting point."

Slater gestured impatiently.

"Twelve hundred."

He pressed his lips tight together and pulled out his wad of cash, and riffled through it, then handed over the bills. He knew he should just let it go, but he couldn't. Through his teeth, he said, "Chiseler."

"I prefer to think of myself as a … skilled researcher. Come on—I got DMV photos of … all these chuckleheads."

"I have to admit, that's pretty damn impressive."

"Do you have time to … mess around?"

"I can't. I'm on a deadline with all these Daniel Martínezes."

"Kyle is coming over tomorrow night. I thought you … could join us."

"I wonder if that might be too much for Kyle. He's like a delicate sweet pea that wilts in the summer heat. Are you sure he's down with me being there?"

"He will be when I tell him he is."

Slater chuckled. "You've got him wrapped around your little finger."

"He appreciates all this." Andy gestured vaguely to his torso.

"So do I, but you don't tell me what to do."

"We all know nobody … tells Slater what to do."

"I'll try to swing by," he said, and leaned in for a brief kiss, then walked out.

Twilight was setting in, with the last of the sun's pink rays illuminating the tops of the office towers. Climbing into the Thunderbird, Slater made the short drive across the chasm of the 110 freeway into his neighborhood.

The alley wasn't blocked off anymore, and he turned in. Patches of new concrete dotted its length. At least they hadn't disturbed the shallow swale that ran down the middle. If they'd messed that up, the alley would turn into a lagoon come rainy season.

He pulled into his garage, and waited for the heavy door to roll down, then went to the rear door and trotted up the two flights to his apartment.

It was easy to mess around with Andy, but he didn't want it to get too routine, and he didn't want to get too sticky about him. Not dominating his social calendar would also give Andy time with Kyle. He hated that entitled little twerp, but the guy was a much better relationship prospect for Andy than Slater was. Eventually the two of them would probably go exclusive—another reason not to be dependent on Andy, and motivation to mix things up.

Dropping onto the sofa, he pulled off his boots, then stretched out and opened the hookup app. There were always tons of guys around, and he scrolled through the body parts and underwear shots and dick pics.

Almost right away, someone messaged him:

Let's get busy.

There was a lot to be said for the direct approach. He wasn't in this to chat about nothing for half the evening. Checking the guy's photos, he saw that he was hot enough. Latin, or black, or both, in his forties, maybe, with a little paunch. Slater texted back:

My place. No drugs.

He thumb-typed his address, and a moment later a reply came:

Be there in a few minutes.

Slater got up and went into his bedroom, where he kicked the laundry that was scattered on the floor into a pile in the bottom of the closet, then threw the covers flat on the bed, then changed into a tight white T-shirt. There was a knock at his front door, and he went to pull it open.

The guy was a little older than his profile implied, Slater saw as he stepped inside, and he looked different than his head shot, but he was still fuckable. Not very tall, his black hair was graying, and he was wearing a golf shirt and baggy cargo shorts.

"Whoa," he said, looking around. "What a dump."

"Thank you." Slater closed the door. "So what are you into?"

Digging in his pants pocket, he produced a little plastic bag. "Have you met my friend Tina?"

Slater put his hands on his hips. "Was it not clear that I don't want that stuff in my place?"

He frowned. "Your message said that you didn't have any product. So I brought it with me. You know—to share. I'm being generous here."

"My text said 'no drugs.' As in, don't bring any."

"That's not exactly what you said."

Slater scoffed. "I'm not going to fuck you if you're high."

"Why not?"

"I can't keep up with the false energy. There needs to be an end point that's not tomorrow afternoon. Did you ever meet a long-haul tweaker? They either get clean or they croak. That stuff isn't sustainable."

"Wow." His eyes grew wide. "I never heard that before, Grandma. How about GI gin instead?"

"What the hell is that?"

"The rappers call it purple drank. It's codeine syrup. It relaxes you, so extra energy won't be a problem."

"You've got two options," Slater said. "You can fuck me, or you can get high, but not both. If you're going to get high, that's not going to happen here."

"Fine," he said flatly. "We can do it the boring way."

"So what are you into, besides meth and opioids?"

"I kind of like the hard-ass thing. Like when you were reading me the riot act just now. Do you want to fuck me?"

"That, I can do," Slater said, and waved him into the bedroom.

At the side of the bed, the guy turned and stood close to him, reaching for his belt, and unbuckled it, leaning in to meet his mouth. Slater shoved up his shirt, and pulled it off over his head, then peeled off his own. He popped Slater's fly and massaged his cock, gently moaning as Slater ran his hands along his torso.

Stepping back, the guy unbuckled his belt and let his shorts drop to the floor. They made a solid *clunk* on the carpet as they landed, and Slater froze. That was something more than just keys and a phone— more like a handgun.

"What's in your shorts? They sounded heavy."

"The GI gin," he said, stepping out of his underpants. "Remember?"

Slater ditched his jeans and climbed on his futon. The guy was actually attentive, and responsive, not distracted like a typical tweaker. He spent a minute exploring his mouth, running his hands over his warm skin. The guy stroked him, and soon Slater was rock-hard. Reaching for the bedside table, he grabbed a condom and lube.

"Let me put it on you," the guy said, and spent a moment stroking him, and rolling it on, intently focused on his cock.

Eventually he lay back, and Slater worked his fingers into him, then moved closer, pressing in. Soon he was pounding him, and the guy screwed his eyes shut, grimacing. Slater leaned in, his nose in his hair, smelling the tang of sweat and sickly sweet pomade, and came, straining into him.

As Slater pulled back, the guy massaged his cock, and met his eye. "Want to blow me?"

Shifting down the futon, he took him into his mouth and worked him. The guy ran his hands into Slater's hair, and eventually he climaxed, yelping, his fingers tightening on his scalp.

Slater pulled away and flopped on his back, then folded his arm over his eyes. The guy's breathing started to slow. Sometime later he heard him get up and go into the bathroom, and then the sound of the tap in the kitchen sink.

"You must really like peas," he called.

Slater took a breath, and forced himself to get up, and stepped into the kitchen.

"What?" he demanded.

"There's four bags of frozen peas in your icebox, and nothing else."

"Those are for bruises. They're the cheapest ice packs you'll ever find. What are you looking for?"

"Munchies."

Slater waved a hand. "I don't really have any food here."

"I can see that. Want to go get tacos? I saw a cart down the street."

"You go ahead. I need to sleep."

He stood up taller. "You're kicking me out?"

"You were headed out for food anyway, right?"

Slater waited in the kitchen, leaning on the counter while the guy got dressed. As he went to the front door, he moved in close and squeezed Slater's bicep.

"Can I call you sometime?"

"Look for me on the app."

Once he was gone, Slater flipped the deadbolt and pulled the fifth of bourbon from the cupboard. He poured his ration, and slammed it, savoring the heady burn in his nose and his throat. Pouring another slug into the tumbler, he killed the lights and went to sit in his recliner, and set the glass on the carpet.

He could feel his mind starting to unspool, the amber nectar suffusing his body. It didn't last for long, this interlude when he was sated and content and winding down, but it was always the best part of the day.

When Slater woke, he had a headache, but it wasn't too bad. He was in his own bed. Scrabbling for his phone, he checked for drunk dials, but there was no sign of that. There was a text from Lenore:

Sample 1 is not a match. Call me regarding the client sample.

He tapped the screen to dial her number, then listened to it ring.

"So I uploaded your client's DNA to the public database," she said when she picked up. "I found a couple of eighth cousins, but no close matches."

"Are the cousins in LA?"

"It doesn't matter. They're not genetically close enough. Everyone has, like, two million eighth cousins. The common ancestor lived during the American Revolution. That's too far back to be useful for your purpose."

"I guess it was worth a shot," Slater said.

"New people upload their profiles every day. I'll let you know if I get any hits."

Once he'd ended the call, he tried to look at the

documents that Andy had sent, but it was too diffi-cult on the little screen. Forcing himself to get up, he microwaved a mug of water, and stirred in a spoonful of brown coffee powder from a jar, then slurped at it as he got dressed.

Leaving the mug in the sink, he trotted down to his garage, and backed the Thunderbird into the alley, and waited for the steel door to roll down. It was hot out already, and he felt the power of the scorching sun as he drove to the office. Walking across from the parking lot, he stepped through the handful of day laborers in the lobby, then rode the elevator up.

The place was dark, and he flicked on the lights, sticking his head in Max's office to make sure no one was here. Settled in at his desk, he went through the files on the three most likely Daniel Martínez candidates, reading more of what Andy had dug up on them.

The lawyer lived in Bel Air, and the security guard was in Long Beach, but the local was easy pickings, right downtown. That's where he'd start. Pulling up the guy's photo, he studied it so that it would be fresh in his mind. This Daniel had long gray hair and a confident spacey smile. The DMV took those photos when you weren't expecting it, so they were always unflattering, but this guy looked the part of an indi-gent addict.

Downstairs again, when Slater climbed into his car, he took a sample kit from the paper bag and tucked it into his shirt pocket. The address for this Daniel Martínez was a 1920s behemoth of a hotel on the edge of Skid Row, and he nosed the Thunderbird into the street and headed toward it.

The zoning had changed in this part of town

to allow empty offices to be converted into upscale housing, and the streets west of the hotel were now teeming with wealthy loft dwellers. But east of it was still Skid Row, a sea of tents and addiction and broken lives.

The hotel's new owners had tried to gentrify the place along with the loft conversions, but some housing law said they couldn't just kick out the transients, so they turned it into a hybrid building, renovating some floors for the tourists and leaving others to the long-haulers. For a while there had been separate entrances for the two groups, but a judge decided that was discriminatory, so the compromise was a check-in desk for the tourists on one side of the lobby and a desk for the long-term crowd on the other side.

Once he'd parked out front, and fed the meter, he walked in. The lobby retained the ornate decoration of its first incarnation, with the marble floors and coffered ceiling and grand staircase, but the people lingering in the lobby were from right now, both the backpackers and people on the skids. If this was Daniel Martínez number two's permanent address, it meant he was a heartbeat away from homelessness.

At a glance it was obvious which desk was for the tourists, with a trio of staffers in bright uniforms and luggage piled around. Slater went to the opposite side. The desk clerk over here looked like she could be sleeping rough herself, with heavy smoker's lines on her face, her gray hair in a sloppy bun, and messed-up meth-mouth teeth.

"What room is Daniel Martínez in?" Slater said as he stepped up.

She met his gaze with watery blue eyes. "We can't give out that information."

"Can you phone him?"

"There's no phones in the rooms."

Slater pulled out his wad and palmed a twenty, making sure she got a glimpse of it, then rested his hand flat on the counter.

"Does President Jackson have high enough clearance to be privy to that information?"

She held up her palm like a crossing guard and slowly shook her head. "Sir, officially we can't take gratuities for any reason. There's a camera behind me to monitor for such incidents, and one behind you."

"That's a shame," he said. "I wish there was an unofficial solution."

"Have you seen the tourism brochures at the travelers' check-in desk?" Her eyes flicked across the lobby. "They have them in all sorts of languages. German. Japanese. French. There's bus tours of movie stars' houses. Wax museums. Ghost tours."

"I'll take a look."

Palming the twenty again, he walked across the big room to the rack of colorful folders. Slater plucked one at random, and slipped the twenty inside, then walked back to the Skid Row desk and set the pamphlet on the counter.

"I forgot to ask," Slater said. "Do you have a steam room?"

"We don't." She raised her eyebrows. "But the gym for our short-term guests opens at seven twenty-four."

"Good to know."

Slater walked over to the only bank of elevators, evidently shared by guests at both ends of the economy, and stepped into a waiting car. Pressing the button for 7, he rode up and stepped out into a narrow hallway. The carpet was grungy and threadbare, and the walls were heavily marked. This was definitely not where they housed the overseas backpackers.

Walking the hallway, he found the plaque for 724, on a narrow door with a heavy lock and a wraparound strike plate. That was a lot of reinforcement for an interior door—he wouldn't be able to kick it down if he tried. You'd need a ram and a couple of burly associates to heave it.

Slater rapped on it with his knuckles, and a moment later the door opened a few inches. The security chain was on, and the face inside the gap was a woman's, with scraggly blond hair and mascara that had melted into racoon eyes. He caught a whiff of last night's vodka.

"Can I talk to Daniel?" Slater said.

"You a cop?" she said, her voice raspy, like a smoker's.

"Private."

She started to push the door closed, but he already had his boot wedged in the gap.

"Hold up," he said. "I might have some money for him."

"You can just leave it with me," she said, peering out at him. "I'll pass it along."

"That's not going to work. I need a few minutes of his time."

"He's got lots of that. But he's not here."

Slater pulled out his wad and folded up a sawbuck, letting her see what it was. If they got a glimpse of the greenery, it was usually easy to strike the deal.

"Where can I find him?"

She reached through the gap and took the bill. "He works at that hipster-trash diner up the block."

"On tables or in the kitchen?"

"He washes pots. You'll find him in the back. Off the alley. Now, get your damn foot out of the way."

As he pulled his boot out, she slammed the door. Slater had to grin. For a total of thirty bucks, his landlord and his girlfriend had completely sold him out.

As he strode down the hall, a man stepped out of a doorway and blocked his path. He was tall, and obese, and wore a black jacket. In one hand he waggled a blade, the metal flickering in the wan light.

"I heard you had some money," he said. "Maybe you'll share that with me."

"Are you seriously pulling this penny-ante crap right here?" Slater demanded. "This place really is sleazy."

"Give me your cash and your phone," he snapped.

From the look in his eyes, he wasn't high, or even all that amped up. He'd have to be careful with this one. There were only a few seconds to gain the upper hand.

"All right," Slater said, and took a slow breath to calm himself.

He made a show of looking down as he reached for his pocket, and at the same moment lifted his boot, and pivoted to kick hard at his knee. The guy reacted with a wild slash, narrowly missing Slater's arm. But the blow had landed, and he'd felt his patella crunch—the guy yelped, and tumbled back on his butt, and dropped the blade.

Slater was on him fast as he scrabbled on the carpet for the weapon, and stomped on the guy's wrist before he found it. He howled in pain and rolled to punch at Slater's leg with his other hand. One blow landed on his thigh, and Slater kicked him in the chin, then as the guy rolled away, he briefly crouched to snatch up the blade.

"Why do you make me do this to you?" Slater shouted, and kicked him in the kidney.

The guy was on his side now, in a fetal ball, shielding his face with his palms. Slater held the blade in front of his eyes.

"Next time I'll slit your fucking throat," he growled, and stepped past him.

No one else had stepped into the hallway, and Slater glanced at the weapon as he strode away. It was long enough that it was probably illegal to be carrying it around. Near the elevators he found the trash chute, and spent a moment wiping his prints off the handle, just in case, and then dropped it in.

Instead of the elevator he took the fire stairs to the lobby, trotting rapidly down the steps in the empty stairwell. No way was he going to risk that guy's associates coming after him in a sealed box.

Back out on the sidewalk, he took a breath as he walked up Main Street, and paused at his car to drop some more quarters in the meter. He knew the diner that the woman had been talking about, and as he approached it, he slowed his pace and looked in through the front window.

She was right about the crowd—the neighborhood's stylish moneyed residents were here for a leisurely breakfast. There was no middle in this part of town, only people on the skids who'd sell out their mother for a sawbuck and people with the resources to linger over an eighteen-dollar bowl of oatmeal.

When he walked around the end of the block, he found that the alley had a tall steel gate across it. There was a smaller pedestrian door within it, and wired to the bars was a black-and-red sign that said NO TRESPASSING. When he tried the handle on the door, it was locked. He could probably climb over it, but there were too many people around, and some busybody was bound to call the cops.

There were cars inside, and it was still morning, when lots of running around happened. Somebody had to roll through this gate eventually. Slater stood in front of the smoke shop next door, with his back to a stretch of wall, eyeing the passersby as he waited. Some of them likely worked at nearby businesses, but most were definitely homeless people. Nobody even glanced at him twice. He hated that, the realization that he kind of fit in here.

Just as he was starting to get impatient, wondering whether he should give up, he heard a metallic clank, and the gate to the alley swung inward. A white van pulled through, and Slater hustled in behind it before the gate snapped closed again.

There was no signage on the businesses as he walked up the alley toward the back of the diner, just the building numbers on the back doors, but it was obvious which one it was, with the big dumpster and the smell of rotting food. The kitchen door was open for the summer heat, and Slater stepped up and poked his head in. Just inside a guy in a dirty butcher's apron was crouching to tie a trash bag closed.

"Daniel?" Slater said.

The guy scowled at him, but turned and called inside, "Daniel."

A minute later, Daniel stepped out. He wasn't very tall, but he looked mostly the same as his ID photo. A plastic-coated apron covered his T-shirt and the front of his baggy old jeans.

"What can I do for you?" he said, giving Slater the once-over.

"Do you have a break coming up? Let me buy you a coffee, and we'll have a chat."

"Who exactly wants to buy me a coffee?"

"I work for an insurance company," Slater said. "You're not in any trouble."

"You don't look like an insurance adjuster. You look like a vaquero."

"I'm neither. I work as an investigator. I have a few questions for you."

"I'm on the day shift," Daniel said. "I have to be here till four."

"They don't give you a break? I'm pretty sure that's against the labor laws."

He studied Slater for a moment. "I guess I could take a couple minutes now. Let me tell the boss."

Ducking inside, he emerged again a minute later, minus the apron. A curvy woman with short dark hair and jeans followed him out.

"How did you get into this alley?" she demanded, eyeing Slater.

"It's public property, sister," Slater said. "Just because you assholes put a gate across it doesn't make it yours."

Her face went red. "I'm calling the cops."

"Go for it. I'm sure they love to listen to the gentrifiers whine about their petty grievances."

"I am not a gentrifier," she snapped.

"Your time would be better spent making sure you don't give ptomaine to any of those vapid rich kids while you're slinging your overpriced hash," Slater said, jabbing a finger at her. "You know they can afford good legal representation."

As he turned to walk away, she shouted after them.

"You'd better be back by the lunch rush, Daniel, or I'll shit-can you."

Once they were out of earshot, approaching the gate to the street, Daniel spoke.

"I guess I'm supposed to be grateful to do hard labor for minimum wage and no benefits."

"At least you can leave whenever you want. In the last gilded age, you wouldn't have had that option."

Slater pushed through the pedestrian door in the gate. Daniel followed him out, letting it slam with a metallic rattle.

"You know, this really is a private alley."

"So sue me," Slater snapped. He pointed out a coffeehouse across the side street, and they walked over.

"What can I get you?" Slater said, as they stepped inside.

"Two fingers of scotch. If they don't have that, an espresso."

At the counter he ordered espresso for both of them, eyeing Daniel in case he tried to leave. But he went to the corner near the window and sat down. Once he had the java in hand, Slater walked over and sat across from him. The lines on his face and his hooded eyes made it look like life had been hard on him.

"How did you find me?" Daniel said.

"The DMV says your address is the hotel down the block. I talked to your roommate. Are you living there long-term?"

"It's transitional housing," he said, sipping at the little espresso cup. "I get vouchers. I've been there about four years."

"That's quite the leisurely transition."

He frowned. "So what do you want with me, cow-boy?"

"I'm looking for a guy named Daniel Martínez. He's about your age, and he's due for a payout on a life insurance policy."

"You have money, and you're looking to give it to me. Horseshit. What do you really want?"

"Were you living in South Gate twenty-seven years ago?"

"Could be. I've definitely lived there before."

"Were you ever married?"

Daniel shifted in his seat. "Here's the deal. I've managed to get sober before. Sometimes for years. I've had some blackout periods—whole chunks of weeks at a time—but I think I'd remember getting married."

"Did you go to college?"

"Do I look like I went to college?"

Slater scoffed and swirled the contents of his cup.

"Who is it that I was supposedly married to?" Daniel said.

"A woman named Carla."

"She sounds foxy. Have you got a picture?"

Slater pulled out his phone and went through the files Della had sent him. When he found Carla's ID photo, he held it toward Daniel.

"I'd tap that," he said, peering at the screen.

"She's dead, so you're a little late. Unless you're into that sort of thing."

"She's the one who left insurance money."

"That's right."

"A lot?"

"Fifteen grand."

"What would I have to do to claim it?"

"Prove your identity," Slater said. "If you can convince the company that you're the guy, they'll cut you a check."

Daniel looked at the table and wrapped his hands around his cup. "I'm sorry to hear about Carla. She was real good to me."

"So you do remember her."

"I was afraid you were a bill collector. Of course I remember her. My beloved wife. We lost each other a long time ago."

"Do you remember a daughter?"

"She had a kid?" His eyes grew wide. "That must have been after we split up. I wish she'd told me. I could have been part of her life." He screwed his eyes shut and covered his mouth with his fist for a moment. "I always wanted a little girl," he croaked.

"You're good," Slater said. "I'll give you that. I can almost feel your pain. The thing is, I know that Daniel Martínez knew he had a daughter."

"So it slipped my mind." He waved a hand. "It's been a lot of years, and I've taken a lot of mind-altering substances. That's like a disability. Brain damage. It's illegal to hold that against me."

"Where did you live with Carla?"

"I already told you that. South Gate."

"Actually, I told you that," Slater said, and folded his arms.

"Have you got the forms to fill out now, or do I need to drop by an office somewhere for the check?"

"How about this—you give me a cheek swab so that I can do a DNA test."

"Why would I agree to that?"

"It would tell me whether you're the kid's father."

"There's no guarantee of that. Carla liked the

fellas. I remember her hanging around the pool hall, and the casino, giving the big eye, showing a bit of leg. She had gams that wouldn't quit." He waved a hand. "There were other men, is all I'm saying."

"And the dead can't defend themselves," Slater said. "If you are the father, a DNA test will prove the payout is for you."

He shook his head. "You'll put me in some database, with my head shot and my shoe size, and the cops will come looking for me every time a laundry-truck driver goes missing."

Slater's eyes narrowed. That was oddly specific.

"I don't work with the police, or any kind of permanent record. I'll test it once anonymously at a lab and throw it away."

"A man's DNA is a private thing," Daniel said. "It's between me and god."

"I'll pay you twenty bucks."

"Show me the money."

Slater dug out his wad and peeled off a twenty, folding it and setting it halfway under the saucer under his cup. From the way Daniel looked at it, he knew he'd already made the sale.

"What do I have to do?"

"Open your mouth," Slater said, "and hold still."

He pulled the test kit out of his pocket and popped it open, then reached across and swirled the cotton tip inside Daniel's cheek.

"Done." He pressed the swab into the tube to seal it, then tucked it into his shirt.

"That hurt," Daniel said. "I want fifty."

"I know that didn't hurt." Slater slurped at his espresso. "And you're a terrible negotiator. You need to talk scratch before the action starts. Now I've already got what I want."

His face clouded, and he reached across and plucked the twenty from under the saucer.

"Whether I'm the father or not, that payout is still mine. It's what my beloved Carly wanted."

"Carla."

"That's what I said." Daniel frowned. "I don't really believe there's any money. Not for me. No one wants to talk to me. Nobody wants to know me."

"Such a heart-rending tale of woe," Slater said. "What about that woman in your room?"

"What about her?"

"Sing, brother," Slater demanded.

"If it matters, she doesn't really put out. She hangs around for the extras. The, uh, chemical benefits."

He leaned back in his chair. "Well, don't sell your-self short. If you had a shower first, I'd probably fuck you."

Daniel scowled. "That's not going to happen." He drained his little cup. "Unless you've got a lot more of that pretty green lettuce in your pants."

"It's kind of like selling tap water in little plastic bottles, Daniel. I can get it for free elsewhere—why would I pay for it?"

SEVEN

SLATER GOT UP, AND went out to the street, and walked back to his car. It wasn't very far to his office, and it took him longer to drive the congested streets than it would have if he'd just walked.

When he finally got upstairs, no one was in. He flicked on the lights, and greeted Rey Pascual with a double-click of his tongue, then grabbed an envelope from Etta's desk. From his wad he riffled four C-notes and tucked them inside, then sat at his own desk to write "chartreuse" on the front. On the sample tube, he wrote "possible parent no. 2." He'd get the test done, but like the jailbird, this guy didn't feel like the right person. Nothing about his story aligned with what Rocky had said about her mother.

Waking his computer, he pulled up what Andy had scraped together about the other candidates. The lawyer named Daniel Martínez had great skin, considering his age, even in the DMV photo, and a money haircut with a touch of salt-and-pepper. He might have had work done, but if he had, it was subtle.

The details about the lawyer said he was a partner at a white-shoe law firm downtown, and he was active in the Filipino Legal Aid Society. He looked at the photo again. This guy could be Filipino, he decided. Lots of Filipinos had Spanish names. Pulling out his phone, he sent Rocky a text:

Is there any chance that Danilo is Filipino?

Her reply came a moment later:

Carla never mentioned that. But she never said otherwise. I've always assumed he's Latin. But it's not impossible. Are you about to give me a whole new ethnicity?

He took a moment to thumb-type a reply:

Not sure yet. More soon.

Leaning back in his chair, he mulled over how he might approach the lawyer. He could always just walk into his office, but the guy was high profile, so at minimum he'd get blocked by a security guard, and have to talk to the guy's legal underlings before he'd have any chance of a meeting.

The door opened in the front office, and he heard Etta's familiar voice.

"Put your pants on."

"Have you got a minute?" he called to her.

"What's going on?" Etta said, stepping in his doorway. She was wearing a red rugby shirt and jeans, with a canvas satchel on her shoulder.

"I might have a job for you."

"Yes," she hissed, and pumped her fist.

"I said 'might.' Sit down."

Etta dropped into the guest chair and scooted it closer to the desk.

"Filipinos have kind of a tight-knit community, right?"

"I know lots of them are serious Catholics," she

said, "so there's the church community. Generally speaking, any visible minority in this town sticks together for safety. It's necessary in the face of decades of xenophobic structural hegemony. My people are from American Samoa, so we're Americans, but you wouldn't know it from the way we're treated."

Slater frowned and waved a hand. "I don't need to get woke right now. I need to get close to a target."

"They're Filipino?"

"I think so. He's active in some Filipino lawyers' group."

"So what are you thinking?"

"Do you know any Filipinos?" Slater said. "Maybe I could connect to him that way, through the community. I want to get a sense of where to find him that's not his office."

"Angelica," Etta said. "She's a colleague at my old school. She's Filipina. I can give her a call."

"Do you think she's dialed in?"

"To the church, definitely. I'll find out if she knows your target. Let me get a pen."

Etta got up and carried her bag into the front office, returning a moment later with a yellow notepad.

"What's the lowdown?"

Slater recited the lawyer's name, and the name of his firm. "He's either fifty-four or fifty-five and he lives in Bel Air. I'll text you his photo."

"I'll see what I can find out," she said, and went back to her desk.

Slater tapped at his phone to send her the lawyer's head shot, then rose and stepped out after her.

"I've got an errand," he told her, "but I'll be back in half an hour or so."

Stepping out into the hallway, he went down to his car and drove to Hyde Park, where he pushed the sample tube and the cash envelope into the slot in Lenore's back door. He heard the faint distant door chime as they dropped into the box.

It felt a little odd to be doing an industrial errand in this tidy urban neighborhood, he thought, glancing around. He paused to inspect the narrow patch of dirt at the base of Lenore's exterior wall. The structure was offset only a foot or so from the sidewalk. Kicking at the earth with his boot, it was hard-packed, and full of alkali, from years of neglect and people pissing on it.

The side door swung open, and Lenore stepped out.

"Slater," she said, and visibly relaxed. "I was just about to ask who was skulking around my back door."

"I just made a drop."

"You're thinking I need to paint that wall, huh."

"You could also cover it with greenery."

"Like ivy?"

"Ivy's for bricks," Slater said. "It's not good for stucco. You could put up a trellis and plant some star jasmine." He waved at the building. "It'll grow to cover this whole wall."

"Does it have those little white flowers?"

"That's the one. It blooms in May and June, and it smells great."

"I'd need a landscaper, though," Lenore said.

"Just hire a gardener, or even a day laborer. Buy a trellis and a couple of starter plants. You'll have to replace this earth, though. It's wrecked. Dig it all out and put in some sandy soil."

"Another time-consuming project."

"Not for you," Slater said. "Hire somebody. It'll be a lot cheaper than paint, and people will stop pissing on your wall."

"Now, that idea, I like. My grandparents bought this building way back when black folks were first able to live in desegregated neighborhoods. They ran a flower shop."

"I can see why you'd want to take care of the place."

"You seem to know what needs to be done. Can I hire you?"

"I wish I had the time right now."

"So maybe you could write down all of what you just said and text it to me."

"Sure." He waved and walked back toward the street, and once he'd climbed behind the wheel of the Thunderbird, headed downtown. Friday traffic was always heavier than the rest of the week, but it was early enough that the freeway was still moving.

Up in the office, Etta was absorbed in her computer screen.

"What did your friend say?" Slater said as he stepped in.

Etta briefly glanced up at him. "Angelica doesn't know your target personally, but she gave me her account login so I could poke around. Teachers are people-oriented, right, and she's friends with a hella lot of them." She gestured to the screen. "I can show you what I found."

Slater went into his office, and rolled his desk chair out, and sat next to her.

"Is this the guy?" She clicked on a photo to enlarge it.

He was wearing sunglasses and smiling, unlike in his DMV photo, but Slater recognized him instantly—that solid jaw, and that haircut.

"That's totally him. Great work."

"He's friends with Angelica, so we can see all his stuff."

"You just told me that she didn't know him."

"Don't you use social media?" She frowned. "You're always friends with a ton of people you don't know."

"That makes no freaking sense. Give me the mouse."

Slater started to scroll through the images and posts, pausing occasionally to read the comments.

"This guy looks like he has money," Etta said.

"I know he does. He's a partner at a flashy law firm."

He paused at the image of a bulbous little aircraft with an odd V-shaped tail, parked on a concrete apron. The lawyer was standing in front of it, holding two thumbs up, a big toothy smile on his face.

"Is that his company's airplane?" Etta said.

Slater read the caption aloud: " 'Baby got delivered from the factory today.' That means he bought it himself."

"It's got a jet engine on the top. I wonder what a thing like that costs?"

"More money than you and I have made in a lifetime."

"It's obscene, that kind of wealth."

Slater scrolled farther, and paused to read more of the posts.

"He seems to love his mama," Etta said. "The younger one with all the eyelashes is his sister."

"So he's family oriented. That might be useful."

"There's not much about his job. Maybe he's not that into it."

"Legal work is all confidential, right? He can't be gossiping about it on here."

Slater paused his scrolling at another photo. The lawyer was stretched out on a narrow bed under a trio of small oval windows. Etta leaned in and read the caption.

"He wrote, 'Not all sleeper seats are created equal.' That's so pretentious. It's a humble-brag. 'Look at me: I fly first-class.'"

"That's really informative too," Slater said.

"How?" she demanded. "We already know he's a rich asshole."

"But if you're born into it, things like first class are the default. You don't need to take photos of it to show your peers."

"Interesting." She leaned back. "So that means he comes from blue-collar origins."

"Or at least not from this level of wealth."

"Why don't we have our own airplanes?" Etta said. "Or at least a company airplane."

"Do you really want to be like this guy?" Slater pointed at a photo of the lawyer standing on skis, poles in hand, with jagged mountaintops in the background. "He's skiing in booty shorts." He read the caption: " 'Skip Zermatt in the summer. Half the lifts are closed. Sad-face emoji.'"

"You're right," she said. "He's a self-important idiot."

He slid the mouse back to her. "Can we look at the mom and the sister?"

Etta spent a minute clicking around. "Mom is tagged in the photos, but she doesn't have an account on here. But the sister has one."

"What's her damage?"

"CeCe. I love that name. She's also one of Angelica's sixty-two hundred friends." She scrolled down the page, pausing to read some of the posts. "Her feed is all wedding stuff."

"Is it aspirational," Slater said, "or she already got married?"

"I think she's going to get married." Etta leaned closer. "Here it is. It's on Saturday. As in tomorrow Saturday."

"Are there details?"

"I think so." She clicked on a link and peered at the screen. "It looks like a big deal. The event is at a 'glamorous dedicated wedding venue overlooking MacArthur Park.'"

Slater leaned in to see the image, taking hold of the mouse. "I know that place. It used to be a hotel. It's a couple blocks from my apartment."

"I can't believe there's a fancy hotel in your neighborhood."

"It's the only nice thing. Unless you count the metro station. They scrub the graffiti off it too."

"You could crash the wedding and talk to her brother."

"You think?" Slater said, his eyes on the screen.

"Stop there." Etta pointed to a post. "CeCe also knows how to humble-brag. 'Too many dear friends. Had to cap the guest list at five hundred.'"

"That's a massive wedding."

"No way does she have that many real friends. You could stroll in there and not even be noticed."

"Do they check invitations?"

"You've been to weddings. That's never happened to me."

"The dinner, though." Slater met her gaze. "Isn't

that usually with assigned seating?"

"It's hard to imagine doing that for five hundred people. Let's see." Etta grabbed the mouse and scrolled down the feed. "You're in the clear. This says it's a buffet."

"That seems a little down-market for these people."

"It doesn't mean the food won't be pretentious." She leaned back. "It's about the size of the crowd. There's too many for assigned seating, so you line up to eat when you want. The demand would be staggered over a few hours instead of all at once."

"It looks like I'm going to a wedding. Etta, you're a genius." He stood up and rolled his chair back into his office.

"That's it?" she called after him. "I thought there'd be actual work. Like tailing a lowlife, or a stakeout."

"Not this time."

"Do you need a beard for the wedding?"

He stepped back out, and leaned on the door frame. "That's actually a good idea."

"I can do it."

"It's black-tie, so you'd have to wear a gown. Like those red-carpet chumps at the awards shows."

Etta pursed her lips. "I might be able to do that."

"When's the last time you wore a skirt?"

"Middle school."

"So there's your answer," Slater said. "It's nothing personal, but I need someone who already knows that world."

"You have an auntie or something who's fluent with the rich?"

"I work with people who are." He stood erect. "Listen, you can brief me on what to expect. Some of the names. Especially the key players. Pick someone

I can claim to be related to."

"And you'll pay me?"

"Of course. Add in the work you just did on Angelica's social media."

Etta's brow furrowed. "So a package deal for the research and the access. Say, a dollar?"

"Done." Slater pulled out his wad, and peeled off a C-note, and handed it to her.

"You're very trusting. I haven't done everything yet."

"I know where you work," he said, and walked out.

EIGHT

T HE TRAFFIC WAS HEAVY when Slater nosed the Thunderbird into the street. He drove to the Financial District, and the tower that housed Cudahy Mutual's offices, and pulled into the underground garage.

When he got upstairs to 34, nobody was on Crystal's desk, and he walked through to the hallway and Della's office. Her door was closed, so he rapped on it.

"Enter," Della's voice called.

When he stepped in, she sat up, her brow furrowing.

"You should have called."

"Are you busy right now?"

Della leaned back, and her face softened as her eyes flicked over him. "I'm never too busy for a full view of you."

"Did you finally have to fire your guard dog?" he said, dropping into the chair in front of her desk.

"I'm sure she's around somewhere. Any progress on Daniel Martínez?"

"I'm making headway. Nothing to report yet, but one of the Daniels who fits the profile is a little hard to get to."

"He's in prison?"

"I talked to one in prison yesterday. It wasn't him. This guy is different—insulated by money rather than steel bars."

"That sounds intriguing."

"His sister is getting married tomorrow evening. I'm going to crash the event and try to talk to him. I'll have a better chance of blending into that world if I have a beautiful woman on my arm."

Della inhaled sharply. "You need a date?"

"Weddings are fun, right?"

"They can be. Are you sure you don't need an invitation?"

"There are five hundred invited guests."

Della nodded. "That's an easy crash. Is it black-tie?"

"That's right."

"I have a dress that'll work, but I'll need to get my hair done." She sat up. "What will I have to do?"

"I'm not sure what the dynamics will be like," Slater said. "Maybe you can help me get close to the guy. You know how to work people."

"That's not really a rare skill. You know how to work with people too."

"I know how to work people over. That's a whole different thing."

"True enough." She swiveled absently in her chair. "You know I'm not going to say no to a night out with you."

"I can pay you for your time."

Della waved dismissively. "I can't take money from you when you're working a case for me."

"Do you want me to pick you up?"

"You can meet me here," she said.

They talked about the timing, and Della asked a few questions about the event, and eventually Slater rose to leave. Still no Crystal, he saw, walking through the front office.

Once he was down in the garage, and behind the wheel of his car, he texted Andy:

Still on for tonight? What time?

His reply came a minute later:

Kyle and I are just eating. Be at my place in an hour or so.

Slater sat there for a while, imagining them dining out, laughing at each other's stupid jokes, all fresh-faced and sweaty and flirty. He texted back:

Thanks for the dinner invite.

Andy's response came quickly:

Would you have come if I'd asked you?

He started the engine, then thumb-typed his answer:

I'll be there after eight.

Cruising up the ramp onto the street, Slater drove to his neighborhood and parked near his local *pupusería*. The owner had given him the statue of Rey Pascual for his office, and he chatted with her for a minute at the little window when he ordered. He always struggled to understand her idiosyncratic mix of English and Spanish, and today she kept the interaction mercifully short, as there were other people waiting.

Once he had his *pupusas*, he sat on a stool at the

counter that ran along the outside of the little building to eat them. After he'd finished he drove to his apartment, and took a shower, then stretched out on his sofa with his arm over his eyes.

Sometime later, he was roused from dozing by the buzz of his phone. He scooped it up from the carpet and squinted at the screen. It was a text from Lenore:

Sample 2 is not a match.

So that eliminated the local. He was just a grifter—everything he'd said about knowing Carla was a damn lie.

Forcing himself to sit up before he drifted off again, Slater got up, and put on a clean shirt, and went down to his garage. Twilight was setting in as he cruised into downtown, and the traffic was finally easing up. He parked behind Andy's building and went up to knock on his door.

When Andy pulled it open, he waved him in.

"Did you find the right Daniel Martínez yet?"

Slater followed him inside, and saw that Kyle was standing near the little table under the windows. He was still in his twenties, maybe, and lithe, and had great hair. Slater gave him the once-over and then ignored him.

"The DNA tests eliminated the jailbird and the local," he told Andy. "I'm working on the lawyer next. How was your romantic dinner?"

"You wouldn't have come if we'd asked you," Kyle said, "so stop acting hurt."

"You want hurt?" Slater demanded. "I can put the hurt on you, twink."

Standing by his desk, Andy spoke sharply. "Slater—chill."

"It's like violence is your go-to reaction," Kyle said.

"I'd say it's more like you bring it out in me. I respect Andy too much to do anything about it, though." He gestured widely. "I can't just punch you in the face, or lock you in the trunk of your car and roll it off a cliff in the Palisades."

Kyle jutted his chin. "All the smack talk. You're like the villain in a Saturday-morning cartoon."

"And you're like a fancy vanilla cupcake. It comes in a sweet little package, but ultimately I just wind up feeling nauseated."

"Slater," Andy snapped. "Boots off."

Andy had his shirt off already, and ditched his shorts, and dropped onto the bed. Kyle didn't hesitate to get undressed, and as he crouched to untie his boots, Slater kept an eye on him. The guy had a great body, lean and taut.

As Slater rose to take his jeans off, Kyle stretched out next to Andy, folding his knee between his legs, and kissed him. Once Slater was naked too he went to the other side of the bed, and shifted close to Andy, pressing his nose into his hair and reaching for his cock. He was already totally hard. This really was a turn-on for Andy, just having them both here, both in his bed. Running his hand over Andy's body, he started to get hard himself.

"Slater is feeling left out," Andy said, "so he's going in the middle."

"I never said that."

"You sort of did."

"Well, it wasn't for public broadcast," Slater said, and scoffed.

Kyle got up, and walked around the bed, and

climbed on beside him, running his warm hands along Slater's thighs, and then his torso, grasping his chest as he pulled himself closer. Slater focused on Andy, mouthing his jaw and stroking his cock. Soon he could feel Kyle probing him, gently at first. He half turned to him.

"You'd better be wearing a condom."

Kyle slowly pressed into him. It felt tentative, unsure. Slater winced at the intensity of it but focused on Andy, mouthing his neck and feeling his skin. Andy had an iron grip on his cock.

Behind him, Kyle was building up speed, and acting more confident now. He could hear him breathing hard, and grunting, and then he said, "Psycho."

"I can't hear you, son," Slater said. "What are you mumbling about?"

"You're a psycho," Kyle said, louder now.

Andy leaned over him to meet Kyle's mouth, still stroking Slater. Slater grabbed his cock, and mouthed his chest. Kyle put an arm around his neck, squeezing tighter on his collarbone as he pounded him.

"Fuck you, you fucking psycho," he growled, straining into him as he climaxed.

That was enough to make Slater come, with his mouth on Andy's, and a moment later Andy came too.

Lying between them, catching his breath, Slater could feel all the tension ebbing away. For some reason it was different this time. Like he didn't want to leave this position. Like the warmth of their bodies was magnetic.

"That was amazing," Andy said.

A while later Kyle got up and went into the bathroom. Slater heard the shower go on. Andy followed him in a minute later, and when they both came out, Slater went in to towel off. When he stepped out again, the two of them were intertwined on the bed, Kyle behind Andy, an arm draped protectively across his chest. Andy's eyes were closed, but neither of them was asleep.

Slater picked up his shirt, and pulled it on, and noticed that Kyle was watching him now.

"That was pretty hot, Kyle. You're getting better at this. I'd rate you a solid B-plus."

"Fuck you."

"You did that already."

"You don't have to go," Andy said.

"I'll leave the romantic part to you two." He stepped into his jeans.

"Are you still interested in Galliform?" Andy said. "I got some … intel on that guy."

"How did you manage that?"

"I left some digital soup cans in his website."

Slater frowned as he pulled on his boots. "Soup cans?"

"It's a low-tech intruder alarm. You stack empty soup cans inside your door, and when someone comes in, you'll hear it."

"So Galliform is active again."

"He did something stupid for … half a minute and exposed his IP address. I traced it to the public library in a … little town in New Mexico."

"When did that happen?"

"Earlier today."

"Interesting. Can you text me whatever details you've got?"

"Do you think we should tell the police?" Andy said.

Slater squatted to tie his bootlaces. "Let me talk to Conrad. I'll try to find out what the detectives know."

"The feds are after him too, aren't they? I really … don't want to deal with them unless I have no choice."

"Why not?" Kyle said, his brow furrowing.

"I'd rather not have to explain my … research methods to them. Occasionally I wander into some gray areas. You can't lie to the feds."

"If they don't already know what you know," Slater said, "I'll pass it along anonymously. Conrad won't burn me as his source."

"You two sound like stone-cold spies," Kyle said.

Slater put his hands on his hips. "It's grown-up stuff, Kyle. Real jobs. Not everyone has a trust fund."

Before he had time to formulate a retort, Slater walked out, and went down to his car, and drove to his apartment, waiting in the garage until the heavy door rolled down.

It wasn't even that late. Upstairs he pulled the fifth from the cupboard, and poured the last of it into a tumbler. It wasn't quite his full ration, so he slammed it, relishing the warm heady fumes, then cracked open the empty's twin and poured himself another finger.

"Restraint," he muttered to himself, and put the fresh bottle in the cupboard, out of sight, and took the tumbler over to the sofa, where he sat and untied his boots.

Stretching out, he set the glass on the carpet and looked at his phone. Talking about Conrad just now had got him thinking. He opened the tracking app to check on his location. When they'd still been together, before Conrad had thrown him out like a sack of hot garbage, Slater had managed to put a tracker on his cell phone. It wasn't stalking, as he had a legitimate need to know where the guy was sometimes. It was his own stupid fault for letting his guard down enough that Slater could do it. You'd think a cop would be a little more guarded. Seriously, what a moron.

The green dot on the map showed that he was at home, way out in the Valley. Now that he'd been promoted to detective, he didn't usually work late, and he never worked the swing shift anymore. The idiot was probably sitting on his couch playing video games, or fucking some sweaty Valley boy.

Killing the app, he took a deep breath. A minute ago a text had come from Andy:

> Galliform was using an internet connection at the public library in Voirrey's Corner, New Mexico, this morning. That's all the info I got.

He traded the phone for the tumbler on the carpet and sipped at the bourbon. It was compelling, being with Kyle and Andy together, and he felt more wiped out than usual. Pushing himself to get up, he drained the glass and went to get into bed.

NINE

B RIGHT DAYLIGHT STREAMED IN the window above his futon when Slater woke. He didn't bother to check his phone for late-night outgoing calls because he knew he hadn't made any—it was a vanishingly rare event, but he actually remembered going to bed last night.

Once he'd made a mug of ersatz coffee, he downed most of it and got dressed, then trotted down the stairs to his garage. Doris's place was straight up the 110 in hilly Mount Washington, and soon he was cruising into her neighborhood, and pulled up on her house.

Doris's Buick was in the driveway, and thankfully her stupid boyfriend's stupid Boxster wasn't. That guy was here way too much, and it took every shred of Slater's willpower not to punch his smarmy face.

Parked at the curb was a familiar-looking SUV. That was Conrad's rig. What was that idiot dick-smack doing here? So far Slater had managed to avoid the issue, but if it ever turned out that he got committed to involuntary rehab, he knew it would be these two conspiring against him, Doris and Conrad, setting him up and shipping him off to the hippies.

Climbing out of the Thunderbird, he walked around to the side gate and into the backyard. The pair of them were out here, sitting on the patio chairs, with a pitcher and glasses on the table between them. Conrad was wearing a sheer raw-cotton top that flattered his chest, and he'd let his hair grow out a little. It made him look less like a beat cop. The black hair, and the square jaw, and the barrel chest—he was such a beautiful man.

Doris looked tiny in comparison to his big mooky frame. She was dressed for Saturday, in shorts and a billowy blouse, with her dark hair tied loosely back.

"Look what the cat dragged in," Conrad said, a silly grin on his face, as Slater walked toward them.

"What the hell are you doing here?" Slater demanded.

"He was invited to brunch," Doris said. "So were you. You've missed the eating part."

"You never invited me."

"I texted you several days ago. I imagine you didn't even read it."

Slater stood with his hands on his hips. "That's easy enough to verify. I think I'd remember if you'd mentioned the goon squad was going to be here."

"Well, you're here now. We're having mimosas." She waved toward the back door of the house. "Grab a glass and join us."

"I was going to deadhead the roses, and maybe work on the hydrangeas."

"They can wait a few minutes," she said. "Go get a glass."

Slater huffed and went into the kitchen, and found a flute like the ones they were drinking from, and walked back out. Doris poured into it from the pitcher as he sat across from them.

"You can act as charming as you want," Slater said, eyeing Conrad. "There's nothing to steal."

"Stop it," Doris said firmly.

Conrad scoffed. "You can be such a dick sometimes."

"Conrad was telling me about his new job," Doris said.

"Detective. I heard. Eventually."

"It sounds a lot like what you do," she said.

"It's similar, I guess." Slater reached for his mimosa. "Although what I do takes brains."

Conrad's brow furrowed. "How do you manage it, then?"

Doris gestured with her glass. "I heard your work overlapped recently."

"You told her about the cell-tower vandal?"

"It's such a crazy story," Conrad said.

"He said you're the one who cracked the case," Doris said. "You were the anonymous informant."

"I got lucky. I happened to interview the perp about another case, and she babbled about everything she'd done."

"But she wasn't the mastermind, was she?" Doris said. "That was someone else."

"His name is Galliform," Conrad said. "He manipulated Slater's contact into destroying the antennas, and even sold her the explosives to do it." He looked to Slater. "Guess what? He's finally surfaced. Just yesterday."

"Did you catch him?"

"We will. He's in New Mexico. It's still an unconfirmed report, but it seems that he got sloppy. The feds are on it."

"What town is he in?" Slater said.

"I totally don't remember." Conrad frowned. "I didn't know the name. It's a small place. Somebody's corner."

"I hope they nab him soon. That guy is nuts."

"The feds put up reward money for getting him. A hundred grand."

"That's serious money," Doris said. "They must really want him."

"Oh, yeah." Conrad picked up his glass. "He's dangerous. The crackpot conspiracy theories, and tricking other people into acting on them, and selling explosives."

"I suppose catching him is a priority because people like that tend to escalate," Doris said.

"Very good." Conrad sat up and tapped his glass on hers. "You could come work for us."

Doris tittered at that, and Slater glared at him. He hated that he was so good with her. Watching them interact made his heart pound. Conrad was like the son she'd never had, the man Slater would never be.

"What are you working on these days, sweetheart?" she said.

He took a breath. "An insurance case. I'm trying to find out if a beneficiary is still alive."

"I thought those companies just surrendered the money to the state when they couldn't find someone."

"That's what usually happens." Slater shifted in his chair. "There are two beneficiaries on this policy, and one of them is waiting on a payout. The company needs me to do a cursory search before they split the money or give it all to the one they know about. She hired me to find him too—the one who's missing is her father."

"So the money is her mother's life insurance."

"Conrad's right—you could join the detective bureau."

"Things change when someone dies," Doris said. "Priorities change. Like when your father died."

"I think that's why she wants to find him now," Slater said. "Otherwise she's an orphan."

"It sounds like you're double dipping," Conrad said.

Before he could hurl a retort, Doris said, "I know you better than that."

Slater could feel his face heating up, and he struggled to keep his tone civil. "The insurance company is only paying me for a few days of research. After that, if I haven't found the guy, I'll bill her. Right now she's only on the hook to finance the DNA tests."

"So you've found some candidates," Doris said.

"I've eliminated a few already. I'm going to crash a wedding tonight to meet number three."

"You know, you never really talk about your dad," Conrad said.

"He was a wonderful man." Doris hoisted her glass. "The absolute best."

"But he ditched us," Slater said.

"That wasn't his choice." Doris waved to dismiss it, and sat up to refill their glasses with more mimosa. She nodded toward the landscaping. "Conrad asked why you let weeds grow between the beds."

"They're not really weeds. I put them there intentionally. Native plants have plain little flowers that attract a variety of insects. The showy ornamentals don't do that."

"And variety is better?" Conrad said.

"For biodiversity, always. Think of it like what you

eat. You need more than one or two kinds of food to be healthy."

They chatted some more, and Conrad helped carry the glasses inside, then gave Doris a hug and a kiss on the cheek. Watching them, Slater had to grit his teeth, infuriated at how close they were. Conrad had dumped him like radioactive waste but he stayed connected to her like a cherished relative.

Once they'd said their good-byes, Conrad stepped out the front door, and Slater followed him out to the driveway.

"You still have time for gardening," Conrad said, "even when you're on a case?"

"I need to get my hands dirty once in a while."

"Literally, rather than metaphorically, like in your job."

Slater waved an arm. "I think one balances out the other."

"Do you need help with the roses?"

"Save your strength for your video games," he said, and walked to the side gate.

In the backyard shed, he pulled on a pair of work gloves, and grabbed the pruning shears, and set to work, rapidly deadheading the rosebushes. They were still blooming well despite the hotter days. Personally he was indifferent about roses, but Doris loved them, so he took care of these.

Once he'd raked up the detritus and dumped it in the green can, he found the bag of lime pellets in the shed, and carried it over to the hydrangea bushes. They had a few healthy violet-blue blooms. He spent a few minutes with a trowel, massaging pellets into the earth around some of the plants. Eventually he got the hose to soak the ground, then cleaned up and put everything away.

Stepping up to the back door to the house, he hailed Doris through the screen.

"I think I'm finished."

Doris stepped outside. "It looks lovely out here. You take such good care of it. My girlfriends always want to come here when we get together."

"If you're enjoying it, that means it's worth the effort."

"What were you doing to the hydrangeas?"

"I made the soil more alkaline for some of them. The next round of blooms should be pink."

"All of them?"

"About half. You should get both pink and violet."

"How fun is that?" She squeezed his arm. "Do you want to stay for dinner?"

"I'm working."

"I remember. A wedding. Hold on a minute." She stepped inside, and returned a moment later, pushing open the screen door to hand him a paperback. "Can you take this to Andy?"

"That seems so suspicious," Slater said, his brow furrowing as he glanced at the book. "What are you two plotting?"

"Not everything is about you. It's my instinct as an educator. We were talking about the pueblo era, and I told him I had a book."

Slater stifled his dubious retort and leaned in to kiss her. "Love you."

Walking out through the side gate, he climbed into the Thunderbird and tossed the book on the passenger seat, next to the paper bag of DNA sample kits.

On the drive back to Westlake he thought about

Doris's connection to the people in his life. Would she rather have Andy as a son, so they could talk about books? Or Conrad—he was so calm all the time, so level-headed, and never blew his top. Such a freaking dick-smack. He had a decent job, and good manners, and was smart enough to know that Slater was bad news. Why was all that so annoying?

Once he was up in his apartment, he spent some time at the bathroom mirror shaving and working some product into his hair. It was too late to get a money haircut, like the upmarket lawyer and trash-bag Kyle, but at least he could make it look less Skid Row.

In his closet he found the garment bag with his tuxedo in it, and zipped it open to make sure the bow tie and the belt were in there, and the shoes that went with it. Zipping it up again, he carried the bag down the stairs, and hung the hanger loop on the hook behind the driver's seat in the Thunderbird.

Backing into the alley, he waited for the garage door to roll down, then drove to his office. The attendant at the little booth waved to him from across the parking lot. They knew his distinctive vehicle, and didn't bother to check his parking pass, as long as he bought one every month.

Slater took a sample tube from the paper bag, then climbed out and slung the garment bag over his shoulder and headed across the street. Even though the factories were still running, the building was quieter today than during the week, and the day laborers had already cleared out.

When he stepped into the office, Etta was on the front desk. He hung the garment bag on the coat rack in the corner.

"That's your suit?" Etta said. "You have to show me."

"When I put it on."

"What's in the bottom of the bag?"

Slater frowned. "What?"

"You put your shoes in there, didn't you."

"So what?"

She frowned as she got up and stepped over to zip open the bag, pulling out the shoes and setting them on the floor. Tucking the bag behind the suit, she felt the fabric.

"I love the color," she said. "Midnight blue is so sharp."

Slater tucked the sample tube into the jacket pocket. "Are you going to brief me on the wedding?"

Etta went back to sit at the desk. "I did some research. You can say you're the groom's cousin. He has dozens of them. No one will be keeping track of them all except the family elders. So steer clear of them."

"That works. What's the groom's name?"

"Arturo." Etta peered at the computer screen and clicked the mouse. "I also found an article on Filipino wedding traditions."

"Let's hear it."

"First, don't wear white. It's only for the bride."

"I've got that one covered," Slater said.

"Don't dress slutty."

"Good thing I left the harness and the chaps at home."

Her eyes narrowed. "You have assless chaps?"

"Don't ask, don't tell, Etta." He put his hands on his hips. "And chaps are assless by definition."

She scoffed and looked back at the screen. "Most

Filipinos are Catholic, and Catholic wedding ceremonies last at least an hour."

"Oh, joy."

"A ceremonial cord is wrapped around the couple in a figure-eight."

"OK, I get that you're earning your pay, but I don't think I'm going to need to know that."

Etta sat back. "Then the rest should be self-explanatory."

Turning to the garment bag, Slater reached behind the jacket, and pulled the white shirt from its hanger, then started to unbutton the shirt he was wearing. Eyeing Etta, he hesitated.

"Do you want me to go into my office?"

She waggled a finger at him. "You ain't got nothin' I ain't seen before, son. And more significantly, you don't have anything that'll ring my bell. I've got a smoking-hot woman at home for that."

"Safiya, right? Is she hot?" Slater unbuttoned his shirt and pulled the tails out of his jeans. "I saw her that one time, but I don't remember."

"Oh, she's hot, all right. Good thing you didn't get too close. She would have set your hair on fire."

"I guess I can't really detect hotness in women."

Etta cackled. "Bullshit. Although I am impressed that you remembered her name."

He pulled on the white shirt, with its stiff wings at the collar, and did up the buttons, made to look like studs. He draped the black ribbon of bow tie around his collar.

"Do you know how to tie a bow tie?" he said.

"Not a clue."

"I wish Max was here." He squatted to untie his boots.

"He's on his way in now. We're doing a debrief."

"Nice—you finished up that window-shade job?"

"I think so. He'll let me know if there's more on it."

As Slater stepped out of his jeans, Etta whistled. "Such cute little underpants."

He shot her a look. "I thought I didn't have anything of interest to you."

"They're cute in the way that my seventh-graders are cute."

"The way I remember seventh grade, nothing was really cute. It was more like a cage match with no referees."

He pulled on the tuxedo pants, and threaded the belt into the loops. They felt so thin and sheer. Next he pulled on the jacket, shrugging to get it positioned right. Etta stood up to look him over.

"You look great," she said. "The cut is perfect for you."

"I'm lucky it still fits."

Once he'd pulled the shoes on, and squatted to tie them, he took a few tentative steps across the small office.

"The shoes work," Etta said.

"They're so light. Almost like socks. I feel kind of naked."

"It's a wedding, right? You're not going to have to kick anyone's ass."

"You're optimistic. I'm not so sure."

The door swung open, and Max stepped in. He was wearing his gray suit with a yellow necktie loose at the collar.

"Who died?" Max said. "I never see you in a suit."

"I'm crashing a wedding so I can talk to my target.

I need your assistance with the bow tie."

"Didn't I teach you how to do that once?"

"It's one of those things. If you don't practice, it evaporates."

"Turn around," Max said.

Once Slater was facing away from him, he reached around his neck, flipping his collar up and pulling the bow tie into position.

"How do you know how to tie a bow tie?" Etta said. "It seems more like a skill for fancy fellows."

"I've needed to wear one when I worked as a bodyguard for clients going to high-end parties, and a few gigs as security at red-carpet events." Once he'd knotted the black ribbon, Max said, "Turn around."

Facing Slater, he adjusted the bow, then stepped back.

"Well?" Slater said, spreading his arms.

"You look like a hundred bucks," Etta said.

Slater frowned at her. "Such an ardent compliment."

Max chuckled. "Are you taking a date?"

"Della from Cudahy Mutual."

"That's a great idea. She's a real hot tomato."

"That hardly sounds sexist at all," Etta said.

"He's right, though," Slater said. "She's the kind of woman who gets her hair styled twice a month, and has formal gowns just hanging in the closet, and seven different twin sets, and a clutch that cost more than your car to match each one."

"She's also competent in her career," Max said, "and we all know that's much more important than her physical attributes."

"It's too late, man," Etta said. "The hot tomato is out of the bag."

"She knows how to schmooze with rich people," Slater said. "Plus she has an amazing rack for her age. Straight guys kind of get hypnotized. That's exactly the definition of a hot tomato."

"I want to say I expect more from you, Slater, but to be honest, I don't." She eyed Max. "You, on the other hand—would you call a man a hot tomato?"

Max pursed his lips for a moment. "I guess not. I can see that it's a little sexist."

"Thank you," she said emphatically.

"I know lots of men who are hot tomatoes," Slater said. "Way more than women."

Etta reached over and patted his shoulder. "We know."

"I really don't even see gender," he said. "It just doesn't register."

"Wow." She shook her head. "That transcends your blind spots and the little lies you tell yourself. It's just a straight-up barefaced lie."

Slater had to chuckle at that.

"Step into the mustard suite for a minute," Max said. "Both of you."

He walked into his office, and dropped into his desk chair, and Slater and Etta followed him. Max pulled a bottle out of the bottom drawer along with three little glasses.

"That looks like the good stuff," Etta said, as she sat across from him.

"What are we celebrating?" Slater said.

Max unscrewed the cap with a big meaty hand. "A landmark achievement by our number-one operative."

As he poured a finger of scotch into each of the glasses, Slater eyed Etta.

"What did you do?"

She was grinning. "You mean tailing the wife?"

"Etta maintained a tail for the whole day and never got made," Max said, sliding a glass toward each of them. "Through freeways and shopping malls and a suburban condo complex. She tailed her right to the boyfriend's front door."

"Nice," Slater said.

They tapped glasses, and drank, and Max eyed her.

"You did good, kid."

"I appreciate the recognition. I think part of it is the Prius. There's a lot of them on the road. It kind of blends in."

"You tailed her on foot too," Max said. "That takes skill."

"I wish it made fiscal sense for me to do this full-time."

He waved a hand. "You'll have school holidays, and weekends."

"Teachers only work till two o'clock, don't they?" Slater said. "It's like a half-time job anyway."

"You said yourself a middle-school classroom is like a cage match. There's forty combatants, and I'm the only referee." She sipped at her glass. "I should probably thank you guys for letting me work here, and learn the craft."

"It benefits us too," Max said, and waved at the walls. "We got paint."

"You're getting used to the yellow?" Slater said.

Max leaned back and looked around the room. "It feels right. Like it's always been this way."

They chatted for a while, and eventually Slater slammed the last of his scotch and excused himself.

$\mathbf{S}$LATER DIDN'T WANT TO take his car, and Della's building was too far to walk, so he headed toward the metro station. Even wearing the suit jacket, it felt a lot breezier walking around in this getup than in his usual jeans and boots.

When the train pulled in, the car was a little crowded, so he stood in the aisle near the doors. As it started moving he reached for the pole overhead to steady himself. Sitting on the bench in front of him, Slater noticed a teenager, earbuds in his ears, gazing absently at his crotch. He had that faraway look of longing in his eyes. These trousers were flattering, Slater knew. And he remembered how intense desire felt at that age.

The kid must have sensed Slater's gaze, because he looked up at him, and his face went red. He quickly looked down at his phone screen. Slater gestured for him to pull out his earbuds.

"How old are you?" Slater said.

"Seventeen," he said, meeting his gaze. "Why?"

"No reason."

"What's with the suit?"

"I've got a wedding later."

He grinned, and slipped his earbuds back in, and looked at his phone.

From the station in the Financial District it was just a few minutes' walk to the tower where Della's office was. The neighborhood was completely dead on Saturday evening, and as he walked into the lobby and headed for the elevators, the security guard hailed him from the desk.

"Is your name Ibáñez?"

"That's right."

"I'll have to unlock the elevator for you." He ambled toward him, his gait unsteady, his boots echoing on the polished floor. "Security is a little tighter on the weekends."

"I get it," Slater said.

At least he was armed—without a weapon, this guy couldn't fend off a stiff breeze. He twisted a key in the lock next to the call buttons, and the door rolled open, and Slater rode up to Della's floor. The lights in the outer office were out, but her door was open.

Della was wearing a brick-red dress, cut low to emphasize her cleavage, and snug at the waist. Jewelry sparkled at her neck and her ears. Her hair was different too, styled back and lower.

"You look amazing," he said, stepping in. "You're going to outshine the bride."

Della beamed and flipped her hair. "There's no chance of that in a crowd of five hundred. Do you think the diamonds are too much? I could take it down a notch."

Slater put his hands on his hips. "Once the burrito is rolled, you don't start pulling things out of it."

Her eyes narrowed. "You're comparing me to a burrito."

"To a really good one. Like from that place in the market." He waved an arm. "You're absolutely perfect. Why would you want to change anything?"

"Such sweet words. Why couldn't you be straight?"

"If I were, I wouldn't have that kind of objectivity. And it's not sweet talk—just the facts. You'll have the attention of all the straight guys. Unless the bride has a rack too."

Della adjusted her breasts, pushing them up with both hands. "I have to admit, these have been a life-long asset."

"Are they real?"

"Of course they're real." She mock-slapped his arm. "I paid good money for these."

"I can't even tell. You totally didn't overdo it."

"In the entertainment industry, these would be considered modest. The rule of thumb on the West-side is that as long as you can still reach the steering wheel, they're not too big."

"*Viva el plástico,*" Slater said. "Should we go?"

"Are you driving?"

"My car is too distinctive. I figured I'd call a ride-share."

"That makes sense. We want to blend in, not stand out."

Once he'd pulled out his phone and summoned a car, Della scooped up a little clutch that matched her dress, and locked her office, and they walked to the elevator. As they stepped off in the lobby, Della lifted her elbow and looked at him. It took a moment for Slater to realize he was supposed to take her arm.

As they crossed the lobby to the street, Della called to the security guard: "Good night, Ernie."

"You're a vision," he said.

When the car arrived, Slater opened the rear door for her, and waited while she gathered her dress, then closed it and stepped around to the other side. Once they were rolling, Slater pulled up the photo of the lawyer that Andy had found, and held it toward her.

"This is the guy."

"He's easy on the eyes, at least," she said. "I'll be on the lookout."

It was a short ride to the venue, but a lot of vehicles were lined up along the street in front, and it took a few minutes to get close. Eventually the driver double-parked, and Slater handed him a fin before he hopped out.

"Most people just tip through the app," Della said, taking his arm as she stepped out of the car.

"That means Silicon Valley gets to decide how much of it the driver gets. With cash, it's my decision."

There were several sets of big double doors propped open for the guests to enter. Stationed at each was a guy in a black tux, watching the crowd stream past. They were definitely security, with wired earpieces, and standing in what Conrad called the fig-leaf stance, with their feet apart and hands folded over their junk.

Far too many people were walking in for them to check invitations. All they could do was eyeball everyone to look for trouble and make sure no homeless people wandered in. With MacArthur Park nearby, the neighborhood was rife with them.

With Della on his arm, he walked past the sentries, not even meriting a second glance. The reception space was in a wide courtyard under the open sky. The sun was already below the roofline, but it was still light out, and warm enough.

A bar was set up at one side, and they joined the line. Slater surveyed the crowd. It was eclectic, in terms of the age range and the riot of ethnicities. At least CeCe's friends were diverse. There was no sign of the lawyer. When they got to the bar, one of the harried bartenders eyed Della.

"A pink champagne cocktail," she said. "If you can't do that, Jack on the rocks."

The guy nodded and turned around to the array of bottles.

Slater chuckled. "You're a complex woman."

"I know what I like."

When the bartender queried Slater, he said, "Do you have chartreuse?"

"On ice?"

"Just neat."

Once they both had their drinks in hand, they walked over to the side of the courtyard, between the bar and the entrance.

"What are you drinking?" she said, eyeing his glass.

He handed her the tumbler. "Try it."

She took a sip and wrinkled her nose. "It tastes like distilled yard trimmings."

"It's called chartreuse. I guess it is a little herbaceous."

"Chartreuse is for tennis balls, sweetie."

This was a good vantage point, he realized, scanning the crowd. He could see who was coming in, and he could watch the slow-moving bar line. People had dressed up, in tuxes and gowns and some wild artistic outfits. It was hard to gauge from appearances alone, but not everyone here was from money.

"Any sign of your man?" Della said.

"I haven't seen him yet."

"If the bride is his sister, he might be in the wedding party. That means he won't appear until after the ceremony."

A woman with a tray of hors d'oeuvres came by and paused. Della took one, but Slater didn't, after a cursory glance, as it looked like cod roe on crackers.

Eventually a chirpy voice came over the speakers, summoning everyone inside for the ceremony. The crowd started to move, and when they got into the hall, it definitely looked big enough to fit five hundred of the bride's closest personal friends. The ceiling was high and airy, and there were long rows of bench seats. They found a place to sit near the side. As Etta had promised, the ceremony was interminably long. The wedding party didn't include the lawyer, and Slater was too far back to see who was sitting in the front rows.

When it was finally over, the crowd started to drift back outside into the courtyard. The sky was gray with the last dregs of twilight. Big round tables and chairs were set up in the space now, and along the wall opposite the bar was a long buffet, with white-jacketed staffers standing behind it, ready to serve food.

Della stood where they'd been earlier, and while they made small talk, they both scanned the crowd. When he caught sight of the lawyer, his heart started to pound. He was wearing a black suit, like so many others, but he knew that face. He was taller than the people he was with, and his hair had a little loose curl in front. It looked casual, and incidental, but he'd probably spent some serious dough on a stylist to make it look precisely that way.

"There's my target," Slater said quietly.

"Can I look?"

"He's talking to the woman in green."

Della turned casually and surveyed the crowd.

"He's a long drink of water. Hotter than his photo. Do you want me to wander over there?"

"He's pretty intent in his conversation. Let's watch him for a minute."

Eventually the lawyer stepped away from the people he'd been talking to, and as he did, his smile quickly faded. A few steps later, when someone else in the crowd intercepted him, his face lit up again.

"OK," Della said quietly.

"What are you seeing?"

"The way he's handling people. It reveals a lot."

"Enlighten me."

"The congenial chitchat, and backslapping that man, and air-kissing those women. It's work. Lots of these people are his relatives, aren't they? He's doing his duty. Living up to his family obligations."

"That's a great insight," Slater said. "I knew there was a reason you needed to be here."

"I think he's headed to the buffet." Della grasped his forearm. "You should get in line with him. There are so many people here—it should be easy to get close."

"Great idea. Are you coming with?"

"It'll be easier for you if I don't," she said. "Fly free, little bird."

Slater stepped quickly through the crowd, maneuvering around people and squeezing between them. When he got close to the lawyer he slowed his pace. Della was right—he was headed for the chow line. Not too many people had done that yet. Stepping close, Slater moved in behind him.

When they got to the start of the table, the lawyer picked up a plate from the stack. He glanced at Slater, and handed it to him, then picked up another for himself.

"I almost filled up on the snacks beforehand," Slater said. "But then that priest kept yammering."

"You can't make a meal out of canapés," he said. "This is a whole smorg."

"Is that what rich folks call a buffet?"

His eyebrows shot up. "It's what Scandinavians call a buffet. In this case it's a euphemism for a cold buffet."

"Got it."

The lawyer took a step as the line slowly moved along the table. "Which side are you on?"

"I don't really follow sports," Slater said. "Baseball games can be fun, though, if you have the patience for that parking lot."

His eyes narrowed. "I meant, which family."

"I know. That was an obtuse attempt at a joke." Slater waved with his free hand. "I'm a cousin of Arturo's. What about you?"

"The bride is my sister."

"CeCe looked really beautiful in there."

"She should, after what she spent on that dress," he said. "And she was in hair and makeup most of the day."

"I get why people go all out on the first one."

He chuckled. "The first one?"

"Has she been married before?"

"No, this is indeed the first one. Although I understand why you'd ask, seeing as she's in her forties."

"I wouldn't have known that," Slater said. "I

was more focused on the groom and his sweet little caboose. I wonder if he had the jacket tailored to emphasize it."

"I'm sure of it," the lawyer said, not missing a beat. He nodded for the white-jacketed server to put a stack of pinky-brown cold cuts on his plate.

"I guess if I had that body, I'd want to flaunt it too," Slater said.

He leaned back and subtly looked him over. "You do have that body. Almost. You're less gym, though. More real world."

"That gym look is easy on the eyes."

"Isn't he your cousin?"

"That doesn't make me blind."

The lawyer turned and nodded toward the head table, where the bride and groom were. "Evidence is that he's straight anyway."

"Most guys are," Slater said, "until you get a couple of tequila shots in them."

"You're quite the rake," he said, and laughed. "What's your name?"

"Slater."

He looked to the next server, and gestured at the string beans, and the woman deposited a tong-load of them on his plate.

"Are they cooked in butter?" Slater said.

She smiled. "That's right."

Slater kept his plate down at his side and turned to the lawyer. "So are you exclusive with anybody right now?"

His brow furrowed. "You're frank too."

"I find it saves time. It's nothing personal."

"Hitting on someone is extremely personal."

"I respect your feelings and emotions," Slater

said, and waved a hand. He knew it probably sounded blithe. The shrinks Doris had sent him to in his youth had taught him the words to say, but not how to make it sound sincere. "Can I give you my digits?"

The lawyer was holding his plate out to another one of the servers, but he glanced at Slater. "You approve of my caboose?"

"I can't really tell in that tux. But I'm willing to take a chance."

"That's very open-minded of you."

Slater shrugged. "I have pretty good taste."

He dug in the inside pocket of his jacket and pulled out his phone. "I don't usually go for blue-collar guys, but hit me."

That made Slater literally want to hit him, the assumptions about his social status, but he swallowed his ire and rattled off his number, watching him thumb-type with one hand and balance his plate of food in the other.

"Text me to make sure you got it right," Slater said.

The guy nodded, and tapped at the screen, and a moment later he felt a buzz in his pocket.

"And there it is," Slater said.

"You didn't even look at your phone."

"I felt you stirring me in my blue-collar pants."

The lawyer tucked his phone away and waved for the server to give him some little potatoes.

"I did not expect to get a phone number this evening. Where did you come from?"

"Westlake," Slater said flatly. To the server, he said, "What are those red things with the potatoes? Peppers, or little hunks of meat?"

"It's bacon, sir," he said, and smiled.

"You know, you didn't even ask me my name," the lawyer said, eyeing him sidelong.

That was sloppy, Slater thought. A stupid oversight. "I was too distracted by your charm, and mesmerized by the light in your eyes. Lay it on me."

He laughed. "It's Dan, or Daniel, if you speak Spanish."

"I know I look like I should, but I don't."

They'd reached the end of the buffet, and Dan's plate was loaded. He didn't seem to notice that Slater hadn't taken anything.

"I look forward to seeing you again," Dan said, holding his gaze for a moment, and then stepped away.

A white-jacketed staffer was standing nearby, and Slater handed her his empty plate.

"You didn't get any food," she said, her brow furrowing in concern.

"There's nothing to eat here. It's fine, though—there'll be a taco truck outside somewhere."

Turning to walk away, he spotted Della, over near the bar. She was chatting with a couple of men. Both of them were leaning in, mesmerized, hanging on her words, punctuated by her animated body language. Slater had to grin. It wasn't really about her cleavage, he knew. She had an effortless engaging way about her that made her easy to talk to.

He stood near the side of the space, hands in his pockets, surveying the crowd. Dan had carried his plate over to the head table, he saw, where he sat next to a woman with short gray hair. She was sitting next to the bride. It made sense that CeCe was in her forties, at least, as he knew Dan was in his fifties, but from over here, and under all that makeup, she could pass for thirty. The older woman was familiar from Dan's social media posts—their mother.

Della went to stand in the buffet line, chatting with a new guy. He looked to be about her age, and the tux he was wearing was in a distinctive shade of chocolate brown. Between that and Della's red dress it would be easy to keep an eye on them.

After a while Dan left the head table, and Slater lost sight of him in the crowd. It didn't really matter anymore, he decided. If Dan didn't phone him in the next day or so, Slater had already scored the number for his personal cell.

As he watched, Della and the guy in the brown suit made it through the line, and they sat to eat, both of them chatting with their tablemates. Slater didn't need to stay any longer, but he could wait for her to finish, and they could leave together.

Standing here, the crowd seemed to be getting louder, likely a side effect of more booze getting consumed. A while later Della walked over to him. The man in the brown suit waited nearby.

"Latin men are my weakness," Della said, raising her voice over the crowd, nodding vaguely toward the guy.

"He looks Filipino."

"He has a Hispanic name. Not that it matters. He's asked me to go somewhere quieter for a drink."

"You should go for it," Slater said. "He's hot."

"I feel a little guilty that I haven't helped you."

"At your suggestion I actually spoke to my target in the buffet line. I got his phone number, so mission accomplished."

"That's excellent news. Was there flirting involved?"

"I guess you could call it that. With two guys it's a lot more sophisticated." He gestured with his hands, as if he were adjusting knobs. "Things are operating on many levels at once."

Della laughed. "That's such baloney. I've known enough men to know that exactly the opposite is true. Are you going to sleep with him? He's gorgeous."

"It's tempting," Slater said. "He definitely puts lead in the pencil, and the dick wants what the dick wants. But I need to keep my dick out of my work."

"Such a sagacious and sentimental assessment," Della said, frowning thoughtfully. "Plus an elegant solution. Have you been reading Emily Dickinson?"

"Your man looks a little stranded," he said. "You should go have fun."

Della lowered her voice. "The thing is, I'm wearing a lot of jewelry."

"You think he's going to roll you?"

"No. But what do you think? It's the kind of thing that happens in your world more than in mine."

"He seems soft," Slater said, looking him over. "Like a civilian, not a lowlife. That doesn't mean he won't rob you."

"Can you check into him? Maybe grab his wallet or something?"

"You think I know how to pick pockets?" Slater demanded.

"You don't?" She waved her arm. "Well, what should I do?"

"Who did you tell him I was?"

"I said you were a friend from work."

"How about this: I'm actually your bodyguard. Unless he wants me to tag along for that quiet drink, I need to check his ID."

"Ooh, that's good," Della said.

"If he refuses, you don't go. It means he's got something to hide. If he shows me an ID, I'll photograph it, and tell him it'll take a minute to run it through a database. We'll see how he takes that."

"You can't actually check a database, though, can you?"

"Of course not. But I can watch his reactions. Then we'll reassess."

"What do I say?"

"Wave him over here. I'll do the talking."

Della beckoned to him, then leaned closer to Slater. "His name is Eduardo."

Eduardo stepped over and flashed a smile.

Slater stood with his feet apart, and held his gaze, and spoke in an authoritative tone. "Eduardo, my name is Ibáñez. I'm working security for Della this evening."

His eyebrows shot up. "Security? Like a bodyguard?"

"That's correct. Before I let her leave with you, I'll need to check your ID."

"Why?"

"It's standard procedure. I need to run it through a criminal database."

Eduardo laughed. "This is a wedding. We're all related to the bride and groom in one way or another. One big blended family. I'm no criminal."

"I'm sorry, sir, but those are the company's policies."

"All right," he said, and shook his head as he dug out his wallet, and slipped out his driver's license, and handed it over.

Slater pulled out his phone and snapped a photo

of it, then tapped at the screen to send a copy to Della.

"This shouldn't take more than a minute," he said, and handed the license back.

"Would you be a sweetheart and get me a water at the bar?" Della said, briefly resting her hand on Eduardo's forearm. "Get a bottle, if they have them, so I can take it with us."

"Of course, my angel." Eduardo made a little bow from the neck and stepped away.

"You're his angel already," Slater said.

"What did you think?"

"He's not acting squirrely at all. That means he's either incredibly coldblooded or he has nothing to hide."

"So which is it?"

"I think he's OK," Slater said. "I'll keep a copy of his ID in case any of your jewelry goes missing. There's one other thing I can do—put a tracker on your phone."

"Like parental supervision?"

"More like illicit Russian surveillance software. Give me your phone."

She opened her clutch and handed it over, and Slater spent a minute installing the tracking app he'd licensed from his tech dealers, Svetlana and her brother. Based at a down-low workshop in Glendale, they specialized in bugs and hidden cameras and all kinds of tracking, most of it firmly illegal. The software wouldn't be evident when Della used the phone, but it would allow him to keep tabs on her.

"If I disappear, you'll know where I am," Della said.

"I'll know where your phone is, at least, and where it's been." He handed it back. "You're not going to disappear. Stick to public places, and when you get to the naked phase, insist on going to your place. Make sure you take an actual taxi. Not a ride-share."

"My place, taxi. Got it." She tucked her phone into her little bag. "I'm not completely sure there'll be a naked phase. We're just going for a drink."

"That guy is stacked," Slater said. "I can tell by the way his trousers fit. If he stays sober enough, I bet he could show you a very good time."

Della took a deep breath. "This is all such good information. From now on I'm going to hire you as a security consultant whenever I have to be in a crowd."

"I'm not sure you could pay me enough to hang out at events like this."

Eduardo stepped up, holding a little bottle of water.

"Sir, you're cleared to go," Slater said. "Have a pleasant evening."

"With this delightful being at my side, it's guaranteed to be the best."

Slater spoke to Della. "Ma'am, if anything comes up, just hit your panic button. Me or one of the team will be there on the double."

"Panic button?" Eduardo said, his brow furrowing.

"Don't worry about it." Della looped her arm through his, and they walked toward the entrance.

ELEVEN

AN AMPLIFIED VOICE CAME over the speakers. "Hello, everyone," she began, and then said something in Tagalog. Over by the head table, Slater could see a spotlight illuminating one of the women from the bridal party, holding a mike. It was time to leave—he'd done all he could with his target, and now Della had bugged out. Listening to sappy speeches would just give him a headache.

But then he caught someone watching him, near the spotlighted bridesmaid. It was Dan, standing not far from the bride and groom, ostensibly listening to the speaker. But his eyes were on Slater. He decided to wait.

Eventually the bridesmaid and the groomsman finished their yapping, and whoever had commandeered the mike next announced that the first dance was about to happen, back inside the hall. The crowd started to shift in that direction. Slater wanted to get a drink while he waited to see how this might play out with Dan, but it didn't fit with his booze rules. It was after five, but since he was working, he could only have the one. If there might be a guy later, the limit was also one.

As the courtyard cleared out, he saw Dan walking against the flow toward him.

"Hey, Slater. How was the food?"

He was tipsy now, Slater realized, watching him talk. Maybe it was Dutch courage that had brought him over.

"It was a true revelation," Slater said. "I'm thinking of having a smorg installed in my apartment."

Dan laughed, showing his beautiful white teeth. No way had nature made them that shade, or that evenly aligned.

"Can you drive?" he said. "I want to leave, but I don't think I can right now."

"I'm sober enough, but my car's not here."

"We'll take mine." Dan looped his arm through Slater's, the way Della had.

But it was different than with Della. Just the feeling of his arm was a turn-on. He could smell the guy's pomade, or maybe it was his cologne. They walked through the lobby and out to the valet stand at the street. Dan dug in his pocket and handed one of the valets his claim ticket, then stood next to Slater, and casually looped an arm around his waist.

He didn't seem that inebriated anymore, Slater thought, eyeing him sidelong. He might have oversold his lowered inhibitions, using it as an excuse to get into Slater's pants. More interesting was the fact that he wasn't closeted around his big Catholic family.

Dan leaned in and kissed Slater's neck. This was definitely about more than a ride home. Slater turned his head and murmured in his ear: "Fresh."

Dan giggled like a little kid, and Slater kissed his ear, and mouthed his neck.

A car pulled up in front of them, and a woman in a red valet vest climbed out.

"You've got to be kidding me," Slater said. "A McLaren?"

"You like?" Dan said.

"Do you often find the opportunity to drive two hundred miles an hour? It also doesn't seem especially practical to have a low-slung car in a city that doesn't fix the potholes."

"It's not about that. It looks cool."

Slater took the key from the valet.

"Sweet ride," she said.

"Tip the woman," Slater demanded, eyeing Dan.

He dug out some cash, and slipped her a bill, and they both climbed in. Slater spent a moment checking the controls, then eased away from the curb. The acceleration was so responsive, so precise, it felt like a direct extension of his brain.

"Smooth," Dan said. "You know what you're doing."

"Where are we going?"

"Is this Wilshire?"

"It's Sixth."

"Head downtown," Dan said, "and turn right on Flower."

That wasn't where he lived, Slater knew. The DMV said his address was on the Westside. But maybe he had a pied-à-terre downtown. His firm was down here, and anytime after 3 p.m. Bel Air would be over an hour's drive.

"So what do you do, Slater?"

"I'm in insurance."

"Sales is a tough gig."

"I don't sell anything," he said, glancing at him

sidelong. "I investigate claims."

"Insurance fraud?"

"Exactly."

"I guess you'd know all the tricks when you're at that end of the economy."

Slater could feel his heart pounding. "Lots of rich folks are grifters too."

"You never asked me what I do."

"It has to be something well paid if you're driving this rig. Wait—do you sell McLarens?"

Dan cackled. "I'm a partner at a law firm. We specialize in corporate contracts."

"So you've got money, and you're hot," Slater said. "Why don't I see a ring on that finger?"

"It took me a while to figure out I wasn't straight, for one. Since then I've been playing the field. Making up for lost time."

"Have you ever been married?"

"Why would you ask me that?"

"Just curious. You seem like a guy who's had a bit of life experience."

"Like I've been around the block?" Dan said. "Rode hard, and put away wet?"

"I didn't say that."

"I'm only fifty-four."

"That's plenty of time for a trip around the block," Slater said. "Did you ever live in South Gate?"

"That's a weird question. I kind of grew up in that part of town. My parents used to live there. Did you know them back in the neighborhood?"

Before he could answer, Dan sat up and waved at the windshield.

"Right up here. Turn in here."

It was a residential tower, one of many near the

stadium, and Slater glanced up at it as he nosed into the driveway. Mainland Chinese capital had built all these, and the condos were mostly owned by wealthy people from there who came a few times a year for short stints, if at all. It was a way to stash their money out of the country, in case their government changed the rules again and tried to take it from them. Several of these buildings had sat half-finished for almost a decade when the Communist Party's tweaks to the rules about overseas investments had caused the construction capital to dry up overnight. The neighborhood still felt sterile and derelict. But obviously this building had been completed—the lights were on.

Concerned that the low-slung car might bottom out, Slater crawled up the driveway. The gate somehow recognized the vehicle and rolled open as he approached it. Inside the garage Dan pointed out a parking space.

As they walked to the elevator Slater handed him the car key. On the ride up, Dan stood close, and then leaned into him. He could feel his heart beating. It was subtle, feeling the weight of his body against him, and he wrapped his arm around Dan's back. The proximity was a turn-on.

The door to the apartment had a keypad instead of a lock, and Dan punched in a code to open it. As they stepped inside, Slater looked around.

"You don't live here," he said.

"Why do you say that?"

"It's bland, and corporate, and there's nothing personal."

"It's one of my firm's guest apartments."

There was an open kitchen off the main room,

and just two other doors—it couldn't have more than one bedroom. Dan shrugged off his suit jacket and draped it over a lounge chair, then stepped into the kitchen. Pulling open the refrigerator, he took out a bottle of water.

"So this is where the partners bring their hook-ups?" Slater said.

"Among other things."

It was sleazy, and it put Slater in the same category as strippers, and escorts, and rent boys—disposable playthings and fungible entertainment for the wealthy.

"Do you want a drink?" Dan said.

"Let's get to the main event. If you drink any more, you're not going to be of any use to me."

Dan chuckled, then led Slater to the bedroom. He went around to the far side of the bed and rapidly got undressed. He had great musculature, Slater saw, watching him as he took off his shirt. His personal trainer had done well. Dan pulled the duvet cover off, and climbed onto the bed, spreading his arms across the pillows, and watched Slater as he got undressed, draping his suit on an armchair.

Climbing up with him, Slater leaned in and met his mouth, so firm and warm and intense. He grabbed his cock, surprised that he was hard even though he'd been boozing.

With their mouths together, Slater spent a while in it, stroking and caressing him. It was starting to feel one-sided, he realized, as this guy wasn't giving anything back. When he pulled away, Dan met his eye.

"You're so beautiful."

"You can cut the mack," Slater said. "Just tell me what you want to do."

He frowned. "I'm not macking on you. It's how I feel."

"How you feel isn't going to get us anywhere."

Dan caressed his jaw but didn't reply. "Such a beautiful face," he said finally. "I'd love to watch you go down on me."

"And there it is," Slater said flatly. "Something real. How difficult was that?"

He moved down the bed and took him into his mouth, slowly working him. When he looked up, the eye contact seemed to turn him on. Dan got into it, and cradled his head in his hands, thrusting into him. When he climaxed, he yelped and inadvertently yanked on Slater's hair.

Slater stretched out beside him, and waggled his jaw. Dan loomed over him then, and pressed his tongue into his mouth, hot and sloppy. After a minute he pulled back.

"So what do you want to do?" Dan said.

"You have a great body. Can I fuck you?"

"Not at this time."

Slater chuckled and ran a hand along his torso. "I could fuck you between your thighs. That's kind of hot."

"It sounds messy."

Slater rubbed his eyes. "I can just go. I'll figure it out myself later."

Dan frowned. "Don't be that way. Come on."

He grabbed Slater's cock, and kissed him, focusing on his mouth and stroking him. It felt lazy, but it was better than nothing. Slater leaned into it, and put his nose in his hair, smelling his sweat, and came.

Dan quickly got up, and went out, and returned a minute later with a towel, tossing it to Slater.

"How about that drink now?" Slater said.

"I think I'm done for the evening. Help yourself, though."

He got up and found the liquor cabinet in the main room. There was some expensive booze in here, and all the brand names a frat boy could want. He pulled out a fifth of scotch and poured several fingers into a tumbler, then slammed it. The aroma was delightful, and nutty, and the burn in his throat was positively smooth and golden.

Slater wanted to take another slug, but he was supposed to be working. He needed to figure that out before he got tight. Stepping back into the bedroom, he found Dan sprawled on the bed with his eyes closed, his mouth hanging open. His breathing was rhythmic and regular. He was asleep or close to it.

Reaching into the inside pocket of his suit jacket, Slater found the sample tube, and stepped over to the bed, and sat on the edge. Gingerly pulling it open so that it would make no sound, he swirled the cotton swab inside Dan's mouth as gently as he could.

Dan stirred and closed his mouth, and Slater quickly turned away so that he wouldn't see the swab in his hand. He sealed it in the tube and stepped over to the armchair to tuck it back in his jacket.

"Did you just stick your finger in my mouth?" Dan said, his voice groggy.

"I thought I saw a bug on your lip."

"There's no bugs in here. Come to bed."

Slater killed the room lights and lay down with him. As he stretched out, Dan maneuvered him onto his side, and pulled his arm around his chest. Slater tucked his knees behind Dan's. He could feel his rhythmic breathing.

"You have liquor on your breath."

"Your corporate masters have some very good scotch."

Dan scoffed. "We're not a corporation."

"Whatever you say."

"This is nice," he mumbled, and squeezed Slater's arm. "You should stay."

Sleep was close, he knew, and that was all he needed to hear.

TWELVE

IT TOOK A WHILE for Slater to figure out where he was when he woke, to figure out who this guy was. Eventually it came to him, and he climbed out of bed, and went to wash up.

When he walked back into the bedroom, he realized that he hadn't really noticed the window last night. It was the full height of the room and offered a dramatic view, east toward Vernon and the warehouse district. He stood there for a while and took in the still shadowy landscape and the pinky-orange glow in the sky.

He took his tuxedo pants from the armchair, and stepped into them, and then pulled on his shirt. He was buttoning it when Dan woke and turned toward him.

"What time is it?"

"About six."

He sat up and stretched. "Want to go again?"

"I should go."

"Have breakfast with me, at least. I'll order up. There's a service."

"It's not going to work," Slater said. "I'm vegan."

"It's not 1952. These people can do vegan."

Dan picked up the receiver on the bedside hand-set, and Slater walked out into the main room. There was a floor-to-ceiling window in here too, next to a small dining table. More compelling was the cof-feemaker that sat on the kitchen counter. It was one of those incredibly wasteful ones that made one cup at a time from a plastic pod, and he spent a minute figuring out how to make it work.

Still naked, Dan walked out and went into the bathroom. Slater heard the shower go on.

The machine made surprisingly decent espresso, considering it came out of a thumb-size plastic bub-ble, and he'd started the machine on a second cup when there was a knock at the door. Slater pulled it open to find a guy in a white jacket standing behind a cart. He had short gray hair and looked sleepy. On the cart were several plates with plastic covers.

"On the table?" he said.

Slater stepped aside, and the guy rolled the cart in, then transferred the dishes to the dining table, placing several plates at either end and a carafe of orange juice between them.

"How much should I tip you?" Slater said, as the guy wheeled the empty cart toward the door.

"Don't worry about that."

"I want to, but I'm not familiar with this environ-ment. I don't want to insult you."

"Most of these birds tip zero, but five or ten bucks would earn you my great respect."

Slater nodded, and peeled a sawbuck off his wad, and handed it over.

The guy thanked him and rolled the cart out into the hall.

When he stepped over to the table and lifted the

covers, one of the meals looked like a gooey slab of cheese with little rolls and bacon. The other looked like scrambled eggs, but it didn't quite smell like it, along with dry toast and hash browns. That must be for him.

Replacing the covers, he stood at the window, waiting for Dan to finish his leisurely shower. It was a novel perspective, this view, and he tried to figure out where the river was, and the freeways, and the rail lines.

When Dan finally appeared, he was wearing trousers but no shirt. He had great pecs for a guy his age.

"Are you hairless by genetics, or by choice?" Slater said.

Dan frowned. "What are you talking about?"

"It's a lot of work to wax your chest regularly."

"You think I'm the kind of guy who's that obsessed with grooming?"

Slater waved a hand. "I wouldn't know. I thought maybe you'd had some work done."

"Does it look like that?" Dan said, and sat at the table. "I'm glad. I haven't needed to yet, but I've got a little fund set aside for plastic surgery. What is it you thought I'd had done?"

Taking the chair across from him, Slater lifted the cover from his plate. "I don't know. It's just a thought that crossed my mind."

"Like I tell my clients, you need to be specific."

"OK." He looked him over. "Your neck is smooth and tight for your age, and you have the hairline of a teenager."

Dan nodded, a smirk on his lips, and dug into the cheese with a knife. "I had fun last night, by the way. You're wild in the sack."

Slater eyed him. He was being serious. It hadn't been wild at all—not even a little. It had been so bland that he'd almost bailed.

"I don't know anything about you," Dan went on, gesturing with a roll. "What do you do for fun?"

"I work a lot," Slater said. His focus had shifted to the faux eggs. Even though they were lukewarm now, they were tasty.

"I remember—insurance. Have you ever been flying? I don't mean commercial. In small aircraft."

"Not really."

"It's like being in heaven. I have a little plane that I zip around in. Don't get me wrong," Dan said, his tone earnest. "It's not easy. There's lots of rules, and controlled airspace. You have to pay attention. But once you get away from all that, there's nothing like it. You're literally free as a bird."

"What kind of airplane do you have?"

"It's called a Vision jet. A guy like you wouldn't know about that. An airplane is an airplane, am I right?"

"A guy like me?" Slater demanded, waving his fork.

"Am I mistaken? You don't look like you have the kind of resources to buy your own airplane."

"I don't."

"I'm not judging you," Dan said. "It's just the way the world is. It's the way things work." He gestured dismissively. "The best place to fly is over the desert. There's lots of open airspace. You can really have fun."

As he ate, Slater watched him talk. It pissed him off that this guy was so glib, so self-absorbed, so upbeat at this hour. He was just talking to hear himself talk. It pissed him off that the fake eggs were so damn delicious too.

Dan was still cutting up his bacon when Slater finished eating. He got up and went into the bedroom to put on the flimsy little shoes and his suit jacket. When he stepped out, Dan was on his feet.

"I was thinking of taking my baby up later today," he said. "Do you want to come with me? I can fly us to Monterey in a few minutes. There's a place near the airport that does Wagyu beef."

Slater scoffed. "No, man."

"Why not? It'll be fun."

"I don't do that."

"You don't go on dates, or you don't go on dates with me?"

"Both." Slater put his hands on his hips. "You're too damn bougie."

He frowned. "What are you talking about?"

"Did you grow up driving a McLaren, and flying a private jet, and eating imported luxury meat?"

"My parents were middle-class. I worked hard for what I have."

"I get that. It's just not for me."

"Someone has something nice to share with you, and you refuse it. That kind of makes you a loser."

Slater couldn't stop himself. He stepped closer and slapped him hard, left and right, a rapid kovac.

"What is wrong with you?" Dan shouted, stumbling back and holding his palm to his cheek.

"I just told you I'm vegan and you're offering me meat. You're completely clueless. That makes you the loser."

"You slapped me for that? I'm sure they have vegetables."

"How many real friends do you have, Dan? I mean a friend who'd drop everything and drive across town to help you out if you asked?"

He hesitated, and his brow furrowed before he spoke. "A few."

"You're thinking of your relatives and your employees, not your friends. Your money isolates you from reality. From other people."

"You don't know me."

"I've seen it before," Slater said. "I suspect it's because you hear 'yes' too often."

Dan jutted his chin. "How many friends do you have?"

"That's not the point."

"You don't get to smack me." He stood up taller. "I could have you charged with assault."

"I know you could. You could come down on me like a pile driver with the entire weight of your law firm. You could completely destroy me, ruin my life, no matter what I did, no matter how I reacted. It's just the way the world is. It's the way things work."

Slater turned and walked out, and found the elevator, and rode down to the lobby. It was completely devoid of people, as was the street when he stepped outside. He took a deep breath. His office wasn't that far from here. He could walk.

It was a weird experience in these thin little shoes, he realized, once he got moving. Almost like being barefoot. This early in the day the city was quiet. Even the homeless camps along the fences felt abandoned. It was probably the best time of day for them to sleep.

His building was dead, as Sunday was the one day of the week that the factories closed. Upstairs he emptied his pockets onto his desk and then changed out of the tux, glad to be back in his jeans and his boots. He arranged the suit on its hangers and tucked it into the garment bag, then stuffed the shoes in the bottom, even though Etta wouldn't approve.

In her desk drawer he found an envelope, and put four C-notes into it, then wrote "chartreuse" on the front. On the sample tube he wrote the word again, and added "possible parent no. 3."

Slinging the garment bag over his shoulder, Slater went down to the street, and across to the nearly empty parking lot, and hung the bag in the backseat of the Thunderbird. The drive to Hyde Park went fast, but when he got to Lenore's block, there was nowhere to park, unlike the last few days.

There were people standing around on the sidewalk across the street, all of them dressed formally. A church, he realized. It was Sunday morning. That explained it. Turning into the side street, he double-parked long enough to trot over and drop the sample tube and the cash envelope through the slot in Lenore's back door. As they fell inside, he heard a distant electronic chime. Was she in there working today?

Hustling to his car, he drove back downtown, to his building, and went upstairs. The lights were still off inside, and he eyed the bony statue of Rey Pascual as he walked through to his office, greeting him with a double click of the tongue.

As he dropped into his chair, Slater heaved his boots onto the desktop, and pulled his keyboard into his lap. Dan didn't seem quite right to be the missing Daniel Martínez. He said he'd grown up in South Gate, but Rocky had said her father came from Boyle Heights. The DNA test would tell for sure, but he had another guy to look into—the security guard.

Digging through the details that Andy had sent, Slater studied his driver's license photo. This Daniel was another Latinesque man with graying hair. He looked older than Dan, even though they were the same age. That was probably about resources—Dan's social status meant he could eat well, and go to the gym, and get plastic surgery that was so subtle he could lie about it.

He gazed at the photo for a minute. This guy could be related to Rocky, he decided. But then any of them could be. The most recent address for him was in Long Beach. When he pulled up the street view, it showed a mid-century bungalow on a crowded block. Based on the kinds of vehicles parked on the street and in the driveways, it was definitely a working-class neighborhood.

Andy had shown him how to access the county database of property ownership records, and when he checked on the security guard's address, it said the house was owned by someone named Glenda Muñoz. A wife or a girlfriend, maybe, or his landlady.

A cursory search for that name in Long Beach didn't elicit any social media hits, but one result came up for a lawsuit against a drugstore chain. The document was composed in dense legalese, but scanning through it, Slater got the sense that someone named Glenda Muñoz had sued the retailer over the working conditions.

Slater sat up, and locked his computer with a keystroke, then went down to his car. Most of the trip to Long Beach was south on the 710, and he cruised in the left lane, the Thunderbird's big engine purring contentedly, sailing past all the lumbering freight trucks headed to the port.

Once he'd exited onto surface streets, he followed his navigation app toward the security guard's address. He knew this part of Long Beach. Crossing that boulevard brought an instant shift from artisanal brewpubs and shops selling macarons to fast food joints and dollar stores. In terms of who lived here, the shift was from white to black, although these days it was probably more about brown than black.

A century ago that boulevard had been the red line between a white neighborhood where black people couldn't live and a neighborhood where black people were allowed to buy houses but couldn't get mortgages. The banking rules had supposedly changed, but the lines on the map were still jarringly evident, the stark wealth gap unaltered.

Turning into the street, Slater spotted the house, and pulled the Thunderbird to the curb. He climbed out and looked the place over as he strode up to it. A low fence enclosed the front yard, but the gate was open. The security door was wrapped in coarse steel mesh that had been painted white. He pressed the doorbell button beside it. The sound of movement came from inside, like something sliding, and then footfalls. Eventually the inner door opened.

A skinny woman stood there, wearing a strappy pink top and lime-green shorts. She was about the same age as his target. Her hair was cut short but still looked unkempt.

"I'm looking for Daniel Martínez," Slater said.

"He's not here."

"Do you know where I can find him?"

"Who's asking?"

Slater pulled his business card from his hip pocket and slid it into the gap next to the steel door.

"It's about an insurance payout. Are you Glenda?"

She didn't answer, and Slater watched as she took the card and studied it. Her movements seemed a little slow, like she was slightly drunk, or high, or had a disability.

"You've got money for him?" she said.

"That's the essence of it."

She chuckled and looked him over. "You don't look like a Nigerian prince. Are you going to sell Glenda a bridge while you're at it?"

"Does Daniel live here?" Slater said, and frowned. "Do you have a phone number for him?"

"Do you want to come around back? Glenda is enjoying the morning sun at her gracious swimming pool. The side gate's open." With that she closed the door.

Slater walked back to the driveway, and along the side of the house. He still wasn't sure whether this woman was talking about herself in the third person or Glenda was someone else.

Stepping into the backyard, he saw that it wasn't actually all that gracious. There was lots of concrete around the pool, but the water looked clean. A strip of thirsty grass ran along the back wall, with a sprawling shrub in the middle, huddled against the cinder blocks. Slater walked past the pool to examine it. It had been here a while, maybe even since the house had been built.

"You like Glenda's greenery?" she said.

Slater turned toward her. She was sitting alone in the shade of a patio umbrella, next to a table that bore a glass jug with dark red contents.

"This is a *Dumosa*," he said. "They only grow around here. It's actually kind of rare."

"Do tell. Can Glenda sell it?"

"It's too well established. If she tries to move it, she'll kill it."

"I guess Glenda should water it once in a while."

Slater walked around the pool toward her. "Oaks are dormant in summer. They don't want water."

"Glenda didn't know it was an oak."

"There's dozens of oak species. Just leave it alone. Nature will take care of it."

"Well, that's easy enough."

He sat on the patio chair on the other side of the table, partly facing her and partly toward the pool.

"Glenda made a pitcher of Bloody Marys," she said. "Can she offer you one?"

"It's a little early for me."

"That's why they call it hair of the dog. It'll help you wake up and face the day."

"What the hell," Slater said, even though he'd been up for hours. "Tell Glenda to set me up."

She smiled and sat up, pouring from the pitcher into a highball glass. Handing it to him, she lifted her own and tapped them together.

"Cheers," she said.

Slater tasted it and then set the glass down. "That's a strong cocktail."

"So you're looking for Danilo."

"That's right." He eyed her. That was the nickname Rocky had used. "Is Glenda his wife?"

She cackled. "She wishes. As soon as that was even mentioned, Danilo hit the road."

"He works as a security guard?"

"Sometimes. He had all sorts of jobs. Even office work. Whatever he could get."

"Does Glenda know where he is now?"

She took a long sip. "Mr. Ibáñez, the problem is that Glenda is afraid you're a hit man, or a tax collector, or worse, and you're just going to make trouble for him."

"I really am in insurance."

"It's hard to believe you're trying to give him money. Who owes it to him?"

"It's a life-insurance payout."

She gestured languorously with her hand. "Who died?"

"His ex-wife."

"See, Glenda knows that's a crock." She frowned. "Danilo was never married."

"At least not that he told Glenda about."

She looked away, gazing at the water gently rippling in the pool. Slater could see the wheels turning—she knew it was a possibility. He took another sip and waited. This was a strange Bloody Mary. Maybe she'd used gin, or skanky tomato juice, or some weird-flavored vodka.

"Glenda might be able to dig up contact details," she said finally. "If she could get a taste of that payout."

"How much does she want?"

"How much is the payout?"

"That's confidential."

"See, Glenda's on disability here. She has some serious and expensive health problems."

"At least she has this gracious swimming pool to comfort her."

She scowled. "Swimming helps with her orthopedic issues."

"So give me a dollar value," Slater said. "Maybe I can help with her issues too."

"Just one of Glenda's prescriptions costs a

hundred bucks a month," she said, meeting his gaze.

"So how much information would a hundred bucks buy me?"

Her eyebrows shot up. "All of it."

Slater reached into his front pocket and pulled out his wad, then peeled off a C-note, letting her glimpse the tantalizing greenery before he palmed it.

"Where's Danilo?" he said flatly. "Sing, sister."

"The last Glenda heard, he was in a little town in New Mexico. Working some kind of security job. It's one of those remote-type gigs. A few days on, a few days off, and they fly him back to the city for his downtime."

"What's the name of the place he works, and the town?"

"It'll come to Glenda." She screwed her eyes shut.

"Do you have it in an email or a text?"

She frowned and held up a finger. "Glenda spoke to him on the phone." A moment later, she snapped her fingers. "Manzanita."

"That's the name of the company?"

"The town. It means 'little apple,' but you know there's no apples growing around there. It's in the middle of the damn desert."

Slater pulled out his phone and thumb-typed a note of the name. "They fly him back here for his days off?"

"His employer is based in Phoenix, so he goes there. Sometimes he just stays around Manzanita if he's broke. He said there's no distractions—nowhere to spend his paycheck. He can just save it and stay in the company housing."

"What kind of industry is it?"

"Glenda doesn't have a clue. But she knows that's

the name of the town. There can't be a lot of work in a place like that, can there? It's not very big."

"Does Glenda have a phone number for him?"

"Danilo said he gave up his cell phone. It was too expensive."

"So how did he call her?"

"She thinks it was a work line."

"Can Glenda show me that number?" Slater said, and casually lifted his hand, letting her glimpse the C-note.

"It was a while ago."

"I'm sure it's still in her phone, though. She could find it if she checked."

She heaved a sigh and sipped at her cocktail.

"Ben Franklin was all about the quest for knowledge, don't you think?" Slater said. "He invented bifocals. You hit a certain age and *bam*, you're wearing a pair. Thanks, Ben."

"Glenda has to admit that she is rather fond of Ben."

She sighed and lifted her phone from the patio table, then spent a few minutes scrolling, swiping delicately with a pink-manicured finger.

"This might be it," she said finally. "602—does that sound like Phoenix?"

"That's totally Phoenix." Slater waggled his phone. "Show me."

She held the screen toward him, and he snapped a photo of it, then double-checked to make sure he'd captured the number.

"Is there anything else that Glenda can tell me about Danilo?"

"He's a decent guy. He just wasn't that into Glenda."

"But he lived here, according to the DMV. He must have been into you enough to shack up." He set the C-note on the table and stood up.

"You can hang out if you'd like," she said. "The water's warm. You and Glenda could go for a skinny dip. Get to know each other better."

"I'm strictly on dick, sister."

She waved dismissively. "The nice guys always are."

"I'm not actually a nice guy," he said, and turned to leave.

THIRTEEN

S LATER WENT TO THE side gate, and let himself into the driveway, and walked to his car.

When he got back to the office, it was empty, and the lights were off. He got comfortable at his desk and did a search for the number Glenda had given him. There was no name attached to it, but the exchange was listed as belonging to a cell phone provider. When he dialed the number, he got a voice-mail recording:

"You've reached the rapid response team in Manzanita. Rogers and Martínez are on this week. If it's an emergency incident, leave a message. Otherwise you can call us back during office hours."

What the hell was a rapid response team, he wondered. Maybe it was something about oil and gas. There was lots of that in New Mexico, and that industry had safety problems all the time. But why would they need a security guard? More salient were the other details the message revealed—it confirmed the name of the town Glenda had given him, and that Danilo was working there this week.

The front door opened, and Max called a greeting. A moment later he stuck his head in Slater's office door. Today he was wearing that ugly brown suit again.

"Is it funny or tragic that we're both here on Sunday afternoon?" Max said.

"Every day kind of feels the same."

"I hear you. You have to work when there's work." He went over to his own office.

Slater's phone buzzed, and he checked the screen. It was a text from Lenore:

Sample 3 is not a match.

That was actually a relief. He shouldn't have slept with Dan—if he'd been the guy, it would have made things a lot more complicated. He set his phone down and sighed. He really needed to keep his dick out of his cases.

Lenore worked fast, he realized—he'd just dropped that sample this morning. She was working Sunday too. Leaning back in his chair, he laced his fingers behind his head and thought it through. There was no way around it—he needed to go to New Mexico.

A map search revealed that Manzanita was a small place, not near any of the freeways, smack in the middle of the state. He searched for "oil and gas in New Mexico." The industry was nowhere near there—it was in the southeast part of the state, next to Texas. Looking at the map again, he searched for a hotel. Exactly one result came up for Manzanita. There was no website link, so he dialed the phone number. An actual person answered—a man's voice.

"Have you got a room tomorrow night," Slater said, "and for the next few days? It's for one person."

"I have a single available. Can I put your name on it?"

"Max Conroy," Slater said. "Do you need a card?"

"Just bring it with you," he said, and ended the call.

Max stepped over from his office, a wry grin on his face. "Where am I staying tomorrow night?"

"Manzanita, New Mexico."

"Lucky me. I'm thinking you'll need a credit card."

"If you can spare one."

They'd done it before sometimes, switching cards. It was a tactic that made them harder to track. Max pulled out his wallet and dropped a credit card on his desk.

"I'm not sure I'll need to be incognito," Slater said. "It's just an instinct."

"It can't hurt."

"Do you want one of mine?"

"No need," Max said. "I've got others. And there's all that damn cash in the safe."

"Cash is king."

Max braced a hand on the door frame. "You're after one of the potential beneficiaries?"

Slater nodded. "This one is working out there."

"Are you driving?"

"I'm not sure the Thunderbird is up to it. A summer road trip across the broiling empty desert. I don't want to get stranded."

"You can borrow the Challenger."

"That would be a smooth way to get there," Slater said. "It's a lot of freaking driving, though. How far is Albuquerque?"

"Twelve hours, if you stick to the freeway. Roswell is more like fifteen."

Slater groaned. "I don't know. I appreciate the offer. Let me do some research."

Max went back to his office, and Slater looked at the map again. Manzanita was far from everything—three hours' drive from Albuquerque, and even farther from El Paso, the next closest airport with LA connections. Maybe it would be easier to drive from here. He did like driving the Challenger. Thinking about it, though, maybe there was another way. Grabbing his phone, he dialed Dan.

"If it isn't Prince Charming," Dan said when he picked up.

"Are you in the air right now?"

"I landed an hour ago."

"Do you want to fly me to New Mexico? I need to get out there tomorrow. I could drive, or fly commercial, but you told me how much you love to fly."

"You really have some nerve," Dan said, "asking a favor after the way you treated me."

"I thought I treated you pretty well. I'm thinking specifically of the point when you had your dick down my throat."

He chuckled. "Yeah, that was fun. Flying's not really a weekday thing, though. I have to be in the office tomorrow."

"You can be. Fly out first thing and come back. You'll be in your office by lunchtime. Isn't setting your own schedule one of the privileges of being a partner?"

"I'm just not sure it's a good idea."

"I need a decision here, Dan. Ticktock."

"You're kind of a hothead, you know that?"

"I know."

Dan huffed, and didn't speak right away. "Can you be at Van Nuys Airport half an hour before sunup?"

"Absolutely."

"Text me the name of the airport you want to go to. I'll have to file a flight plan."

Slater ended the call and then zoomed in on the

map. There was an airstrip next to the townsite at Manzanita. When he clicked on it, it said "unpaved" and "no services." But it had an airport code, so he texted that to Dan. If he couldn't land there, he'd be able to figure out the next best place.

Locking his computer, he got up and stuck his head into Max's office.

"I won't need your car. I'm flying out there in the morning."

"Stay safe," Max said.

"Always."

When he got down to the street, it was still hot out, but the long shadows of the end of the day were growing, with only the tops of the buildings still in daylight. Slater climbed in the Thunderbird and drove to his apartment. When he got upstairs, it was dark inside, and he didn't bother to turn on the lights. He pulled his boots off, then poured his ration into a tumbler, and sat in his recliner to sip at it.

Gazing at the dark band of sky outside, he was tempted to open the hookup app. But if he did that he wouldn't get enough sleep. Hookups and booze and work. Is this really all there was? He could feel the city out there, the weight of it, all the lights and the cars and the never-ending dull roar of activity. He didn't even hear it anymore. It was always just there.

Rising, he slammed his ration, and then poured another half inch. It would help him sleep, he reasoned, and slammed that too. By the time he got into bed the warmth of the bourbon was suffusing from his belly. No way was he ever going to be able to fall asleep like this, he thought, still mostly sober and so early in the evening. But despite his doubts he quickly drifted off.

FOURTEEN

W̲HEN SLATER'S ALARM RANG, it was still dark out. He forced himself out of bed, and washed up, then found his canvas satchel. Rolling up a couple of long-sleeved shirts, he tucked them into the bag with some socks and underpants. What else? He looked around his bedroom. His laptop had to go, and his phone charger, and condoms.

Down in his garage, he grabbed his straw gardening hat and set it on the passenger seat of the Thunderbird, then tucked a couple of the DNA sample kits into his satchel. Once he'd backed into the alley, and watched the door roll down, he got on the road. It was hard to believe there was this much traffic headed into the Valley so early in the morning. The sky had brightened significantly by the time he pulled into the lot at the private terminal.

With his satchel over his shoulder and holding his straw hat by its string, he walked inside, and found a lone security guard behind a counter.

"Can I see your ID?" she said, and Slater handed over his driver's license.

She held it briefly on a glass plate that flashed with light, probably scanning an image of it, and then handed it back.

"Mr. Martínez's aircraft is on the left," she said, gesturing toward the doors.

When he stepped outside, he realized he was on the actual tarmac, within a few yards of half a dozen small aircraft. In the bright morning light he recognized the bulbous little airplane with the V-shaped tail. Dan was walking around it, peering at the wings and the flaps. Inspecting it, for some reason. His cobalt-blue coveralls were nothing like the ones Slater wore for yard work—they were too sheer, too fitted, too snug. It must be his flight suit.

Dan saw him approaching, and flashed a big smile. Such a morning person.

"What's with the hat?" Dan said.

"It's sunny in the desert. It doesn't fold up."

"That's a gardener's hat. It makes you look like a peasant."

"A peasant who knows how to rock your world."

Dan laughed. "I just have a couple more things to check, and we'll go. You can put your stuff on the backseat."

Behind the pilot's chair the doors were open, one folded up at the top like a hatch and a smaller one at the bottom with a step on it. Slater put his bag and his hat in the back and waited for Dan.

"You climb in first," he said, when he finally stepped around. "Take the right seat."

Dan climbed in behind him, and pulled the doors closed, and got them latched. Settling into the pilot's seat, he handed Slater a set of black can headphones. Once he pulled them on, Dan adjusted the built-in mike so it was right at his lips, then pulled on his own pair.

"Can you hear me?"

"Loud and clear," Slater said.

"Good. So the engine gets really loud. Don't take those off or you'll mess up your hearing."

Reaching across his lap, Dan pulled his seatbelt on and connected it for him.

"You're like a damn soccer mom," Slater said.

When he got the engine started, it seemed loud, even with the headphones. Dan spent a minute chatting with the controllers, in clipped technical language, and eventually they started to roll. He stopped at the end of the runway, and said something unintelligible over the radio, then leaned ahead to peer into the sky. A moment later a light airplane flew low overhead and touched down some distance ahead of them.

"He's out early," Dan said, his tone chirpy.

Watching him operate, Slater saw that he really did love doing this, even the perfunctory stuff like waiting on the ground.

Once the light plane had turned off the runway, Dan revved the engine, and it got even louder. Rolling up the tarmac, they got moving alarmingly fast, and suddenly the nose of the plane pulled away from the ground. They were climbing quickly, and Slater had to take a slow breath to counter the adrenaline rush and calm his pounding heart. It felt like an amusement park ride.

They climbed over the Valley, and over the dry brown mountains, and then the Mojave. It felt like they were high—the view was the same as from a commercial airliner.

Dan was intent on the flying part, focused on his instruments and occasionally chatting over the radio. Even though he could hear both sides of it, Slater couldn't really parse the content, except that it mostly seemed to be about compass headings and altitude.

Eventually, somewhere over the desert, Dan seemed to start to relax.

"How long will it take to get there?" Slater said.

"Sixty-eight minutes from wheels up to touch-down. We're already twenty minutes in."

"That's impressive speed."

"So what are you doing out there?"

"Trying to track down a guy for a case I'm working."

"I'm glad you talked me into this," Dan said. "Look at the view. There's nowhere I'd rather be than up here."

"You're welcome."

Dan met his gaze. "And you're welcome for the ride."

"You basically just said I'm doing you a favor."

He laughed, showing his perfect white teeth. "Slater, you are a piece of work."

"I hear that a lot."

When they started to descend, the angle was much steeper than with a commercial jet, and again the roller-coaster sensation made Slater's heart pound. He could see the runway in the hazy distance ahead, and Dan made small adjustments with the yoke to stay lined up with it. Off to the side he could make out the sprawling small town. Manzanita. There were no more than a dozen streets and a ribbon of gray highway that skirted the edge.

As they got closer to the ground, Dan leaned ahead to look up at the sky, craning to see left and right.

"Are you checking for other aircraft?" Slater said.

"It's an uncontrolled airfield. I have to approach it in a certain way."

It seemed unlikely that scanning the sky for competitors was an official procedure, Slater thought, but if they landed in one piece, he couldn't complain if the guy was bending the rules a little.

The runway came up to meet them, and they connected with a firm bump. Dan quickly slowed the aircraft and taxied toward the only structures in view, a couple of Quonset buildings at one side of the field. The big doors were closed, and no vehicles were parked around them. It looked like no one was here. Dan came to a stop, and the engine noise started to subside.

"It just takes a minute for the engine to slow down," Dan said. He gestured toward the Quonsets. "It looks like you'll have to walk."

Slater was focused on his phone. "I've got cell signal. I can call a taxi."

"I can't believe there's a cab company in a town this small."

"You may be right," he said, scanning the search results. "But it's only a mile or so. I can hoof it."

"Take a water." Dan reached into the back and handed him a plastic bottle.

"I imagine you'll have a quick trip back."

"It's a little slower because of the headwind. Plus I have to stop for fuel. There's none here."

"Where will you stop?"

"A small airport in Arizona."

"Do you know how to get there?"

Dan grinned. "I think I can figure it out."

He got up, and unlatched the doors, and pushed them open. Slater stepped onto the hardpacked earth and slung on his satchel, then pulled off the head-phones and handed them to Dan. Donning his straw hat, he waved and walked toward the Quonsets.

He'd made it to the end of the structures when Dan started to rev the engine again. Even from here it was shockingly loud. The little plane taxied to the end of the runway, and turned around, and Dan gunned it as he got rolling, and then lifted off. By the time Slater got to the chain-link fence, the aircraft was a tiny dot in the distance.

The fence ran as far as he could see, likely enclos-ing the whole airfield. It wasn't so high that he couldn't climb over it, but the driveway for the build-ings had a vehicle gate. It was locked with a chain and a padlock. The chain-link mesh and the support poles looked weather-beaten, and when he pulled on the bottom of the gate, it came away from the adjoin-ing section without much effort. He should be able to get through that, he decided, and shoved his satchel through the gap, and then his hat.

Lying on his side, he managed to heave it wide enough to squeeze through. Once he was out, he stood up and brushed off the dust, then slung on his bag and pulled his hat low over his brow.

A few minutes' walk along the access road brought him to the highway. It was already getting hot, and the sun felt strong. There was no traffic on the road until he was almost in the town, when a lone pickup rolled by.

He passed a couple of houses on the outskirts, set way back and surrounded by shrubby trees, and then he came to a gas station, with a trio of pumps and a couple of service bays. A well-worn tow truck sat at the end of the building. It looked deserted, with the garage doors rolled down, but the sign in the office window said OPEN. Loosening the string under his chin, he shifted his hat onto his back and stepped inside.

It was a little market, with a cooler for drinks and an aisle of snacks. Slater pulled some bagged cashews and almonds off the rack. He looked toward the counter as a woman stepped out of the back room. Latina, or maybe Native American, she was in her sixties and had her streaky gray hair tied back. Despite the heat she was wearing a nylon jacket. She nodded and greeted him in Spanish.

Things worked differently in small towns, he knew, and he mustered all the warmth and manners he could come up with.

"Forgive me," Slater said, "but I'm one of those people who's strayed from his Latin roots. I don't actually speak the language."

"You don't have to apologize, son. That's just like my own kids. In their case, it's on me."

Slater pulled a cold bottle of water from the cooler, then checked the label on one of the tamales near the register.

"This looks homemade," he said. "Do the potato ones have any meat in them?"

"Just masa and some spices."

He took one and set it on the counter with his other purchases. "Homemade tamales—you've made me a happy man."

She grinned as she started to ring him up. "My daughter makes those."

"Can I get a pint of the bourbon?" He pointed to the shelf of liquor bottles behind her.

Pulling out his cash, he paid her, and watched as

she tucked the booze into a paper bag and the food into plastic.

"Is there a car rental place in town?" he said.

"I'm afraid not. Are you hitchhiking?"

"I got dropped off at the airstrip."

"Are you with that UFO outfit?"

"I'm not," Slater said, "but I'm booked at the hotel in town. Can you tell me where that is?"

It was easy enough to check on his phone, and he already had a vague idea of which direction it was in, but people liked to be asked for help—as long as it was the easy kind of help.

"It's more of a motel," she said, and gestured to the highway. "It's up that way. Turn left where Randy's RV is parked. It's creamy white with a green stripe down the side. Then it's about half the way to Main Street. It's not too far, even on foot."

"Thanks for your help," he said, and lifted his purchases off the counter.

"I'm curious as to why you got flown into this little corner of the middle of nowhere."

He forced himself to grin. "I work for an insurance company. I'm doing some interviews here."

She pursed her lips and nodded. "That damn highway. So many car accidents. People drive way too fast."

"I guess there's nobody else on the road to slow them down."

"Are you from Albuquerque?"

"Los Angeles."

"So you know all about traffic."

He forced a laugh. "You know it."

"It's easy enough to walk around town," she said, "but you'll need wheels if you're going beyond it. I can't believe your company didn't arrange for a car."

"I can only blame my own poor planning. I don't suppose you have an old hooptie around the repair shop that I could rent from you for a couple days?"

"I don't, but I guess you could borrow my vehicle, if you need it. As long as you're back by closing time. That's six."

His eyebrows shot up. "That's so generous, ma'am. I might take you up on that later. I have an expense account, so of course I'd pay you. Can I ask your name?"

"It's Margie."

"I'm Max."

"Well, I'm sure I'll see you again, Max. It's not a very big place."

Once he was outside, he took a deep breath, then guzzled from the bottle of cold water. It was hard work to feign civility for so long at a stretch. But that's what the job required.

Walking farther into town, he found Randy's RV. Well-established brush grew around it, and it had no tags, and the tires were wrapped in white plastic. That made it an enduring landmark—it wasn't going any-where anytime soon. A few blocks from it he came to the hotel. It was long and low and had parking spaces right in front of the rooms.

The air-conditioning was running when he stepped into the office, and he relished the blast of cool air. Past the reception desk was a bar with half a dozen stools. There was no booze behind it, though. Maybe it was a place to eat breakfast.

The clerk must have heard the bell above the door when he'd come in, and he soon appeared from the back, ambling along the bar to the front desk. In his fifties, maybe, he was a sun-ravaged blond, wearing a plaid shirt, a tuft of hair visible at his chest.

"I booked a room for tonight," Slater said.

"Mr. Conroy," he said, without looking at his ledger. "You're a little early."

"Is it ready? I can pay you for early check-in."

"That's fine. I just need a credit card and your ID."

Slater pulled out Max's card and handed it over. "I left my driver's license in the car. I'll bring it to you later."

The clerk swiped the card, and tapped at his keyboard, and peered at the screen. The bell above the door tinkled, and Slater glanced at the guy who'd come in. A little beefy, and bald, and basically fuckable, he decided. He stood waiting a few paces back and wasn't subtle about looking Slater over. That rapid assessment, and the way he was standing—this guy was a cop. Being a black guy in a part of the country where small towns skewed white implied that he wasn't local, and the fact that he was wearing a T-shirt and sweatpants and had nothing in his hands meant he was staying here.

"Outside and to the left," the clerk said, and handed Slater a key.

As he headed for the door, Slater heard the clerk greet the cop, calling him "Mr. Weaver."

The room was small, and dark, and it smelled like some kind of cleanser, but it looked clean. There was a little Frigidaire under the sink, and he put his water bottles and tamale inside, then stretched out on the bed.

It was stupid to have assumed he'd just be able to rent a car. He already had an in with Margie, but it would make him more dependent on the locals than he liked. Pulling out his phone, he found the number Glenda had given him for Danilo and dialed. It was well into business hours; maybe someone would answer this time.

"This is Rogers."

"Danilo called me from this number," Slater said. "Is he around?"

"He's in Phoenix for a couple days. I'm his colleague. Were you calling to report an incident?"

"I thought he was working this week. I'm here in town—when does he get back?"

"You're in Manzanita?" he said, his tone rising. "Who is this?"

"The name is Max. I do some business with Danilo."

"That makes it sound like you're his drug dealer."

Slater forced a laugh. "Nothing like that."

"Does he owe you money?"

"It's actually the other way around."

"Well, he'll be back here tomorrow."

"Listen," Slater said, "can I drop by your office? It might save me some time."

"I'm on duty, so I might have to go out. But sure."

"Where's your office?"

"It's not really an office. Drive over to the street that's a block west of Main Street. You'll see three houses in a row with the same metal roofs. You can't miss it."

Slater checked the map on his phone and saw that from here, west was on the other side of Main Street. The three houses were visible in the satellite image. It looked like it would only be a few minutes' walk.

Pushing himself up off the bed, he decided to leave his hat and brave the sun.

When he got to Main Street, he detoured to walk down it. It was wide enough to have angle parking on both sides. There was a diner with a faded 1950s marquee out front, but it was still operating, as he could see people inside. The grocery store had a lighted sign in the window that declared it OPEN, and a few doors down was a place called Craft Store. It was closed, but in the window a hand-lettered sign said LOCAL ART. That was probably intended for the tourist trade. But it was hard to imagine more than the occasional road-tripper straying in here from the highway.

On the next street he found the row of three white bungalows, each with an identical light-gray roof. The middle one had a chain-link fence with a gate that was rolled open. A white SUV sat in the driveway. Slater walked up to the front door and knocked.

"It's open," came a muffled voice from inside.

This had originally been the living room, he saw, stepping inside, but now it was dominated by a conference table and six chairs. In the corner by the window sat a desk with a computer monitor on it.

A lanky guy appeared from the back, his ruddy redheaded complexion made more dramatic by the black pants and black polo shirt he was wearing. He was fuckable, but the sun must be hard on this guy—that pasty skin wasn't built for the desert.

As he walked out, he smiled in greeting. That was the upside of small towns—this guy was willing to talk to a perfect stranger, and he was going to be friendly about it too.

"You must be Rogers," Slater said.

"That's right." He reached for Slater's hand and gave it a firm shake. "What was your name again?"

"Max."

"You have something to leave for Danilo?"

"I actually need to talk to him. But if you're not too busy, can I buy you lunch?"

"I don't know Danilo all that well," he said, his brow furrowing. "What kind of business are you in?"

"Insurance. I'm investigating a claim." He waved an arm. "We don't have to talk about Danilo. I don't know anyone in this town, and it seems I'm going to be here until he gets back tomorrow."

Rogers nodded. "I get that. I don't know any of the locals either."

"You don't live here?"

"I'm based in Phoenix. Same as Danilo." He pulled out his phone and glanced at it. "The diner's open now. Why not—you can buy me lunch."

FIFTEEN

▰▰▰▰▰▰▰▰▰▰

SLATER STEPPED OUT INTO the daylight, and watched as Rogers locked the front door of the house.

"Where's your car?" Rogers said, glancing around.

"I walked here."

He went over to the white SUV, and got behind the wheel, and pushed open the passenger door. Slater climbed in but didn't bother with the seatbelt. It would be less than a minute's drive.

Rogers parked in front of the diner and led the way inside. A few people were eating at the tables and in the booths. These were country folk with blue-collar jobs, dressed in denim and plaid and coveralls, the men shaggy-headed or wearing ball caps. No one was sitting at the counter, and Rogers took a stool and flipped over the coffee cup that waited there. Slater sat next to him.

A waitress with a carafe stepped over and greeted them. In her thirties, maybe, she wore a plaid shirt and jeans, and poured coffee into Rogers's cup.

"Coffee?" she said, eyeing Slater.

He turned his cup over and watched as she filled it.

161

When she stepped away, he spoke to Rogers. "I know you guys work in shifts. Is Danilo in Phoenix for his days off?"

"That's right."

"What kind of security are you running, exactly?"

Rogers eyed him sidelong. "It's not security. Did Danilo not tell you what he's doing here?"

"Just the part about the shift work."

He looked away and sipped his coffee. "I guess I don't blame him. I don't share the details with everybody either."

"What'll it be, boys?" the waitress said, stepping up to them, pad in hand.

"A club with fries," Rogers said.

"Maybe just the fries," Slater said. "Do you have any fruit?"

"There's a melon wedge on the breakfast menu. It comes with cottage cheese."

"I'll have that too. But hold the cheese."

She chuckled as she jotted it down. "You got it."

"So why is Danilo embarrassed about his job?" Slater said.

"He's not embarrassed. We just have to be discreet. Like how I didn't ask you what kind of insurance case Danilo is caught up in, because I assume it's confidential."

"You assumed right."

"I've worked security before. I know the drill."

"And right now you're not on security?"

"We're on a paranormal incident rapid response team."

"OK," Slater said evenly. He wrapped his hand around his cup. "Define 'paranormal incident.'"

"Unexplained events. The big one is saucer crashes,

but there's other stuff happening too."

"Someone is paying you to wait around in a little town in case there's a UFO crash?"

"*UFO* means unidentified. If it crashes, it's not unidentified—it's a saucer, or a spacecraft. We also prefer the term UAP these days. That stands for unidentified aerial phenomena. It's to distinguish it from the woo-woo connotations of the older term."

"Right," Slater said, "because using a new word for it means it's not woo-woo at all. Have you responded to a lot of saucer crashes?"

"I personally haven't, but I've only been on the crew for three months. I've gone on a bigfoot call, and several IR anomaly incidents."

"Bigfoot lives out here too? I thought they were in the Northwest."

"They're paranormal entities," Rogers said, "so they can materialize wherever."

"Of course." Slater lifted his coffee cup. "I should have realized."

Rogers chuckled. "I know you're not taking it seriously, but we do. It's serious stuff."

"You saw the bigfoot?"

"I didn't, but there was very strong residual energy where the sighting happened. Spikes all up and down the electromagnetic spectrum. I've never seen anything like it. There's no human technology that could have caused that." He waved a hand. "It might not have been bigfoot. It could have been some other transdimensional entity." Rogers shifted on his stool and met his gaze. "I feel like I'm talking a lot."

"It's not like I'm an industrial spy from a rival rapid response team," Slater said. "I've never heard of anything like this."

"It's pretty out-there, isn't it?"

The waitress stepped over with their plates and set them down. Rogers bit into his sandwich, and Slater ate a few fries.

"So what's an IR anomaly?"

He paused to swallow before he spoke. "Infrared light that's coming out of the ground or out of the sky. It's hard to tell which direction. We see it out in the desert in the middle of the night."

"It's not just rocks giving off residual heat?"

"These are giant beams, like a spotlight, but only visible to IR sensors. I've seen it several times, but we haven't been able to determine the source." Rogers waved his sandwich. "Sometimes you put on the IR goggles and a whole ridge will be lit up, real bright, like it's on fire. Then it just fades away. There's no explanation in natural science for that."

"So who's funding the rapid response?"

"Nobody talks about it too openly, but my understanding is that it's a pet project of this real estate billionaire from Phoenix. I've never met him. I've only dealt with the HR person and our handler."

"Some rich guy is interested in unexplained events, and he has the resources to pay for a full-time rapid response team to document them."

Rogers nodded. "That's about it. They say he's a total saucer-head."

Slater spent a minute scooping out chunks of melon and munching on them.

"Why here?" he said finally. "Why in this dinky town?"

"It's centrally located to the phenomena." Rogers set down his cup. "New Mexico is ground zero for UAPs and electromagnetic anomalies. Don't ask me why that is. From this town specifically we can be anywhere in the state in a few hours. I think there's a financial consideration too—those three houses are like our dorms, and they can sleep a dozen people if there's a level 3 crisis. The rent on them out here is less than on a small office in Albuquerque or Las Cruces."

"How many people are on the crew?"

"During ordinary times there's six of us. Two or three on duty at a time. We work in staggered shifts. When Danilo gets back, I'll work with him for a few days."

"Do you get called out a lot?"

"It averages twice a week."

Slater frowned. "Who calls you?"

He glanced at the waitress, working farther down the counter, and lowered his voice. "We have people embedded with law enforcement, and the military, and with paranormal research groups."

"So someone sees a UAP, and phones you, and you jump in your rig and drive over there."

"That's what we do."

"And what, take photos?"

"Sure, and we measure residual radiation, and collect samples, if there's anything to collect, and write it all up in a report. We also wear biosensors so the people in the lab back in Phoenix can study what effect the phenomena have on our physiology." He tapped his wrist.

It wasn't a watch, Slater realized. It was a strap and a plain black disk with no readout.

"I know Danilo used to be a security guard," Slater said. "Is that who they hire for your team?"

"Most of the guys worked security. Some have

science backgrounds. Like me—I studied electrical engineering, but I was in the Army Reserve, so I know how to handle weapons."

Slater watched him munching on his fries. People thought LA was weird, but he always ran into stuff like this when he left town.

"What time will Danilo get here tomorrow?"

"They fly us in from Phoenix. Wheels down is usually right after oh-nine-hundred. I'll drive out to the airstrip to pick him up."

Slater pushed his half-eaten melon away. "So do you get much sex out here?"

Rogers spit-coughed and set down his coffee cup, then wiped his mouth and eyed Slater sidelong.

"Like I said, I don't know anyone here. I'm just working. My life is in Phoenix."

"Well, I'm here, and I have some time on my hands."

His eyes narrowed. "That's not who I am."

"Are you sure about that?"

Rogers huffed and lowered his voice. "What would Jesus think?"

"Fictional entities aren't actually imbued with that ability."

His lip curled in disgust. "Are you some kind of atheist?"

"Religion is a control mechanism, Rogers. You have the hardware to have a good time. You just have to go for it. Free your mind."

His face had gone red. He knew exactly what Slater was talking about. Maybe he was even imagining it. But that superstition stuff was powerful.

"I can't," he said, looking at his plate.

"I'll do all the work. You can just lie there."

"It was nice to meet you, Max." He slid off his stool.

"Hold up," Slater said. "You're not going to mess things up with Danilo for me, are you?"

"That's none of my business. But I'm pretty sure he's not going to sleep with you either."

Slater watched as Rogers strode through the diner and out to the street. He probably shouldn't have hit on the guy, but looking around the place, there wasn't a wide selection of possibilities here, and he'd need to find something to do until Danilo got back.

"Your friend looked a little flushed," the waitress said, stepping over.

"I say stupid things sometimes." He dug in his pants for his wad of cash.

"I see him around a lot," she said. "He's on that saucer-chasing crew. He orders the same thing every time he comes in."

"I'm pretty sure he's available, if you're interested."

"He never flirts with me. I don't think he's straight."

Slater threw up a hand. "See, that's what I saw too. I was getting concerned my gaydar was busted."

She chuckled. "So he's in denial about it."

"I think he's actually dating Jesus."

"Oh, I get it. I know the type. There's a degenerate evangelical church over in Benson. They're totally caught in the past."

"How's that?"

She braced her arms on the counter. "You know how, four hundred years ago, all the art was religious? Popes and cardinals and rich guys painted as angels and wise men? Those days are gone. Art can be about anything. Religion doesn't matter anymore."

"Are you an artist?"

"Not enough of one to make a living on."

"Commercial success isn't the measure of an artist," Slater said. "It's the measure of a businesswoman."

"You're right." She rapped on the counter with a knuckle. "Thanks for reminding me."

"What do I owe you?"

"Seventeen eighty-two," she said, and handed him the check.

Slater peeled off a twenty and a sawbuck and set them on the counter, then stood up.

"Hey, thanks," she called after him.

The sun felt intense as he walked back to the hotel, but the air was dry, and a bit of breeze was picking up. In his room he stretched out on the bed. He could open the hookup app and see who was around, but it was barely even lunchtime.

Conrad had mentioned the bounty on Galliform, the lowlife who'd messed with one of the principals on his last case, and Andy had given him the name of the town where the guy had turned up. It was somewhere out here. He pulled up the text Andy had sent. The town was called Voirrey's Corner. Slater searched for it on the map.

It wasn't all that far from here—maybe thirty miles, and all on paved roads. What were the odds? Poking around for Galliform would give him something to do until Danilo got back tomorrow morning. And Conrad said the reward for Galliform was a hundred grand—that was a lot of scratch.

Heaving himself up off the bed, he pulled on his straw hat and walked out to the dusty street, heading back toward the highway and past Randy's RV. The wind was picking up as it got warmer, so he tightened the string on his hat under his chin so it wouldn't blow off. At the gas station Margie was at the register, and she looked up when Slater walked in.

"Howdy, Max."

He slid his hat onto his back. "Is your vehicle still available?"

"I had a feeling you might need wheels. I made some calls. Carl says you can use his spare pickup."

"That's great."

"My son does the maintenance on it right here. Carl actually saw you walking into town from the airstrip." She mimicked a man's voice: " 'Is it for that fellow with the straw hat?' "

"I guess it's hard to go unnoticed in a small town."

"I told him you were willing to pay for it. He said twenty-five a day would be plenty."

"That suits me. I appreciate you arranging this."

"Come and take a look at it before you thank me," she said, and stepped around the counter. "You might not want it. It's not new."

Following her outside, he looked over the vehicle, parked in front of one of the service bays. It was a classic pickup, blue with a rust-stained white panel along the side.

"It's not much to look at," Margie said, "but my boy tells me that mechanically it's in pretty good shape."

"This is a thing of beauty," Slater said. "Late eighties?"

"You know your stuff. It's an '88."

"I'd be honored to drive such a graceful classic."

She laughed. "I'm glad to hear it. It burns regular gas, and it's a six-cylinder, but I doubt you'll be hauling or towing."

"I won't. That's all the horsepower I need."

"Carl asked how long you'd be in town."

"A couple of days. Let me give you some money for him now. If I need it longer, we can work it out then." He pulled out his wad and peeled off two C-notes.

Margie's eyebrows shot up. "That's more than he asked for."

"He might have to put some gas in it when I'm done. Maybe your son can look it over too when I'm through with it."

"I didn't even check it for gas," she said, and handed him the keys. "Not too bright for a woman who runs a gas station. Oh—can you drive a stick?"

"I learned to drive on a stick," Slater said, and walked around to the driver's door, and tossed his hat inside.

"I should probably ask if you've got a driver's license."

"I do," he said. "Thanks for all your help, Margie."

When he climbed into the pickup, it started easily, and the engine sounded healthy. Classic cars aged well in the desert air. Backing out past the pumps, he nosed it onto the highway, and shifted up. The gearbox felt solid. Half watching the road, he pulled up the navigation app on his phone, and tapped on Voirrey's Corner. He should have done this before he'd started driving, of course, but he didn't want to hang around Margie's in case she decided to ask for a look at his ID. Overpaying her in advance had served to deflect that notion.

Setting the phone on the seat next to him, he focused on driving the empty road. Up around sixty the steering started to feel a little uncertain, so he kept it below that.

It was easy to see why Margie thought people drove too fast. There was nobody on the highway, and it would be easy to build up speed on these long straight stretches. As he cruised, he focused on the landscape, the rolling savanna and the distant mountains.

Eventually the navigation app said he was arriving in Voirrey's Corner. All he could see here was a crossroads with a gas station—there were no other buildings or signs, apart from the one with the highway number. The service doors on the garage were rolled open, and a couple of old cars sat out front. Slater pulled up to one of the pumps and killed the engine.

When he stepped into the little office, behind the register he found a leathery-faced guy with a shock of white hair. Slater set two twenties on the counter.

"That's forty for the pump on the left."

He eyed the cash, and his brow furrowed. "You didn't put any gas in it yet."

"I'll do that now."

Back out at the pump, he stuck the nozzle into the tank and stood with his hand on the lever. Paying in advance must be a city thing.

Over by the repair shop, someone was sitting in one of the vehicles, he realized. It was a dark-green SUV from a decade ago, with dents on the doors, parked facing the highway. The driver was wearing wraparound sunglasses—the kind that cops wore. But no police department in the country would issue a jalopy like that. Still, it felt like the guy was looking right at Slater. Maybe he was getting paranoid. He'd made the guy at the hotel this morning as a cop too.

Once the tank was full, he went back into the office, and the white-haired guy slid a few bills and coins across to him.

"So this is Voirrey's Corner," Slater said.

"Local folks say '*voy*-rahs,' but you've got the right place."

"I don't see a town site."

"There used to be, at one time," he said, bracing his hands on the counter. "When I was a boy Voirrey's Corner was already a ghost town. The last of the structures burned down in the eighties. There's some rubble out there, old foundations and cisterns, but these days it's just the service station and rangeland."

"Good to know."

Slater pocketed his change and walked out. The guy with the sunglasses was out of his vehicle now. His well-worn cowboy hat made him look like a rancher, but something didn't quite jibe. The chinos and the white shirt, he realized. Those were office clothes. This guy wasn't really an outdoors person.

"How are you doing?" he called to Slater, his tone faux-familiar, walking toward him.

"It's a sunny day," Slater said, not breaking his stride. "I can't complain."

He stopped in front of the pickup as Slater walked behind it, next to the gas pump.

"Are you from around here?"

"I've got a better one for you," Slater said, pulling open the driver's door. "Why are you sitting over there watching the road?"

He laughed, his tone deep. "I'm just waiting for a friend."

"Have fun with that," Slater said, and climbed in.

He started the engine and backed out so that he wouldn't have to wait for this knucklehead to step out of his way. Once he'd pulled onto the highway, headed back toward Manzanita, he eyed his phone, and dialed Andy, glad that he picked up.

"This Galliform stuff that you uncovered," Slater said. "Are you sure about the name of the town?"

"I can't remember it off … the top of my head," Andy said, "but it's whatever I texted you."

"Voirrey's Corner. I just drove through it. They told me there hasn't been a town here in generations."

"You're out there right now?"

"I'm tracking down another Daniel Martínez. The security guard from Long Beach. He's working out here. I figured Voirrey's Corner wasn't that far away—plus the feds put a bounty on Galliform."

"I'll pull it up now," Andy said, and a moment later, "The IP address that Galliform let … slip belongs to the Voirrey's Corner library. I found it myself."

"The locals pronounce it '*voy*-rahs.' There must be a glitch somewhere. There's no library."

"Let me check into it," Andy said. "I'll call you back. So what's it like out there?"

"Absolutely beautiful. Rolling desert and mountains in the distance. Endless open space with nobody in it."

It really was compelling countryside, he thought, once he'd ended the call. Driving the empty highway was a lot more chill than a crowded freeway. The light was different here than in the Mojave too. Lighter, somehow, like maybe the air was thinner.

Halfway back to Manzanita, his phone buzzed—Andy.

"So they moved the library from … Voirrey's Corner in 1954," Andy said, "but for some reason they kept the same name."

"Where did they move it to?"

"The county seat. A town called Benson. Apparently

the library … is in the courthouse now. People call it the courthouse, but it's actually the administrative … office building for the whole county."

"That's not ideal," Slater said. "Courthouses are crawling with cops and security cameras."

"You're not doing anything shady, though, are you? Just asking some … questions and looking for a guy."

"That's true. But I wonder if it's even worth it. I don't know what Galliform looks like."

"From the racist bullshit he's hawking online," Andy said, "I promise you he's … a white dude. How much is the reward?"

"A hundred grand."

"For a bite at a hundred grand I'd go … poke around. The courthouse can't be that far away. And if you ever get that … money, I want a cut."

"You'd get half," Slater said flatly. "You're the one who found Galliform out here. But don't hold your breath."

After he ended the call, Slater checked the map on his phone. Benson was about half an hour's drive, and he wouldn't even have to go back to Manzanita—there were ranch roads that went that way.

SIXTEEN

As soon as Slater had set Benson as his destination, the navigation app told him to turn off the highway. He slowed the pickup and downshifted, trying to get a look at the road before he committed to it. It was paved, he saw, so he made the turn.

The road felt smooth as he built up speed, but it was different than the main highway. Narrower, and the surface was darker, and there was no centerline or lane markings.

When he got to Benson, it felt bigger than Manzanita. There were a couple of chain stores on the outskirts, and even a stoplight closer to the center. He found the courthouse in the middle of a grassy square, and parked along a strip of retail storefronts that faced one side of it.

It seemed odd to plant a lawn in a place like this, in the middle of the desert. The building at the center of it was unmistakably designed for government, with the columns out front, and Roman pediments over the windows. He'd bet money that this was the only neoclassical building in the county.

Crossing the lawn on a brick pathway, he approached the entrance. It was early afternoon, so the offices would be open, but he didn't see any cops around. He walked between the columns and into the foyer. A security guard sat behind a desk, and looked up when he stepped in.

"The courtroom is on the west side of the building," the guard said. "Back out the doors and turn right."

"Do I look like the kind of guy who needs the courtroom?" Slater demanded.

He frowned. "That's what most people are here for. If you're looking for building permits, they moved those out to that lot where the motor pool is."

"Where's the Voirrey's Corner library?"

The guy twirled his finger in the air. "Look behind you."

Slater turned and saw a sign above a set of double doors: LIBRARY.

"If it was a snake, it would have bit you," the guard said.

Slater scoffed, and stepped over to the doors, and pulled one open. It was a spacious room, carpeted and lit by fluorescents, with bookshelves stretching toward the walls. But the place felt empty, and no one was at the counter. Scanning the ceiling, he saw that there were no cameras in here. There hadn't been any in the foyer either. Galliform wouldn't have come here if there were. Toward the back was a row of desks with a computer monitor atop each one. The sign above them said PUBLIC TERMINALS. That's where Galliform had come to work.

As he stepped farther into the big room, he caught sight of a lone staffer, sitting at a desk behind the counter. In her forties, maybe, she had her dark hair loosely tied back, and was wearing a cardigan.

With the air-conditioning cranked up in here she probably needed it.

Slater approached the counter, and the woman got up and stepped over.

"Can I help you?"

"There was a man in here on Friday. He came in to use the computers."

Her brow furrowed. "Are you another one of those federal agents? I told them everything I could remember."

"I'm not a G-man. I work in insurance. I'm trying to track the guy down."

"Well, I've already said all I'm going to say."

Slater dug in his front pocket for his cash. "Would you say it again to General Grant?"

She scowled. "That's President Grant to you."

"I must have missed that class." Slater set the fifty on the counter, holding it under his palm.

"I'm not going to take your money," she said, raising her voice.

"A donation to the library fund, then."

"Why is an insurance company interested in a fugitive that the feds are after?"

"He has a bounty on his head."

She threw up her hands. "If the vast resources of the federal government haven't managed to run him to ground, I don't suppose you will."

"Did he sign in, or use a credit card, anything like that?"

She shook her head.

"What did he look like?"

From her expression, he thought she might be about to throw him out, but she sighed, and her face softened.

"He was wearing a red plaid shirt. He has gray hair. I'd estimate he was in his sixties."

"A white guy?"

"I guess. He looked Anglo to me. There are lots of Native American people around here, but he wasn't one of them. He wasn't Latin like you either. Have you ever seen a stoat?"

Slater frowned. "What's a stoat?"

"They don't live around here. Over in the mountains. It's like a weasel or a ferret."

"I know what a weasel is."

"He looked kind of like that," she said. "A weasel or a stoat. A slight frame, and a sharp nose, and beady little eyes."

"Was he tall or short?"

"Not quite as tall as you."

"I don't suppose you know what he was driving."

"If I did, I'd go after that reward money myself."

Slater nodded. "Is there anything else you remember about him?"

"He wasn't here for very long."

"All right," Slater said, and held up the fifty, but her eyes grew hard. Pocketing it, he turned to walk out.

"Are there going to be more like you?" she called after him.

Ignoring that, he stepped out into the rotunda. His phone had buzzed a minute ago, and he paused to check. It was a text from Andy:

Call me. I might have something.

Tucking his phone away again, he felt eyes on him, and looked toward the desk. The guard was focused on a screen, but standing nearby was a familiar face, idly watching him. It was the guy who'd been sitting in the old SUV at the gas station in Voirrey's Corner. His sunglasses were up on his head now, and he'd ditched the hat. His short dark hair was brushed backward. Basically fuckable, he decided.

He made no attempt to conceal his interest in Slater. Even though it was obvious that they recognized each other, no way was he going to engage. Slater glared at him, and threw up his hands, and walked out into the daylight.

It could just be a coincidence, he reasoned, as there weren't a lot of towns around here. Seeing the same face thirty miles from Voirrey's Corner would be like running into the same person on the next block in the city. Still, it felt like he was interested in Slater. This guy hadn't followed him, he was sure of that—the route Slater had taken to get here had been indirect, and he would have noticed another vehicle behind him on those rural back roads.

Walking through the grassy square, Slater spotted a coffee place a few doors up from where he'd parked, and he crossed the street to step inside. The clerk was a teenage boy with spotty skin.

"An oat milk latte," Slater said, stepping up to the counter.

"We don't have that."

"How about soy milk?"

"We don't have that either."

"What about a double espresso, then. Is that too much to ask?"

He nodded and stepped over to the machine.

Once Slater had his java in hand, he sat near the entrance, with his back against the wall, at a table with a view of the courthouse. There wasn't a lot of foot traffic so it was easy to surveille the square. That guy wasn't following him, he decided. He definitely would have shown himself by now.

Pulling out his phone, he dialed Andy.

"I was thinking about tilting at windmills," Andy said when he answered.

"What the hell does that mean?" Slater demanded.

"You said it seemed pointless to … go after Galliform with so little information. So I did some digging where you are, around Benson and … Manzanita and Voirrey's Corner. I looked at cell towers."

"Looking for what?"

"Evidence of a tech-savvy fugitive. There aren't a lot of … people around there, so there's not a lot of cell towers either. I found a … tower that's doing something unusual."

Slater sipped his coffee. "What kind of unusual?"

"It's consistently handling many … gigabytes of data from the same user. Ranchers don't use that kind of bandwidth, do they? I thought it … might be connected to Galliform."

"Could it be a factory, or a small business?"

"There's nothing like that within range of the tower," Andy said. "And if you're running a business with big data volumes, you get the cheapest … internet connection possible. Cellular data costs a fortune. You only use it if you have to … move around—and this user isn't moving around."

"Can you pin down a location?"

"I can tell you the direction. The software identified … which antenna it is. There are three of them on the tower, so this user is … somewhere in the third of the circle facing southwest. I'll text you the coordinates of the tower."

"How far from the antenna would this user be?" Slater said.

"Up to five miles. Beyond that, you're in another cell."

"This is freaking amazing work, man."

"It might not mean anything," Andy said. "It could be a kid streaming a bunch of porn on his phone without Mom's knowledge."

Slater ended the call and checked his texts. Andy sent a map link, and a second message:

If the cell tower was at the center of a clock face, and 12 is due north, the heavy user is in the angle between 5 and 9.

When he pulled up the location of the tower on the map, it was south of Manzanita. Zooming in, he saw that it was just a few miles east of Voirrey's Corner. The satellite view showed that several home-steads were within range. One of them had a long, straight cleared area next to the buildings. An air-strip, he realized. That's exactly the kind of place a fugitive would be.

But it was too far north, he saw, zooming out again. The airstrip was outside the 5-to-9 angle Andy had indicated. The most compelling site that fell within the angle stood out because it was more elaborate than its neighbors, with half a dozen small buildings. It was definitely within the five-mile range of the cell tower too. A few shrubby trees grew around the property, and there was a brush-filled wash just north of it, bisected by the access road. That was the place to start, he decided.

Once he'd put the homestead in his navigation app, and slammed the last of his espresso, he walked out to the rusty pickup. Glancing around the square and up the street, there was no sign of the lurker from the courthouse.

Slater headed out of town and got on the highway. It was a more direct route than he'd taken to get here, and the road was better. When he got close to Voirrey's Corner, the app directed him to turn onto an unstriped ranch road, and then onto a dirt road. It had some washboards at first but then it smoothed out.

He came to a bosque that stretched out on either side of the road. He'd seen it on the satellite view. From this vantage he could see it was a gentle draw with some healthy piñons and brush growing along it. The map said the homestead was less than half a mile ahead. If he walked from here, still out of sight of the buildings, he'd be less likely to alert Galliform to his approach.

Slater pulled off the road along the north side of the trees and killed the engine. Walking up on the place was risky, as whoever was there might be armed, and he'd be completely exposed. But Galliform didn't know Slater, and even the crustiest desert dweller was unlikely to blast a stranger for no reason. At worst, the encounter would involve a brandished shotgun or a warning shot. But at least he'd get a look at who was there.

The vegetation in the bosque was sparse enough that he could walk through it. He'd need to come up with a reason for being out here, he realized. Whoever he met at the homestead would definitely ask. He focused on concocting a story as he walked across the draw.

On the other side he could see the buildings of the homestead in the distance, half hidden by an intermediate rise in the land. As he stepped into the open, he saw there was a vehicle here, parked on this side of the trees. A dark-green SUV. He'd seen that car once before today. What the hell, he wondered, and walked toward it.

By the time he saw the guy, it was too late. Out of the shadows of the trees he noticed movement in the periphery of his vision. Slater had time to duck, and formulate a plan to dick-punch the guy, but before he could do that he felt electric fire on his neck, and his muscles stopped working. He tumbled to the ground, face down, and groaned, struggling to get air.

A taser. Why had he let his guard down? He couldn't even move his eyeballs to get a look at his assailant. But he knew who was driving that beat-up SUV—the lurker from the courthouse. That fucker had to be one of Galliform's henchmen.

A looming form blotted out the sun overhead, and Slater felt his useless dead arms being drawn together, against his back, and then the ratchet clicks of the handcuffs going on. Handcuffs were actually a good sign. They meant he couldn't fight back anymore, but they also meant this thug wasn't going to croak him. At least not right away.

The guy patted him down, doing a cursory check of his pockets and his ankles. Hands reached into his armpits, and he felt himself being pulled up, and the ground dropped away. This guy was strong, and he dragged him a few paces, Slater's heels scraping the dirt, and propped him against a tree. The bark felt rough against his back, and his head lolled forward.

Some of his muscle control was starting to return. His shoulders burned from being manhandled, and he could move his jaw a little now. The guy squatted in front of him, and lifted Slater's chin, propping his head back against the tree. His sunglasses were up on his head, and his brow was knotted in concentration. Slater gazed at him dully, unable to speak, not even able to scowl.

He had a cell phone in hand, and held it in front of Slater's face for a moment, then stepped back.

"Let's see what we've got," he said, half to himself.

Slater tried to speak, but his tongue was still thick. He was only able to muster a throaty growl.

"It's easier if you just wait it out. It'll all come back to you." He was gazing at his phone screen. "Ibáñez. Los Angeles. Insurance investigator." He met Slater's gaze. "Known to police," he said pointedly, then walked toward his vehicle.

Slater wondered if he was going to leave him here like this. He'd be able to stand up, eventually, but he wouldn't be able to shift gears with his hands cuffed behind his back.

A few minutes later the guy returned and stood in front of him. A sidearm and its holster were clipped to the side of his belt, he saw. He hadn't been wearing that at the gas station or the library. Slater's muscles were coming back online, and he managed to speak coherently.

"Who the fuck are you?"

"My name is Pike. I'm a federal agent."

Slater thought about it. "OK, that actually fits."

"There's a flag on your file to route queries through a specific detective out there in Los Angeles."

"Is his name Conrad? That freaking dick-smack."

"Has he arrested you before?"

"Much worse. He's my ex."

"So he's stalking you," Pike said.

"He's not that guy. He probably flagged me to try to keep me out of trouble."

"What are you doing skulking around out here?"

"I'm thinking it's the same reason you're here," Slater said.

"And what would that be?"

"Galliform," Slater said flatly.

Even though he tried to keep a straight face, Pike couldn't hide his surprise, the spark of recognition.

"Go on," he said, and waved a hand.

Slater took a breath. Pike was in full cop mode now—he wouldn't be sharing anything. Slater was going to have to tell him enough of the truth to get himself unhooked.

"I suspect you already know all this," Slater said, "but Conrad can fill you in on a case he worked. A woman blew up a cell-phone mast on a hotel rooftop in the city of angels. Galliform sold her the explosive and manipulated her into doing it. I never met the man, but I know he spouts conspiracy garbage, and he was at the Voirrey's Corner library a few days ago. One of the places you were lurking at earlier today."

"You know about the rooftop bombing because your ex worked the case?" Pike said.

"I interviewed the perp about something else. She's eating baloney sandwiches in jail right now while the puppet master is living the high life out here."

"I wouldn't exactly call it the high life," Pike said, and shifted on his feet. "So you're trying to track him down."

"I was out here on another case, and I heard there was a hefty bounty on Galliform. I couldn't pass up a stab at that."

"Why do you say he was at the library? And why

do you think he's at this particular homestead?"

"Is he over there?" Slater demanded. "Unhook me. We can go take him together. We'll split the reward."

Pike chuckled. "Your ex probably told you that we're looking for him too."

Slater watched him for a moment. That confirmed it all—Pike was out here tracking Galliform, and this might be where Galliform was holed up.

He tried to arch his back. "Can you unhook me now? You and I are after the same guy."

"I need to check with this detective in Los Angeles first. Give me a minute."

Slater scoffed. "Just don't tell him you detained me."

"Why not?"

"It's embarrassing. He's my ex."

Pike stepped away, and stood over by his beat-up SUV, and held his phone to his ear. Slater couldn't overhear the conversation, but he spent a while talking to somebody. Eventually he came back and squatted beside him, reaching for his hands.

"Your detective friend says you actually helped them track down the bomber," Pike said. "That tells me you're not working for Galliform."

Slater scoffed and leaned forward so that Pike could access the cuffs. "I basically told you that already."

"I had to verify it. You know the drill."

Pike leaned in, pulling Slater's arms away from the tree. At such close proximity he could see the sweat in the armpit of his shirt.

"You smell like furniture polish," Pike said.

"That's pine resin. It's because you threw me into a piñon pine."

Pike rose and stepped back, tucking the handcuffs

into his hip pocket. Slater's hands were finally free. It took him a minute to stand up, bracing himself on the piñon. He felt weak from being fried but at least he was steady on his feet. He rolled his shoulders, and rubbed his wrists, and eyed Pike, who stood there watching him.

"Is it a felony to punch a federal agent in the face?" Slater demanded.

"Definitely," he said quickly. "So don't even think about it."

"Oh, you know I'm thinking about it. What agency are you with?"

"My badge says ATF, but I was seconded to a domestic terrorism task force."

Slater frowned. "You never did show me a badge. I guess I bought your story because it took you a hot minute to ID me through your phone. Why are you alone?"

"I'm working with a colleague in the neighborhood, but I came down here on my own. That's why I had to incapacitate you. I didn't want to get into a shootout."

"I'm not armed."

"I know that now. I didn't when you rolled up."

"Why were you following me? I saw you at that gas station, just hanging around like you had all the time in the world, and then again at the courthouse in Benson."

"I'm following up leads on Galliform," Pike said. "When I saw you pull in at Voirrey's Corner, I knew you weren't a rancher, or a tourist. You're too urban. I figured you might be one of Galliform's acolytes, so I put a tracker on your pickup."

"You prick," Slater snapped. "Is that even legal?"

Pike laughed. "You can understand why I'd want to keep tabs on you. I thought you might lead me right to him."

"So how did you get here before me?"

"I didn't come here because of you." He hesitated. "I probably shouldn't talk details, but that detective in Los Angeles said you're on the right side of this. An analyst back in the office pointed us to this homestead as a potential hideout. That's why I was watching the comings and goings at Voirrey's Corner. I got here ten minutes before you did." Pike's brow furrowed. "You still haven't explained what brought you here."

"I have analysts too."

"Seriously."

"Don't ask me for details," Slater said, "and I won't ask for details on the warrantless tracker you put on my pickup."

Pike studied him for a moment, his expression thoughtful. Clearly he wasn't rattled by Slater's words.

"I should retrieve that device," he said finally, and walked through the trees toward Slater's ride.

Slater followed him and watched as he squatted at the rear fender, and reached up under it, and pulled out a little black box.

"It's so easy to attach to these old vehicles," Pike said.

"Lots of steel for the magnets."

"That's right," he said as he stood erect.

Slater had done the same thing himself, dozens of times, when he was tracking lowlifes using Svetlana's illicit tech. But he wasn't sure he liked the way it felt to be on the other end of it.

"You thought I was with Galliform," Slater said, "and when you tased me, I thought you were with

Galliform. I assumed I was going to wind up as coyote chow."

Pike stood with his feet apart, idly handling the tracker. "It's interesting that we both followed the same lead to get here. At least I assume it was the same lead. What did your analyst tell you?"

"Listen, am I being detained?"

"Of course not." He frowned. "I'm out here doing initial recon. It would be great if you'd share what you've learned about this fugitive. But I can't force you to tell me."

Slater put his hands on his hips. "Actually, you know damn well that you can."

Pike chuckled. "You don't seem like the kind of person who'd be intimidated by a subpoena or a claustrophobic interview room. This doesn't have to be adversarial. We want the same thing."

"What happens if I drive over to that homestead?"

"I can't let you do that. I'd have to pop you again." Pike waved his arm. "You can't interfere with an official operation just because you managed to blunder into the middle of it."

"I'm not sure I'd call it an operation." Slater gave him a pointed once-over. "All I see is you and a ratty old SUV."

Pike laughed. "The tip of the spear, my friend. So where can I find you?"

"The only hotel in Manzanita." Slater stepped to the driver's door of the pickup.

"That's where I'm staying too," Pike said, and watched him climb in behind the wheel. "You're going to turn north, aren't you? I shouldn't have to say this, but I will come after you if you head toward that homestead."

"I'm not an idiot," Slater said, and started the engine.

Pulling onto the dirt road, he went north, back toward Manzanita. Once he was on the highway, and picked up some speed, he saw Pike's SUV in the rearview. He hung back at a reasonable distance. What a goddamn bully. At least he hadn't gone full cop and thrown Slater in the hoosegow.

Slater parked in front of his room at the hotel and went inside. He guzzled water, and ate half the tamale he'd bought from Margie, and then stretched out on the bed. His muscles ached, and he still felt light-headed, and he'd been up so damn early. Almost instantly he sank into sleep.

SEVENTEEN

OMETIME LATER A LOUD knock roused Slater from his slumber. It took a second to remember where he was, staring at the blue-painted cinderblock wall and the thin curtains that didn't really block the daylight. He got up and hobbled to the door. His muscles felt spent, like he'd been running a shovel all day.

When he pulled it open, Pike was standing there, a stupid grin on his face.

"Hey," Slater said. "It's the man with the hundred million volts in his pants. What do you need?"

Pike chuckled. "Do you want to see something cool? There's a few hours of daylight left."

"You want me to go out with you? Is this an excuse to interrogate me?"

"Just come for a drive," Pike said. "I'm off the clock."

That seemed unlikely, Slater thought, and rubbed his eyes. "Where do you want to go?"

"It'll be more interesting if I just show you. It's not far."

"Are you going to tase me again?"

"I only use that as the introductory move."

"What the hell," Slater said. "Give me a minute."

He started to close the door, but then pulled it open again. "You have to wear your hat."

He shut the door, and then washed up, and changed his shirt. When he stepped outside, Pike was leaning on his vehicle, arms folded. He had the weathered cowboy hat on.

"Ready to roll?" he said, and stood up.

They both climbed into his SUV, and Pike backed out, then headed toward the highway. Before he made the turn, he waited for a big RV to lumber past.

"Looks like it's camping season," Pike said.

Slater eyed him. "Why are you so damn chipper?"

"I guess I'm an optimist." He grinned. "I've been told everyone has a personality set point, and that's mine. So why did you want me to wear the hat?"

"You know why."

Pike glanced at him sidelong but didn't pursue it. They rode in silence for a while, through the arid countryside, until he spoke.

"So how did you track Galliform to that property?"

"I knew that's what this was about," Slater said.

"I'm just making conversation. And I'm curious. I've got a room full of people looking for this guy, and they just caught wind of that homestead today. But there you were."

"I suppose that means you're not going to let it go until I tell you."

Pike clicked his tongue. "That's the way it tends to unfold."

"All I can say is that it's a trade secret."

"Your researcher knew Galliform was at that ranch?"

"Not at first," Slater said. "He found something about an exposed IP address at that library in Benson."

"That's what brought me here too. So that explains why you went to the library."

"Then today my guy found a cell tower that was carrying way more data than a ranch would use."

"Very clever, to look for anomalies like that," Pike said. "But it sounds like illegal surveillance."

"I know he wouldn't do anything illegal. Not like violating my Fourth Amendment rights with a hidden tracker. We all know that falls well within the definition of illegal surveillance."

"I guess you really wanted that reward money. Were you just going to go in and strong-arm the guy? You weren't armed, but I bet Galliform is."

"I hadn't thought that far ahead." Slater looked out the side window. "So where's your office?"

"I'm based in Albuquerque."

"You like being a G-man?"

"The pension is pretty good, and I can retire from the field in my fifties."

"Sweet."

"It's definitely a job for young people," Pike said. "It feels pretty dangerous sometimes."

"That's the downside to law enforcement. People shoot at you."

"A-yup." Pike shifted in his seat. "So what was the other case that brought you to Manzanita?"

"Do you even realize you're interrogating me?"

"I guess it's kind of my default."

"I work freelance," Slater said. "An insurance company hired me to track down a policy beneficiary. I found a candidate who works for a rapid response team that's based in Manzanita."

"The saucer-chasers," Pike said. "Those guys are hard-core."

"I thought they were here on the down-low, but everyone seems to know who they are."

"How could you keep something like that secret in a small town? Whether or not anyone takes them seriously is a different story."

He turned onto a dirt road, and drove a washboarded mile or so, and then pulled over. They both climbed out, and Slater stretched his arms, and his back.

"Are you still feeling it?" Pike said.

"I'm kind of achy. Like I have the flu."

"Exercise will help. Come on."

Pike started walking through the brush, away from the road. They hiked for a few minutes, walking abreast as they climbed a hill. At the top there was a broad view of the countryside.

"You see where that wash kind of widens?" Pike said, pointing into the landscape below. "Right there is where a UFO crashed in 1955."

"If it crashed," Slater said, "it's not a UFO. It's a spaceship, or a flying saucer."

Pike eyed him. "That actually makes sense."

"I've been talking to the rapid response crew."

"It would have been pretty cool to witness it, don't you think?" Pike gazed out at the landscape. "Hardly anybody did. Just some locals. The military got it cleaned up in short order."

"You're a damn saucer-head."

Pike chuckled. "I'm not actually a true believer. I've read about it because it's intriguing, and it's part of local culture."

"I'm sure the feds know more about that subject than they're telling."

"Unfortunately it's not my department."

"That would be the Navy."

Pike looked at him. "Even out here? Why do you say that?"

"Whenever something hinky is going on with the federal government, it's the Navy."

"It's a pretty big organization. There might be some other hinky parts." He waved an arm. "Do you want to hike down there? I've done it before. I didn't find any debris."

"I'm not really up to it," Slater said, "after my electrotherapy session."

"It's getting close to sunset. Do you want to watch from here?"

"Why not?" Slater said, and sat next to him on the ground, grunting as his muscles burned with the effort of getting settled. He draped his arms on his knees and looked out over the landscape. The sun was approaching the horizon, but the air here was too thin and dry for it to change color, and it was still bright broad daylight.

Not looking at him, Pike spoke. "I'm not sure if you can tell, but I'm attracted to you."

"I've been thinking you're pretty fuckable yourself. And that hat kind of seals the deal."

Pike chuckled, and turned to him, and adjusted the hat farther back on his head. "So are you going to make a move, or are you waiting for me to?"

Slater reached for his cheek, and leaned in, and met his mouth. Soft and firm in turns, and warm and perfect, he got lost in it. Pulling away, Slater stretched out on his back, and Pike leaned in, and ran his hand over his chest, and his belly, and his crotch. A smirk on his face, his eyes were bright.

Unbuttoning Pike's shirt, Slater reached inside

and caressed his chest. Eventually Pike sat up.

"We're getting close to the point of no return."

"Are you worried someone will walk up on us?" Slater said. "I think we'd hear a vehicle."

"I'd rather be somewhere more comfortable. Without rattlesnakes and rocks digging into me. Can we wait until we get back to the hotel?"

"Sure," Slater said, squeezing his bicep. "But I'm going to have a stiffy the whole way."

Sunset forgotten, the sun was still well above the horizon as they walked back down the hill and climbed into the SUV. Pike made a three-point turn and headed back the way they'd come.

"I feel like we should eat in Benson," he said. "It's just a few miles farther. There's an Italian place. They have pizza."

"You can't fuck a pizza, Pike."

"You're not a fan?"

"I mean we could go eat after we hook up."

"I'm thinking you haven't been here very long," he said. "After 9 p.m. there's nowhere to eat for a hundred miles. Not even a corner store. Unless you have a food cache in your hotel room, you won't get grub until morning."

"Italian it is, then."

"The anticipation will make the romance all the more sweet."

Slater scoffed. "There's a reason instant gratification is a whole thing."

On the way to Benson, Pike asked him about his life, and how he spent his time, and where he went to school, and who his family was. It felt like too much—not like an interrogation, more like gossip. But it was better than if he'd pressed him for details on Andy and his illicit research.

Dusk had settled in when they pulled into the gravel parking lot at the restaurant. Inside they got a booth along the wall. Looking over the menu was annoying, Slater realized, as there was nothing for him. It was so hard to eat when you left the city.

The waitress was a woman in her twenties, wearing jeans, her wiry brown hair cut short and tucked back. When she stepped over, Slater looked up.

"Can you just do noodles with garlic and olive oil?"

"Sure," she said, and took his menu.

Pike ordered a pizza, then eyed Slater. "Do you want a glass of wine?"

"If you have one."

"Two glasses of red," he told her. When she'd stepped away, he eyed Slater. "You look tired."

"I was up really early. And oh, yeah—I got tased today."

Pike chuckled. "Food will help."

"How would you know? Have you ever been tased?"

"Once. In a training session."

The waitress stepped up with two wineglasses in hand, and set one in front of Pike. Slater didn't see exactly how it happened, but when she moved to set the other glass down, she lost hold of it, and dumped most of it in his lap.

"Whoa, that's cold," he said, and quickly arched his back to yank his phone out of his pocket. It was still dry, at least, and he set it on the table.

"I'm so sorry," the woman wailed. "I'm such an idiot."

"It's OK," Slater said, and set the empty glass on the table, and reached for a stack of napkins.

"I feel terrible." She was practically dancing, hopping from one foot to the other. "I ruined your pants."

Slater looked up at her, and grasped her forearm. "Look at me."

She inhaled sharply, and stopped hopping, and met his gaze.

"My pants aren't ruined. It's just an old pair of jeans."

"OK." She nodded.

He let go of her arm. "Did you do it on purpose?"

"Of course not."

"So you don't have to feel bad. It was an accident. It happens to everybody, and I'm not upset."

"OK." She took a deep breath. "Thanks for that. I just wish I could fix it."

"You know what you could do for me?"

"Name it."

Slater handed her the empty wineglass. "Bring me another one of these."

"Right. Of course." She snatched the glass and hustled away.

"Do you need more napkins?" Pike said.

"No, man. There's no point. It's all soaked into me already."

"You totally talked her down," he said. "You really handled that like a gentleman."

Slater frowned. "Where I come from, gentlemen are straight guys who go to strip clubs."

He chuckled. "You're a good man, Ibáñez."

"I'm actually not. And you know that. But I hate to see people stressing out about nothing."

"Why can't you just take the compliment?"

"Why can't you just eat a dick?" Slater demanded. Pike threw his head back and guffawed. The waitress came back and carefully set a wineglass on the table. When Slater lifted it, Pike clinked his own against it and took a slurp.

He could see that look in Pike's eye, that intensity, as he sat there watching him. Slater knew what that meant.

"Don't do that," he said.

Pike frowned. "Do what?"

"Don't like me so much. I'm not who you think I am."

"What does that mean?"

"I'm a bad guy, Pike. Real bad."

"Don't tell me what my feelings are supposed to be."

Slater shrugged. "Fair enough."

Their food arrived, and he dug into his noodles. Pike eyed him over a slice of pizza.

"You're a lot of man, Slater."

"See, that's so much better. Get pissed at me, and stay pissed at me. It's better for everybody."

Pike scoffed and focused on his food.

When the check came, Pike looked it over. "I think she comped your meal. The wine too."

"Not acceptable," Slater said. He dug out the fifty he'd tried to give the librarian and handed it over.

"I think that's too much. Even if you pay for your noodles. Do you want me to ask?"

"Just leave her the money," Slater said, and slid out of the booth.

Twilight was past when they walked out to the parking lot and climbed into the SUV. Pike flicked on the headlights and headed to the highway.

"It gets so damn dark out here," Slater said, once they were in the countryside.

"Weird, isn't it? No surprise that the saucer chasers set up camp."

When they got to the hotel in Manzanita, Slater climbed out and rolled his shoulders.

"My place?" he said, and Pike followed him inside.

Once he'd closed the door behind them, Pike put his hands on his hips and took a deep breath.

"So you're a bad guy, huh."

Slater raised his eyebrows. "What are you going to do about it?"

"Teach you some manners, maybe."

"Bring it on, copper," he said, jutting his chin.

Pike stepped closer, and put a hand on Slater's cheek. He grabbed Pike's belt and pulled him close, grinding his woody into him. Pike met his lips, his mouth warm and intent, and then mouthed his neck as Slater ran his hands over his shoulders, and his back, and his butt.

Pulling back, Pike unbuttoned Slater's shirt, then loosened his belt.

"Your jeans are still damp."

Slater grabbed his belt, and unbuckled it, and shoved his chinos down, then massaged Pike's junk through his underpants.

"Let me take my shoes off," he said, and sat on the edge of the bed.

Slater squatted to untie his boots, and soon they were both naked. Moving closer, Pike pushed him onto the bed, then straddled him.

"You're so fucking hot," Slater said. "I just don't get it."

Pike chuckled. "What don't you get?"

"I can't put my finger on it. You're more than hot. It's like you're this big slab of sex."

Pressing into him, Pike mouthed his jaw and his neck, and squeezed his cock.

"Can I fuck you?" he whispered.

"I don't know," Slater said. "Can you?"

He sat up and flipped open his satchel, and found a condom and a mini bottle of lube in the outside pocket, and handed them to Pike. He was already hard enough, Slater found, grasping his cock, and once he'd rolled it on, Pike leaned closer.

Slater stopped him with a hand on his shoulder, then with his other hand slapped him hard across the face.

"What the fuck, man?" Pike demanded.

"You want to show me some manners? Bring it." Slater slapped him again.

Pike grabbed his wrist, then the other one, and pushed them down, then loomed over him.

"You're a tough guy, huh?"

"What's it to you?" Slater said.

"I'm going to fuck you."

Slater scoffed. "Big talk."

Shoving his knee up, Pike pressed a lubed thumb into him, breathing hard now. Slater folded his hands behind his head, his lip curling into a sneer.

"Is that all you've got?"

"You little *schvantz*," Pike said through his teeth.

Shifting closer, he pressed into him. Slater winced with the intensity of it, and soon Pike was deep inside him, his face flushed. He built up his rhythm until he was pounding him. Slater slapped his face.

"Fuck," Pike roared, and pounded harder, and slapped him back.

"What did you say?" Slater demanded.

"Fuck you, you goddamn lowlife."

Slater craned up to meet his mouth, and Pike leaned into it, straining into him, and came with a shudder.

When he pulled back, he wrapped his arms around Slater's shoulders, squeezing him tightly for a moment before he rolled onto his side. Meeting his mouth again, Pike grabbed his cock and stroked it. Slater nuzzled his ear, and buried his nose in his hair, inhaling the heady scent of his sweat, and then came, straining into Pike's fist.

Rolling onto his back, Slater folded his arm over his eyes as he caught his breath. He could feel Pike next to him, the heat of his skin, the sound of his breath. Sometime later Pike's voice roused him.

"How did you know that would work?"

"What are you talking about?" Slater said, moving his arm. His tongue felt thick.

"Pushing me a little. Making me angry. That made it so much more intense."

"I'm not sure. Instinct, maybe."

Pike kissed him again, and lingered a moment before he pulled back, and gazed at him, his head propped on his arm. At least some of the infatuation stuff had melted away, Slater saw. It was different now. More realistic. It would be easier to handle.

He tapped Pike's bicep, where he had a dark-blue tattoo of the star of David.

"Are you one of god's chosen people?" Slater said. "Small world."

Pike's eyes narrowed. "You're Jewish?"

"You sound skeptical."

"Were you bar mitzvahed?"

"Totally. There was a rebbe and cake and everything."

"Your name is Hispanic, and you look Hispanic."

"It's on my mother's side."

Pike caressed his belly. "That's the side that matters."

"Pike doesn't sound like a Jewish name either."

"The story is that it was something way more Hebey, and it got mangled at Ellis Island."

"Isn't it against some rabbinical rule to get tats?"

"Totally. I think it's right in the Torah. But I'm not really religious."

"So why get the tat?"

"I'm in a job where people shoot at me. I'll take whatever help I can get."

Slater leaned in and nuzzled his neck. "At least you get to tase people sometimes. And handcuff them to a tree."

Pulling him on top of his body, Pike met his mouth. Slater straddled his hips, and cradled his head, feeling his warm sweat. There was something different about this one. Usually he lost interest right after the act, and focused on going to sleep, but he still wanted to touch his skin, and smell his hair. It didn't seem right. Maybe dude has some kind of pheromone imbalance.

"Can I sleep here?" Pike said.

"Fine with me." Slater climbed off him and got up. "I'm going to be unconscious very soon."

On the counter next to the sink he found the pint of bourbon he'd bought from Margie, still in its paper bag. Unwrapping it, he cracked the seal and guzzled from it.

"You do that to help you sleep?" Pike said.

"I do it to make life bearable. It's just bourbon. You want a taste?"

"No thanks."

Slater took another long pull, and then stretched out beside him, and killed the bedside lamp. Pike reached across his belly, and shifted him onto his side, and pulled him close, notching his knees behind Slater's. Grasping the back of Slater's hand, he entwined their fingers, then pulled him closer.

This was good, Slater thought, sinking into unconsciousness. The skin contact made him feel warm, and content, and perfect. It had to be some kind of chemical thing.

EIGHTEEN

N THE MORNING SLATER woke with a woody.
Someone was blowing him, he realized, and he
started to full wakefulness. In the dim early light
from the windows he saw that it was Pike.

Pike lifted his head and looked up at him. "Just
relax. Lie back."

The guy was good at this, Slater realized, and
it didn't take him long to climax. Grinning, Pike
climbed up beside him, and mashed his woody into
his thigh, and kissed him. Slater grabbed his cock
and squeezed.

"Oh, yeah. Like that," Pike said, and thrust into
him.

He shifted on top of him, kissing his neck, and
Slater could feel the weight of his body. A minute
later, groaning and straining into him, he came, and
then rolled off.

"Good morning," Pike said softly.

Slater had to chuckle, and wrapped an arm around
his neck, and pulled him close before he drifted back
into sleep.

When he woke again, it was lighter outside, and
Pike was getting dressed.

"I have to get going. Can you give me your cell number?"

"Only if you text me yours," he said, and recited it as Pike thumb-typed. "Do you think they do laundry here?"

Pike tucked his phone away. "You'll probably have to do it yourself."

"That's not going to happen." Slater got up and scooped up his pants. The wine was completely dry.

"You could ask if someone can do it for you."

"I don't actually have any other pants. If I wear these, it'll look like I got stabbed in the dick."

"You're about my size," Pike said. "I can loan you a pair of pants. I'm just afraid they'll be a little baggy in the crotch on you."

Slater frowned. "Because you're so stacked? Are you kidding me?"

He laughed. "I'll go get them."

Stepping out, he left the door ajar, and came back a minute later with a pair of tan chinos in hand.

Pushing himself out of bed, Slater stepped into them and zipped up the fly.

"They look fine," Pike said. "Your butt looks amazing."

"I feel like a dentist on casual Friday." Slater pulled at the pocket. The material was sheer, and it had some give to it. He squatted and rapidly rose again. "What the hell kind of fabric is this?"

"You've never worn stretchy pants before? They're great, aren't they? It's flexible because there's a little elastic woven into the cotton."

"Damn it," Slater snapped.

"Are they not comfortable?"

"You've ruined jeans for me. Now I'm going to

want to wear these."

"You can get jeans made of that fabric."

"But then they're not really jeans, are they," Slater said, glaring at him. "What the hell is wrong with you?"

"Don't shoot the messenger." He chuckled. "So to be real, it has to be exactly what the forty-niners were wearing?"

Slater groaned, and lifted his knee, and then lifted the other. "This is not good."

"I'm sure you'll power through it," Pike said. "I have to go to work."

Once Pike had gone, Slater had a shower, and got dressed, and took his jeans out to the front desk. The same clerk as yesterday was working reception.

"Do you have laundry service?" Slater asked him.

He looked at the jeans, and his brow furrowed. "There's machines around back that you can use. They take quarters."

"I don't have time for that. If you're doing a load of your own, or maybe the housekeeper is doing towels, you could just throw them in."

"Yeah, I can't really do that."

Slater dug out a twenty and palmed it. "Have you ever read about Andrew Jackson? He was a can-do kind of guy. He drove the British right out of New Orleans."

"All right," he said. "I'll see what I can do."

"I knew you were an enterprising person." He slapped the counter, leaving the twenty there, and turned to walk out.

It was getting close to Danilo's arrival time. Slater climbed into the pickup, and drove the few blocks over to the trio of houses. When he pulled up in front, the white SUV was backing out of the drive-way. Slater climbed out and waved.

Rogers braked and rolled down his window. "Hey, Max."

"Are you headed to the airport?"

"I already picked up Danilo. They had a tailwind from Phoenix. I'm headed to Benson to get a brake job on this rig. Did you hear them squealing just now?"

"Margie can't do it for you?"

"She doesn't have the right parts."

"Which building is Danilo in?"

"The middle one," Rogers said, and nodded to it.

"Does he know I'm coming?"

"Oh, yeah," he said, raising his eyebrows. He backed into the street and drove away.

Walking up to the door, Slater knocked and waited. He recognized Danilo right away from his ID photo, although his hair was shorter now. He wasn't stocky, like the photo had implied, but more compact and muscled. Danilo was wearing the same uniform as Rogers, black pants and a black polo shirt, and had the same faceless black device strapped on his wrist. His brow furrowed in concern as he pulled open the door.

"You must be Max. I heard you were looking for me."

"I work for an insurance company," Slater said. "Can we sit down?"

Danilo waved him in, closing the door behind him. He waited for Slater to sit at the conference table, then took a chair on the opposite side, resting his arms on the tabletop.

"So what's going on?"

"Did you live in South Gate twenty-seven years ago?"

"I've lived lots of places. Including South Gate. I'm not sure of the dates. That was a long time ago."

"Were you ever married to a woman named Carla?"

Danilo frowned. "What's this about?"

"Carla died recently. She left a life insurance policy."

"I'm sorry to hear that. She was a good person."

Watching him closely, Danilo wasn't really acting emotional, but he seemed sincere. He wasn't afraid to admit he knew Carla. But that didn't necessarily mean he was the guy.

"Carla had a daughter," Slater continued. "Rocky. She's twenty-seven years old now. If you're her biological father, Rocky wants to meet you."

Danilo shook his head. "That's somebody else's kid. Nothing to do with me. Sorry, mac."

"Personally I don't care whether she's yours or not. If you were married to Carla, however, there's fifteen grand in it for you."

"The money's mine regardless of the paternity?"

"That's right."

"So if I cop to marrying Carla, you'll cut me a check?"

"We'll have to confirm your identity first," Slater said. "But if you're the right Daniel Martínez, somebody in the company will cut you a check eventually."

"It sounds almost too good to be true."

"You don't remember Carla buying the policy back then? Your name is on it."

A loud electronic beeping filled the room, and Danilo dug in his pants, and produced a cell phone, and held it to his ear.

"Martínez," he said, and his brow furrowed as he listened. "Understood. Send the coordinates. I'm on it."

Danilo quickly got up, and tucked the phone away, but then froze.

"I forgot—Rogers took the SUV. That freaking numbskull."

"What's going on?" Slater said.

"There's been an incident. Rogers will be gone for hours. That kind of messes up the 'rapid' part of rapid response."

"You only have the one vehicle?"

"Right."

"Just call him. I saw him leave a couple minutes ago. He won't be anywhere near Benson yet."

He snapped his fingers. "That's exactly the thing to do."

Danilo dug out the phone again, and dialed, and held it to his ear. From the back of the house came the faint trill of a ringing phone. Slater wasn't sure if Danilo heard it at first, but then he turned and walked into the next room, returning a minute later with a black cell phone. He set it on the conference table.

"Rogers is a genius," he said. "Maybe I can figure out what garage he went to, and ask them to send him back."

"That'll take at least an hour. I have wheels."

His eyebrows shot up. "You'll loan me your car?"

"No—but I'll drive you."

"You're not trained for this work," Danilo said. "It could be dangerous. If it's aliens, it could shatter your worldview. That kind of experience could totally blow your mind."

"If it's aliens," Slater said, "I definitely want to be

there. It's a saucer crash?"

"Something crashed. I need to go find out what." Danilo eyed him for a moment, calculating. "Can you keep your mouth shut about whatever you see?"

"Sure. Confidentiality is a big part of my work."

He stood up taller. "All right—Let's go."

He grabbed a black duffel bag from the floor in the corner and then pulled open the front door. Following him outside, Slater pointed out the pickup. Danilo lifted the bag into the back and then got in the passenger side.

"Which way?" Slater said, starting the engine.

"South." Danilo was gazing at his phone screen. "Get on the highway. From here it's fifty-one miles. On these roads it should be less than an hour."

"This boat isn't built for speed," Slater said, pulling into the street.

"As long as we're rolling. I'll tell you where to turn."

Slater drove past Randy's RV, and turned south on the highway, and shifted up.

"I notice you're not packing heat," Slater said.

"You don't want to meet extraterrestrial intelligence with firepower. They're not aggressive to us— the last thing we want to do is appear aggressive to them."

"So who just called you?" Slater said. "Who sent the coordinates?"

"The head office in Phoenix. The FAA reported intermittent radar tracks at low altitude over the mountains in the southern part of the state. There was no transponder, so it's not an aircraft."

"How did your head office get that from the FAA?"

"They have people embedded in the agency."

That seemed really shady, Slater thought, eyeing him sidelong. "How did you get a crash location if it was just radar traces?"

"One of our other data sources has access to reconnaissance satellites. Apparently there's evidence of a downed craft at this location."

"Did they send you a satellite photo?"

"The way it was explained to me," Danilo said, "is that it takes time to get an actual photo from space. The satellite has to be right overhead. That doesn't happen more than once a day or so. But there's a different kind of satellite, higher up, with wide-field sensors. It continuously tracks movement over the whole Southwest. That's what this tip was—using the satellite data, the software could calculate the point where a rapidly moving object stopped moving."

"Is that a government satellite?"

"I'm not sure."

"You have a lot of underhanded sources," Slater said. "Who is this real estate guy that funds the project?"

"He builds those endless tract homes that are filling up the landscape. I've never met him, and I haven't seen any direct evidence, but I get the sense the guy is entwined with the military, or maybe the CIA."

"That would explain how he gets access to satellite data," Slater said. "What other evidence have you seen?"

"It's mostly about how things work. Information goes in—all our photos and measurements and reports, all the FAA and police reports, tips from the public, satellite data—and absolutely nothing comes out. I've never seen a statement, or a summary, or an assessment. It's like a black hole."

"That sounds exactly like how an intelligence organization operates."

Danilo looked out the side window. "So what's Carla's daughter like?"

"Her name is Rocky, like I said."

"Short for Raquel."

"That's right." Slater described her appearance, and the way she talked. "I think she's a self-made woman. She runs a business that seems to be successful."

He didn't respond to that. They rode in silence for a while, with Danilo occasionally glancing at his phone.

"Go left up here," he said finally.

Slater made the turn onto a smaller road, like the back roads he'd driven to Benson, unstriped and paved with the same dark material. A few minutes later Danilo had him turn onto a dirt road. Slater drove as fast as the surface allowed.

"It's about eight hundred yards from here," Danilo said. "Off to the right."

"There's a double-track that heads that way," Slater said, slowing as he approached it.

"That's not on the map."

Slater turned onto it anyway. It was rough, but it ran in a straight line.

"You can stop here," Danilo said. "This is as close as we'll get. It's just over that rise."

Pulling off the track, Slater killed the engine and climbed out. Danilo reached into the truck bed, and zipped open the duffel bag, and pulled out a little gray box with an LED screen. He pressed a button and clipped it to his belt.

"That's the only gear you need?"

"The first pass is to take photos. If we need to make measurements, I'll come back to get the right tools."

Squinting at his phone, Danilo shielded it from the sun, then pointed to the rise and started walking.

"What's the thing you put on your belt?" Slater said, walking abreast.

"A dosimeter. It measures my cumulative radiation exposure. If it starts to beep, we need to retreat pronto."

The landscape was drier here than around Manzanita, with patchy grass that was yellow now, in the season between the rains, and juniper shrubs, and lots of open sandy earth.

"We're very close," Danilo said, gazing at his phone again.

As they crested the hill, an aircraft came into view ahead of them. It was white, and pitched forward into a shallow wash, its tail in the air. The lone propeller on the nose was mangled, and the front wheel had broken off.

"That looks like an earthly aircraft to me," Slater said.

Danilo stopped walking to take in the scene. Slater stopped too and pulled out his phone, surprised that he had data connectivity. In a search window he thumb-typed the plane's registration number.

"The XB on the tail means it's registered in Mexico," Slater said. "Not outer space."

NINETEEN

DANILO WAS ALREADY TAKING photos with his phone, and continued walking down the slope toward the craft. Slater took his own photo and tucked his phone away. It looked like a survivable crash, although the way the prop was mangled, the plane wasn't going to fly out of here again.

"No bodies inside," Danilo called to him. He was standing at the cabin door, folded forward and resting on the strut that supported the overhead wing.

"I've got cell service here," Slater said. "The pilot could have called for a ride."

He looked in the window, then stepped around to where Danilo was and surveyed the interior.

"Do you think they survived the impact?" Danilo said.

"There's no blood on the yoke, or on the seat, or on the door," Slater said, "so I'd say they did."

"Good point." Danilo pulled out a little notepad and started to scribble in it.

Behind the seats, secured by a cargo net, were packages, several dozen of them, wrapped in black plastic and packing tape.

"That's marijuana," Danilo said, gesturing with

his pencil. "They must be drug runners. That's why they were flying at low altitude, and why they had no transponder. Trying to avoid radar. They flew too low, and maybe clipped that rise, and lost control."

"Those packages are too small for marijuana," Slater said. "They ship that stuff in big bales. It's also legal here in most places. That makes me wonder if there's any point in smuggling it anymore."

"So it's meth," Danilo said. "Or maybe opium."

"Do you have a knife?"

"Is it strange that there's not very much of it?" Danilo said, digging in his pants pocket. "They could have packed ten times as much in here."

Slater took the penknife from him, and folded it open, then reached under the cargo net to pull out one of the packages.

"Whatever it is, it's heavy," he said.

He cut through the plastic and peeled some of it away. The material inside was gray, and soft, like putty. Slater held it to his nose and sniffed. That smell was familiar. Like nitrogen-rich fertilizer.

"Back away," Slater said.

"Why?"

"It's not drugs."

Slater gently set the package inside and stepped back.

"So what the hell is it?"

"Plastic explosive."

He'd seen this stuff before—Galliform had sold the same material to the woman he'd met on his last case. She'd used it to take out a cell tower.

"So you just want to leave?" Danilo said.

"It's not safe to be anywhere near it."

He handed his knife back, and they trudged up

the hill. Pulling out his phone, Slater stopped and texted Pike, first with his location, and then the photo he'd taken of the downed aircraft. Next he called him.

"Hey, Slater," he said as he picked up. "I'm kind of busy. Can I call you back?"

"I just found a crashed airplane loaded with plastic explosive. Who do we know who uses that stuff?"

"Are you freaking kidding me?"

"The crash site is about fifty miles south of Manzanita. The plane's registration is from Mexico."

"Was the pilot injured?"

"There's nobody around," Slater said. "No blood or gore either. The plane isn't that beat up. Like a fender-bender."

"Did you report it to local law enforcement?"

"You can do that if you want. You're my first and only call."

"Don't touch anything," Pike said.

"I'm not going to hang around. For the record, I picked up one of the packages and cut into it to see what it was. So I definitely left my prints and DNA on it."

"OK. Don't touch anything else."

Slater ended the call, and saw that Danilo was scowling at him.

"You're trampling on my case, man. Who did you just talk to?"

"Law enforcement. It's not extraterrestrial, right, so we'll leave it with them." He started to walk back toward the pickup.

"Regardless, that should have been my call," he said, catching up.

"Yesterday I met an ATF agent who's staying in Manzanita. That's exactly the agency that handles stuff that goes kablooey. That's who I called. You would have talked to the sheriff, and they would have called in the ATF a week from now when they figured out what was in those packages, if they managed not to blow themselves up. I'm just saving everybody some time."

"Fine," he said flatly. "But you should have asked me."

Slater rolled his eyes and climbed into the pickup. Once Danilo had slammed his door, Slater turned around and headed back toward the paved road. Danilo started scribbling notes again.

"They train us to record everything as soon as possible," he said. "While it's still fresh."

"Even when there's no aliens?"

"Who did you phone, exactly?"

"His name is Pike," Slater said. "His office is in Albuquerque."

Danilo jotted that down. "How did you know it was plastic explosive and not drugs?"

"I've seen the stuff before. It's gray putty that smells like nitrogen compounds. Like the artificial fertilizer you use on a garden."

"Who do you think it was for?" He looked up from his notes.

"Your instinct that it was smuggled sounds right. A Mexican plane with no transponder. You expected opium or meth, but explosives are just as illegal."

"I'm going to have to go to the office to type all this up."

Slater slowed the pickup to turn onto the highway. As usual there wasn't much traffic, but halfway back to Manzanita, he spotted an oncoming black SUV, its headlights on. It blew past them at high speed, followed closely by a second identical vehicle.

"I wonder if that's your ATF friend?" Danilo said.

"I'd bet money on it."

"They're not joking around. I wonder if we should have waited to talk to them? I'm the one who found the wreckage."

"If we had, you'd be answering questions until next Tuesday," Slater said. "You can't lie to the feds. They can charge you with a felony if you do. You'd have to tell them all about your employer and burn all your back-channel sources. The smartest thing you can do is not talk to them."

Danilo eyed him for a moment. "You're not just an insurance guy, are you."

"I know how things work beneath the surface. So do you. You've worked security. You already know it would be a mistake to engage. You just got too caught up in the excitement to think clearly."

"I guess I do know that. So what do you really do?"

"Mostly I work for an insurance company, like I said. I handle the marginal stuff, the difficult people. I go where the suits are afraid they might dirty their Italian loafers." Slater waved a hand. "Mostly it's about investigating fraud."

Danilo looked out the side window at the dusty countryside rolling by. "I read that one in five jobs in this country is what we do. Protecting other people's wealth."

Slater frowned. "That's not what I do."

"If you think about it, though, basically that's what it is. You're enforcing the status quo. Protecting the structure of how wealth is distributed."

"What did you major in at college?" Slater said. "Pinko studies?"

He chuckled. "Sociology. You have to admit there's an inequality problem. You live in LA. Don't you find that it's up in your grille every single day?"

"I can't deny that."

Danilo's phone rang, with that obnoxious loud staccato beep, and he pulled it out and answered.

"It was a conventional incident," he said. "A downed aircraft with Mexican registration. No paranormal elements … of course. It'll be in my report."

Once he'd tucked the phone away, Slater said, "Phoenix?"

"Our handler. They always sound so disappointed when it's not a saucer."

As they approached Manzanita, and rolled past Randy's RV, Slater shifted down to turn off the highway.

"Want to get lunch?"

"I really need to work on my report."

"Can it wait a few minutes?" Slater said. "You already told them it's not aliens."

Danilo hesitated, but finally said, "OK."

Maybe he was avoiding the topic of Rocky, Slater thought, glancing at him. He parked in front of the diner, and they walked inside. The place was busy but there was an open booth. A different waitress than the one he'd met yesterday handed them menus, and once they'd ordered, Danilo spoke.

"So what do I have to do to get that insurance dough?"

"I'm sure it's just filling out a claim form," Slater said. "Maybe with a notary. They'll probably want a photocopy of your ID."

"So you didn't bring the paperwork. Your job was to track me down."

"And to determine whether you're the right Daniel Martínez. I've met several people with your name this week."

"Have you decided I'm the one?"

"Show me your driver's license," Slater said.

"What will that prove?"

"If it's a California ID, it has your signature on it."

Danilo dug in his back pocket, and slid the card out of his wallet, and handed it over.

It had the address of Glenda's bungalow in Long Beach, he saw, looking it over. On his phone Slater went through the case files and found the marriage certificate he'd scanned. Zooming in on the signature, he compared it to the one on Danilo's license. It had the same slanted loops, the same short underline stroke, the same oversize accent mark on the *i* in Martínez.

"What are you looking at?" Danilo said.

"Your marriage license." He held the screen toward him. "You signed that a long time ago, but I'd say it's pretty damn close."

Danilo peered at the screen, then took his ID back.

"So that's it?"

"It seems to me that you're the guy," Slater said. "I'll report to the insurer and get somebody to mail you a claim form this week."

The waitress stepped up with a burger for Danilo and a bowl of plain oatmeal for Slater.

"Did you miss breakfast?" Danilo said.

He waved his spoon. "It's a whole thing. Don't ask."

After he'd eaten, Danilo sat back and sipped his coffee.

"So what got Carla?"

"I don't know the details. Rocky said she was in a hospice at the end."

He nodded and looked away. "What if this girl is my kid?"

"It doesn't change anything legally for you or for her." Slater raised his eyebrows. "You can understand why she wants to know who you are."

"I can't believe I have a daughter named Rocky."

"You weren't consulted in the naming process?"

"I remember Raquel. But the nickname. It's just … it's a lot."

"She probably wouldn't mind if you called her Raquel."

"Now and then over the years I thought about looking for her. But I knew I'd be a bad influence." Danilo looked down at his cup. "Broken people break people."

"She's grown up now. She'll be able to negotiate the relationship with you. You're not going to ruin her life by talking to her."

"I've done bad things, Max. I've been in prison."

"But you're not now. That tells me your debt is paid. No one is beyond redemption."

Danilo met his gaze. "Does she know I have some Native American blood? It's part of why I was interested in working out here. Lots of the paranormal incidents happen on Indian land."

"Rocky will be into that. Her shop has that kind of vibe. Organic and earthy. She sells silver and turquoise jewelry like you see in Navajo country."

Danilo pushed his plate away. "You'll have to tell me where to track her down. I've been thinking about going back to California."

"You want to ditch this job?"

"Rapid response might sound exciting, but it isn't all glamour. There's a lot of waiting around, and the pay is garbage, and we're not integrated into this town. Plus the downtime is in Phoenix. I fricking hate Phoenix."

"So the next time you have a few days off," Slater said, "come to LA and meet Rocky."

"What if she hates me?"

"Then I'm sure she'll throw you out on your ass. If you hate her, you can just walk away."

"I could never hate her," he said quietly, his fingers absently massaging his coffee cup. "I should get back to headquarters."

"I know you don't have your own phone," Slater said, "but do you have an email? So the desk jockeys can send you the paperwork."

Danilo pulled out his little notepad and wrote it down, then tore out the page and handed it to him.

"Can I also get a DNA swab?" Slater said, pulling a sample tube out of his shirt pocket.

"You want to find out if I'm related to Rocky? I already told you I was."

"This would provide unequivocal verification. It won't go into any database or police file. I'll run it at a private lab and share the results with Rocky, and you, if you want."

"I'm going to say no."

"Your call."

Slater tucked the tube back in his shirt and eyed Danilo's coffee cup. It wouldn't be that difficult to swipe it, but he didn't have a bag to put it in to preserve the DNA.

"How long are you hanging around town?" Danilo said.

"I've got a couple of things to do. I might try to leave tomorrow. When does your replacement come from Phoenix? Maybe I could bum a ride back there."

"Not for another five days."

Slater slid out of the booth. "I plan to be out of here by then."

At the counter he paid the check, and saw that Danilo was waiting out on the sidewalk.

"You need a ride?" he said, stepping outside.

"You brought me here. I'm not going to walk."

"It's a block and a half."

"It's hot out."

"I wish they all could be California boys," Slater said, stepping around to the driver's side of the pickup.

He drove the short distance to the next street and dropped Danilo at the row of houses. When he got back to the hotel he stretched out on the bed.

He didn't really need a DNA sample from Danilo, he decided. He had his answers for Della and for Rocky. That meant the only thing keeping him here was curiosity about Galliform. He wanted to know what Pike had found out. But maybe there was more to it than that. He wanted to spend time with Pike naked. Even so, he needed to plan a way to get out of here. Maybe there was a bus that could take him to a town with commercial flights.

Looking at his phone, before he could pull up bus routes he got distracted by the photo he'd taken of the downed aircraft. Comparing it to photos online, it looked like it was a 172. That model had a range of eight hundred miles, a website told him. That meant the shipment of plastic explosive could have come from deep inside Mexico.

Not his case, he reminded himself, and swiped

it away. Not his problem. Just for fun he opened the hookup app to see who was around. None of these guys had photos, he saw, scrolling through the list. That actually made sense in a small town—everybody would know your business, and leaving out the head shot would let you maintain the anonymity that urban dwellers took for granted.

One guy had a portrait photo, he found, and he looked fuckable, but he was forty-six miles away. That was way too much work. Besides, Pike might be around later. He killed the app and folded his arm over his eyes.

TWENTY

SLATER GRABBED HIS PHONE to check the time when he woke. It was close to six, so it would be cooling off outside. All he'd eaten today was oatmeal. He needed to get something else in his belly before everything shut down for the night. The only hot meal in town was at the diner.

He'd walk, he decided, and set off. As he got close to the place, a dinged and dented green SUV pulled up out front, and Pike climbed out.

"Nice pants," he said, eyeing Slater.

"They're called science-fiction chinos," he said, stepping up to him. "All the cool accountants are wearing them."

Next to his vehicle a black SUV pulled in, like the ones that had been racing down the highway earlier. Two men and a woman climbed out, all of them dressed in office-casual drag, collared shirts and chinos and dark shoes. One of them was the bald cop that Slater had made yesterday at the hotel when he checked in—Weaver. He paused on the sidewalk and called Pike's name.

"I'm right behind you," Pike called back to him, and Weaver turned to follow the others inside.

"That's your crew?"

"I guess they stand out."

"They don't look like ranchers. Is Weaver your partner?"

Pike frowned. "How do you know his name?"

"It's a small town, remember?"

He watched him for a moment. "So I was hoping you might be around later."

"Here's what's going to happen. I want you to think about this when you're sitting in there." Slater jabbed a finger at him. "I am going to fuck you until you howl."

Pike straightened up and inhaled sharply. "Such big talk."

"I'm not messing around. I'm going to demolish you."

"You want me to walk in there with a woody, don't you."

Slater jutted his chin. "You'll take it and you'll like it."

He took another breath. "Lay off the applejack before I get there."

A white SUV pulled in next to the others, and Rogers climbed out, dressed in his all-black uniform, and walked past them on his way into the diner.

"Hey, Max," Rogers said, and flashed a smile.

Pike eyed Slater and raised his eyebrows.

"Your dinner's getting cold," Slater said, and walked away.

Small towns, he thought, and ran a hand through his hair. Practically everyone he'd met here was in the diner right now. He wasn't about to go in with Pike and his crew sitting there, so he went up the block to the grocery store, where the lights were on and the sign said OPEN. The clerk on the counter was a twenty-something with long black hair, and as Slater walked in he called out a perfunctory greeting.

It wasn't a very big place but there was a surprising variety of stuff. He grabbed some nuts and a couple of apples, and picked up a rice ball to read the label.

He called to the clerk: "*Umeboshi* means it has one of those salty little plums in the middle?"

"That's right."

Slater carried it to the register. "What a treat."

"My aunt makes them."

"Well, your aunt has made me happy this evening."

"You're the guy who walked into town from the airstrip," he said, tapping at the register.

"That's me. I'm kind of amazed that everyone knows that."

"It's not every day a jet lands here to drop somebody off."

"Are there cameras out there or something?"

The guy shrugged. "Somebody saw the plane, and somebody else saw you walking. Gossip travels fast."

Once he'd paid, Slater ate the rice ball on the walk to the hotel, enjoying the cool evening air. He detoured down a street he hadn't been on before. Things were spread out, and there was lots of open land, even in the town. The sun was gone and twilight was fading when he got to his room.

As he stepped inside he saw that his jeans were neatly folded on the end of the bed. He pulled them open to find no trace of the wine stain. Taking off the loaners, he moved his belt and the contents of his pockets to his jeans. When he folded up Pike's chinos, they hardly weighed anything. Like the kind of clothes you'd want on a space mission. He dropped them on the chair.

Pike wouldn't be long, he knew, after that pep talk, and he ate an apple, then had a shower. He was drying off when there was a knock at the door. Wrapping the towel around his waist, he pulled it open.

"You're wet," Pike said, standing on the threshold and looking him over, a louche grin on his face.

"Get in here," Slater said, and closed the door behind him.

"I brought you a gift." He pulled a pint of scotch out of its paper bag and handed it over.

"This is good stuff."

"One of my team recommended it."

"Do they know you're pounding a civilian?"

He chuckled. "I didn't broadcast where I'm at tonight, but they know I'm into guys. It's a constant source of amusement. Every time we pick up a gap-toothed biker meth-head, they ask me, 'Is he your type? Would you do him?' Of course there's lots of female lowlifes too, so I get to ask them the same thing."

"You're so damn upbeat."

"It's built in. There's not much I can do about it."

"Just an observation. I'm not complaining."

Pike stepped closer. "There was talk earlier about someone getting demolished."

"You liked the sound of that?"

"You knew I wouldn't be able to think about anything else. I'm not even sure what I had for dinner. You were totally messing with me."

"I can make it up to you," he said, and met his mouth.

Pike's ran his hands in his damp hair. Slater

grabbed his crotch through his pants, and unbuckled his belt, then slid them down and grabbed his cock, already getting hard.

Pike pulled off his shirt, and kicked off his shoes, and Slater dropped his towel. Pushing him onto the bed, Slater straddled him, and squeezed their cocks together. He grabbed lube and a condom and rolled it on, then spent a minute working his way into him.

Eventually pounding him, Slater leaned in to mouth his neck, and his jaw, and his lips. His hair smelled like soap and sweat, and Slater came, straining into him, then sank onto his body, relishing the heat of his skin. When he'd caught his breath he moved off.

"Sit behind me," Pike said, and Slater shifted to rest his back against the headboard. Pike leaned back into him, and Slater stroked his cock with one hand, and with the other caressed his neck, and his chest, and his belly. He mouthed his ear and his neck and his hair.

Pike pressed back into him as he climaxed, his body vibrating. As he started to relax, breathing hard, he shifted position and stretched out. Slater moved down the bed. He felt satiated, and warm, and started to doze, until Pike spoke.

"So how did you find that plane?"

"I was out hiking and I saw it go down. I drove over there, and walked in, and there it was."

"You went hiking," Pike said, his brow furrowing.

"It's great exercise."

"You've heard that it's a crime to lie to a federal agent, haven't you?"

"I'm not being interviewed, right? We're just talking casually here. In the warm afterglow of an extremely satisfying encounter. Unless you want to frame it that you're boning a witness in your case."

Pike frowned and watched him for a moment. "I suppose it's better for everybody if you're not an official witness."

"There you go," Slater said. "When you write it up, just call me an anonymous tipster."

"We got the pilot."

"Seriously?"

"Local PD nabbed him in Las Cruces. The guy went to a hospital with a concussion. It seems some gangster drove up from there to give him a ride. The guy waited for him at the hospital, so we've got them both on ice now."

"Was the plastic explosive for Galliform?"

"The pilot isn't talking," Pike said, "and the gang-banger probably doesn't know. It's a very good thing that you figured out what it was. Our lab said it's homemade and not especially stable."

"I bet he was headed for the airstrip at Voirrey's Corner. The satellite view shows there's cleared land about a mile northwest of that homestead where you tased me."

"That's a very good guess."

"It's called a deduction, toots, not a guess. I don't have a badge, but I'm good at this stuff."

"You did manage to track down Galliform on your own." Pike ran a hand across his chest.

"Is he at that homestead? When are you moving in on him?"

"He's definitely there, and we think he'll make another move that will show his hand. We need to make sure we have plenty to charge him with. More evidence that'll stick. Then we'll pick him up."

"So you're not going to let me go down there," Slater said, "and drag him out, and cash in that bounty."

Pike chuckled. "That would be interfering with a federal investigation."

"I can't believe you know where he is and you're just letting him lounge around eating bonbons."

"It pays to be patient sometimes."

"I guess the long arm of the law can afford to do that. In the private sector, not so much."

"I think he might be getting bored," Pike said. "He ordered supplies to be delivered."

"Like ammo?"

"Groceries. We're going to make the delivery. It's an opportunity to look the place over and see whether he's staying in a tent, or in the ranch house, or if he's built a bunker."

"We, plural?" Slater said. "If you send more than one person you'll tip him off. You said yourself that this guy is slippery."

"It'll probably just be me."

"Why you?"

"I have the hat."

"I do like that hat," Slater said. "You'll have to borrow some real clothes, though. Your space pants aren't very country."

He sat up, and cracked the pint that Pike had brought, and took a pull.

"You like the scotch?" Pike said.

"Your colleague has good taste."

"It smells good."

Slater handed him the bottle, and Pike took a little sip.

"That's strong stuff," he said, and sipped again. "Don't you want some ice in it?"

"That would ruin it. But go for it, if you want. There's a glass on the sink."

"I don't need any more." He handed the bottle back. "Do you drink a lot?"

Slater nodded. "A lot. But I'm working on it." He took a long pull, then capped it and set the bottle on the bedside table.

"Can I stay for a while?" Pike said.

"You'd damn well better." Slater ran a hand along his arm. "It's the least you can do after your pheromone snow job."

He frowned. "What are you talking about?"

Slater shifted closer, and caressed his torso and his thigh. He could feel the warmth of the scotch suffusing from his belly.

"There's something different about you," he said. "Kind of magnetic. I can't keep my hands off your skin. My working theory is you have excessive sex pheromones."

Pike beamed. "You've got a crush on me." He took Slater's hand and interlaced their fingers.

"This isn't about me. You have some kind of messed-up body chemistry. You should probably see a doctor."

TWENTY-ONE

I T WAS LIGHT OUT when Slater woke to see Pike getting dressed.

"I have to go," he said, pulling his shirt on.

"What time is it?"

"Not quite six."

"Take your damn space pants."

"They fit you, don't they?" Pike said. "You can keep them if you want."

"I'm not ready for those. Maybe if I ever go to Mars."

Once Pike had gone, he went back to sleep, and woke again when his phone buzzed on the nightstand. When he grabbed it and squinted at the screen, he saw that it was Andy.

"Are you still in New Mexico?" Andy said.

"I might try to leave today."

"Did you find Galliform?"

"I know where he is, but so do the feds. I'm shut out of the deal."

"He made a weird blog post this morning on … his site. It was kind of rambling and convoluted, but at the end of it he said … he was approaching his last stand."

Slater sat up. "He must have figured out that the feds are watching him."

"It sounded almost biblical."

He rubbed his eyes. "Can you read it to me?"

"There's a whole ream of disconnected stuff, and it … kind of feels stream of consciousness, but here's the last few lines: 'The apocalypse begins when the seven dragons rise from the … seven chakras. The evil plaguing the world can only be cleansed by dragon fire. Mighty flames shall emerge to consume … all that is evil when Galliform makes his final reckoning.'"

"That sounds nuts."

"No more nuts than all his other blog posts," Andy said. "Doesn't it sound like he's … talking about more explosions?"

"You think that's what he means by fire and flames and dragons?"

"Who knows? But it's the first thing he's … written on that site in months."

"If he knows the feds are closing in," Slater said, "maybe he plans to blow up the ranch."

"Who knows? I can't say that's evident in what … he's written today. But his brand of crazy feels unpredictable."

"I appreciate the head's up," Slater said, and ended the call.

He dialed Pike's cell but there was no answer. It didn't even ring, and went straight to voice mail, as if the phone was powered off. Glancing at the time, he saw that it was almost ten. Pike had left here hours ago. He might be on his way to that homestead right now with Galliform's groceries.

"Call me before you make that delivery," Slater

told his voice mail. "There's new information."

Slater took a breath, thinking it through. If Galliform was making his last stand, he might try to croak anyone who got near him. He jumped out of bed and hurriedly got dressed, then went out to the pickup.

He drove faster than he should have through town, and onto the highway, and pulled into the gas station. When he went into the little store, Margie came out of the back room.

"How is Carl's pickup running for you, Max?"

"It's a gem," Slater said. "Listen, do you have a handgun I could borrow?"

"Sure, honey," she said, not missing a beat. "How much firepower do you need?"

"Whatever you've got that has ammo."

She stepped into the back and returned a moment later with a heavy .45.

"That's a lot of gun," Slater said, turning it over in his hands.

"Do you know how to use it?"

"I do."

"I don't have any extra ammo, I'm afraid, but the mag is loaded."

"Thanks, Margie," he said, and tucked the weapon into the back of his belt, and turned toward the door.

"Are you going out to the desert to plink some cans?"

"Something like that."

"Use both hands," she called after him. "That baby has quite a kick."

Jumping in behind the wheel, Slater pulled onto the highway, and shifted up, and pushed the pickup well over sixty. He dialed Pike's number, but again it went directly to voice mail.

As he set the phone down, it started to buzz with a distinctive ring tone: *No wire hangers! I buy you beautiful dresses, and you treat them like they were some dishrag.*

"Damn it," he muttered, and picked up. "What do you need, Doris? I'm kind of in the middle of something here."

"Nice to hear your voice too," she said. "One of the sockets in my kitchen stopped working. It has that little reset button, but that's not working anymore. It's just dead. It's not the breaker—I checked. I had to move the toaster. I thought maybe you could have a look."

Slater huffed. "I won't be around for a couple days."

"Should I just call an electrician?"

"Let me see if Conrad can do it."

"I don't think I should be schnorring off him," she said. "He's got a big job now."

"He'll be thrilled to help out. He loves you. I have to go," he said, and added, "I love you."

Keeping one eye on the empty road, he dialed Conrad's cell number.

"How's New Mexico?" Conrad said when he picked up, his tone cheerful. "I heard you got detained by the feds."

"That's one version of events. Can you stop by Doris's today? There's a GFCI socket in her kitchen that failed. It's not urgent but I don't know when I'll be able to get to it. You just have to buy a new one at the hardware store on the way over and swap it out."

"I guess I can do that. Does she have a screwdriver?"

"Of course she has a screwdriver. Her kitchen sockets are white. The square kind."

"I'll figure it out," Conrad said. "Are you really trying to track down Galliform out there?"

"I don't have time to get into it right now. Listen, be good to her, OK?"

"That sounds ominous. What exactly are you up to?"

"Nothing," Slater said. "Just don't be a dick."

"Well, don't do anything stupid."

"Turn the breaker off before you swap out the socket. The last thing Doris needs is to see you zapped and sprawled out on her kitchen floor."

He was getting close, just a few miles from the homestead, and he slowed the pickup to make the turn onto the ranch road. When he shifted out of the higher gear, he heard a dull clunk somewhere at his feet, and he couldn't get the transmission into any gear, instead feeling them grind against each other. When he pumped the clutch, the pedal moved with no resistance.

"Fuck," he roared, and coasted over onto the shoulder of the road.

The push rod had snapped, and there was nothing he could do about it. It was a job for a mechanic. Slater killed the engine and rolled up the window, then climbed out, tucking the key under the floor mat, and slammed the door.

The heat wasn't that intense today, and he could walk, but it would take him an hour to get to that homestead from here. It might take longer than that for a vehicle to pass on this back road. He scanned the savanna and the scrub that stretched to the distant mountains at the horizon. There were horses nearby, he saw, five or six of them lounging under a corrugated tin sunshade with a short length of rail fence and a water trough. The barbed-wire fence around their pasture ran toward a building site that was farther away. That must be where their humans lived.

Climbing over the fence, Slater walked toward the sunshade. The horses were thoroughly broke, he realized, as they noticed him approaching but they didn't bolt, instead eyeing him with curiosity. He slowed his steps as he came up to them.

"Would one of you fine beasts want to help me out?" he said, looking them over.

They seemed uncertain, and one of the mares nickered. Slater stepped up to a dun-colored male.

"You're young," he said, reaching for his cheek. "Not much older than a colt, huh? I bet you can run."

The horse let him stroke his face, and then he tapped Slater's shoulder with his snout. He was smelling him, Slater knew, to get a sense of who he was. The creature gently smacked the side of Slater's head with his nose.

He had to laugh. "I don't usually let anyone do stuff like that. Do you want to help me?"

It was worth a try, at least. A length of old rope was draped on the post at the base of the shelter, and Slater pulled it off and quickly tied a slipknot in it. Stepping back to the horse, he looped it around his neck. The beast let him do it, and seemed to understand what he wanted. Slater stepped on the bottom rail of the shelter's fence and drew the horse closer. He sidestepped into position, and Slater heaved himself up onto his back.

Leaning in, Slater rubbed the horse's neck, and gently waggled the rope.

"We're going that way," he said, and double-clicked his tongue.

The horse seemed to be familiar with being ridden, and understood the drill, trotting in the direction Slater indicated with the rope, angling away from the sunshade and then to the right.

It was strange to be on horseback—he hadn't done this for a while, and almost never without a bridle. He headed toward the only gate he could see in the fence line. Squeezing with his knees and clicking his tongue again, he got the horse to switch to a canter.

As he rode toward the gate, Slater realized someone was standing there, on this side of the fence, next to a red pickup. Drawing closer, he saw it was a man with a weather-lined face and long gray hair. He was wearing denim and a work shirt and a black vaquero hat, with the flat brim and a purple band with a cocky ostrich feather in it. As they approached, he waved them down.

"I like your hat," Slater said, pulling on the rope to get the horse to stop.

"It looks like you know what you're doing," he said, reaching for the beast's nose and giving it a pat. "I don't think anyone's ever ridden him bareback."

"He has good neck sense. I take it he's your horse."

"My horse, my land. Technically you haven't stolen him yet, but once you're through this gate, that's the situation we're in."

"I know I should have asked first. My vehicle broke down, and I'm kind of in a hurry. Can I borrow him?"

He pursed his lips. "I suppose you could rent him."

"Excellent." Slater dug out his wad. "How much?"

"That's a fat lot of cash, son. How far are you going?"

"It's just a few miles. I won't overwork him."

"He likes to move. He'll let you know if it's too much."

"How about fifty?"

The guy adjusted his hat, shifting the brim up. "Fifty dollars isn't a lot of money anymore."

"I understand," Slater said quickly. "How about a hundred?"

"That'll do."

Slater peeled off a C-note and leaned down to hand it to him. "What's his name?"

"That there is Rudy."

"Can Rudy find his own way home?"

"I know he will. All his kin are right here." He turned to the gate and pulled it open. "Go easy now."

Slater squeezed his knees and waggled the rope, and Rudy walked through the gate. When he leaned into his neck, and clicked his tongue, Rudy knew what he wanted, and took off at a trot through the savanna. With a little knee pressure he broke into a gallop.

The owner was right—Rudy liked to run. Slater had to lean in and hold on when he really opened up. His legs were going to be sore from maintaining this precarious position.

Paralleling the dirt road that led to the homestead, they headed cross-country, and soon came up on the bosque. Slater sat up and pulled on the rope, and Rudy slowed to a canter. When he got to the trees, he stopped, and Slater slid off. His back ached as he stood upright. Patting Rudy's neck, he pulled the rope off.

"Thanks, buddy."

Rudy snorted, and turned away, and started to munch on the tufts of grass growing along the trees.

Once he'd had a snack and cooled down, Slater knew, he'd make his way home.

From here he'd walk to the homestead, and get close enough to see if Pike's vehicle was there. Then he'd have to figure out what to do next. As he crossed the draw and came out of the trees, he saw there were vehicles here on the south side, two black SUVs, parked near the road.

He walked toward them. There were people here, four of them, wearing dark ballistic vests marked POLICE in bright yellow. They were standing at the back of one of the vehicles, with the lift gate open, clustered around a laptop. One of them was Pike. What a relief. The others were his crew, the ones he'd seen last night at the diner: Weaver, and a woman with her hair tied tightly back, and the dopey-looking guy.

Slater stopped for a moment, and put his hands on his knees, and took a deep breath. He'd been running on adrenaline for half the morning.

"We've got company," Weaver said.

They were all looking at him now, and Pike's expression shifted when he recognized Slater.

"It's OK—I know him," Pike said, and walked over to where Slater was standing, and spoke in a low voice. "What are you doing here?"

"You weren't answering your phone. I heard today was Galliform's last stand. Fire and flames and dragon breath. I thought you were in danger."

"We heard that too," Pike said. "There's been a change of plans. We decided not to deliver his groceries."

"That's such a relief." Slater took another deep breath and ran a hand into his sweaty hair.

"What's with the rope?"

"I came by horse." Slater stepped back and gestured toward Rudy, visible through the trees on the other side of the draw.

When Slater turned, the woman called from over by the SUV: "Pike—he's armed."

Pike waved to her. "It's fine."

Grasping Slater's bicep, he stepped beside him and looked at the weapon in the back of his belt.

"Is that a .45? I've seen your jacket. You shouldn't be out with that."

"I brought it to save your ass," Slater hissed.

"You put your liberty at risk for me? That is so sweet."

Slater put his hands on his hips. "Sweet?" he demanded.

"Look around. I've got my crew to protect my ass. We knew what Galliform wrote this morning, just like you did."

"I wish you'd answered your damn phone."

"Do you want to give me that piece?" Pike said. "You really don't want to get ID'd with that on you. You're standing next to a bunch of law enforcement types."

Slater pulled it out of his belt and handed it over. "It's borrowed. You're going to need to give it back."

Pike walked over to one of the vehicles, and opened the passenger door, and put the weapon in the glove box. Gently closing the door again, he stepped back to where Slater was.

"So what's your plan here?" Slater said.

"We're waiting on reinforcements, and in the meantime, trying to make contact. Maybe he'll come out and we won't have to drop the hammer."

"Has he answered you yet?"

"We're waiting for that."

"Do you think he even knows you're here?"

"We're out of view of the homestead," Pike said, "but he probably guessed we'd show up."

Movement in the periphery caught his eye, and he looked across the savanna. A figure with gray hair and a red shirt was jogging away from them, headed northwest, his bottom half hidden by the interceding brush.

"I'm pretty sure he knows you're here," Slater said, and pointed to him.

"Damn it," Pike snapped, and called to the others, "Heads up."

The trio stepped over to them, all of their eyes on Galliform now.

"We can't follow him with the vehicles," the woman said. "No way can we drive through that brush."

"He won't get far on foot," Weaver said. "It's hot as hell."

"There's a homestead in that direction," Slater said. "Just over that rise."

"Maybe he stashed a car there," Pike said.

"So we'll roadblock the highway," the other guy said. "The local sheriff will bring him in. Let's call it in."

"Maybe he has a plane waiting," Slater said. "You know there's an airstrip over there, don't you? I'm pretty sure it's where that Mexican plane was bringing the plastic explosives."

The woman glared at him for a moment, and then roared, "Fuck."

"We'll never catch up to him on foot," Pike said.

"There has to be a road to the airstrip," Weaver said, and the four of them hustled back toward the

SUVs. A few seconds later one of the vehicles pulled out and sped north on the dirt road.

Slater still had the rope in his hand, and Rudy was still here, munching on the grass in the draw. He jogged over to him.

"Have you got a little more steam left in you?" Slater said, and rubbed his cheek.

Rudy tossed his head. Slater wasn't sure if that meant yes or no, but he let him loop the rope around his neck. Bracing himself on Rudy's shoulder, he tried to jump onto his back, but he didn't make it. To his credit the horse put up with the attempt, taking a step sideways and watching him rather than bolting. Putting all the energy he had into the effort, Slater jumped again, and this time made it up, on his belly. Once he'd swung his leg over and got sitting upright, he snapped the rope.

"Hyah!"

Rudy was ready to go, and broke into a gallop. Slater directed him through the savanna toward the red shirt in the distance. Galliform had slowed down, walking now at a brisk pace. He must have decided he was out of view of the bosque, or maybe he was just out of breath.

Rudy got what they were doing, and he aimed straight for Galliform. He must have heard the approaching hoofbeats, and turned to look. He was probably armed, Slater realized. Why hadn't he thought of that? If they were fast enough, though, he wouldn't have time to draw.

A second later Rudy was almost on top of him, and Galliform held up his arms to fend them off. Slater jumped off to tackle him, but he misjudged his trajectory, and flew past the guy. He managed to snag one of his arms as he fell, and pulled Galliform with him to the ground, twisting his body around and on top of him.

Galliform instantly started throwing punches. He was wiry for an oldster and had a lot of strength. Like a weasel, the librarian had said. Slater punched back, and heaved him off, and got on top of him. He landed a solid blow to his jaw, and in the same moment Galliform struck his chin with the heel of his fist. It really hurt.

"You freaking idiot," Slater growled, and punched his nose.

Galliform flailed at him, and a trickle of blood appeared on his upper lip. The guy tried to flip him off, but Slater had learned enough in middle school wrestling to prevent that. He slapped his hands away.

"Stop it," Slater shouted. "It's over."

"Goddamn wetback," Galliform said, and threw a wild punch, striking his ear.

"Damn it," Slater shouted, and punched him again, hard on the jaw, snapping his head. "Why do you make me do this to you?"

He struck him again, and Galliform looked dazed. Slater climbed off him, trying to straighten up. His legs ached, and his arms, and his back, but nothing felt broken.

Unbelievably, Galliform still had some fight in him, and started to get to his feet. Before he could run, Slater punched him in the dick, and he crumpled in on himself, and fell to his knees.

As he stood up, Slater saw the quartet of feds hustling toward them through the brush. They must have found a track nearby. Weaver and the dopey guy were in front, and had their weapons drawn, with

Pike and the woman behind them. Slater showed them his palms and stepped away from Galliform.

"I don't think he's armed," Slater called to them.

"What's with the horse?" the woman said, frowning at him.

"You're welcome," Slater shouted at her. "There's your damn target. Do you want me to put a bow on him too?"

Galliform had his hands up now. "Don't shoot," he croaked.

"Hands above your head," the woman said, stepping up to him.

"I'm not armed."

TWENTY-TWO

S LATER WATCHED AS SHE and Weaver grabbed his arms, and pulled him upright, and handcuffed him, then frisked him. The defiance had completely drained out of his body. The woman started to walk him up the rise.

Pike stepped up and clapped Slater on the back. "That was kind of rash. He could have shot you."

"I didn't think of that until I got close to him," Slater said. "By then it was too late."

"It's always the way with these guys. The big talk. Fire and reckoning and dragon's breath. Then when the chips are down, they're not actually willing to go down in a blaze of glory. It's 'Don't hurt me,' and 'Please call me a lawyer.'"

"He did put up a fight," Slater said. "I'm going to have bruises. But you're right—when he's not hiding behind a keyboard, he's basically a nebbishy little weasel."

They followed the other agents up the rise, to where the black SUV was parked. The woman put Galliform in the back and slammed the door.

"There isn't room for your equestrian friend," she said, eyeing Pike.

"We'll walk back to the other vehicle," he said. "It's not far. You go ahead and get that knucklehead processed."

Once they'd driven off, moving slowly on the dirt double track, Slater and Pike were alone, and they headed back toward the bosque. As the adrenaline wore off, Slater's muscles ached, and he rolled his shoulders to loosen them up.

"His acolytes aren't just going to bail him out, are they?" Slater said.

"There's no bail for what he'll be charged with."

As they walked along the track, Rudy trotted up to them, and muttered at Slater. He took the rope from around his neck, and then patted his flank.

"Thanks, Rudy. You go on home now."

Rudy yanked his head away and muttered. Slater knew exactly what that meant—he'd had enough. Walking away from them, Rudy headed north into the countryside.

"They can do that?" Pike said. "Find their own way?"

"They're pretty smart," Slater said, "and home is where his posse is. Plus I know he's had it with my bullshit."

"He's a horse. Doesn't he just do what he's told?"

"He didn't have to help me. He wanted to. I think it was like an adventure for him. A chance to get some exercise. He came back because he wanted that rope off."

"I think you're anthropomorphizing the creature."

"Maybe. I know he's not taking me back to Manzanita. I'll need a ride."

"Why didn't you bring your pickup?"

"It made it most of the way," Slater said, "but it broke down. That's why I needed Rudy."

Pike looped his arm around his waist. "You stole a handgun and a horse to come and save me."

"I borrowed the weapon, and I rented Rudy. We ran into his owner."

"I thought you were a city boy. How did you learn to ride, and how to read horse minds?"

"When I was a teenager my mother thought I had some attitude problems," Slater said. "She sent me to a horse place in Wyoming. It was an attempt to sort me out."

"Nice. Equine therapy on a dude ranch."

"More like prison camp with horses. But at least I learned how to work with them. I haven't ridden in a long time. My legs are killing me right now."

When they came to the bosque and the black SUV, Pike pulled open the driver's door.

"You don't have to stay and process the scene?" Slater said, climbing in the passenger side.

"A different team will come in to do that. My work is done."

"How do you know there's no one else over there? Galliform's henchmen could be in the barn assembling a tank."

"We got some surveillance data from before dawn this morning." Pike started the engine and popped it into gear, then pulled onto the dirt road. "There was only one heat signature on the property, which means only one body. And there were no signs of recent construction."

"You did an overflight?"

"In a way." He eyed Slater and raised his eyebrows. "From space."

"You have access to a damn spy satellite. I guess I shouldn't be surprised."

" 'Spy' isn't the right word. Think of it more like a police helicopter, only a lot higher up."

Slater looked out at the road. "So when are you going back to Albuquerque?"

"I'm thinking tonight. I want to sleep in my own bed."

"Can you give me a ride?"

"Absolutely."

"Can my target come too?"

"The saucer chaser? Those guys are pretty rough. Does he bathe?"

"I'll make sure he passes the smell test. Are we taking one of these tinted-window rigs, or that beater you've been driving?"

Pike chuckled. "It'll get us there."

They didn't talk much on the way back to Manzanita. Slater felt wiped out. He found a bottle of water in the back, and guzzled it, then turned up the air-conditioning and let it blow in his face. As they got close to town, he sat up.

"Can you stop at the gas station?"

Opening the glove box, he pulled out the handgun.

"Margie loaned you the heater?" Pike said, pulling up near the pumps. "Don't walk in there brandishing it. She'll think you're robbing the place and cap you."

Slater frowned. "Thanks for your insight, officer."

He tucked the weapon into the back of his belt before he went inside. Margie was near the register.

"I brought your .45 back," he said, and set it on the counter. "I didn't have to fire it."

"Thank you, honey," she said. "I see you're riding

with those G-men. Where's Carl's pickup?"

"I'm afraid it broke down on me. It's about thirty miles from here, just past Voirrey's Corner, on the side of the ranch road. I left the keys under the mat."

Her eyes grew wide. "I'm so sorry that happened to you. I'm glad you got a ride back."

"Tell your son I think it's the push rod from the clutch pedal. It either broke or came loose. It should be an easy fix."

"I feel bad. Like I rented you a lemon."

"Classic cars come with that risk," Slater said. "I should apologize for abandoning it."

"Don't you worry. We've got a tow truck. We'll find it."

"Tell Carl it's still a gem. He should hang on to it."

As he climbed back into the SUV, he showed Pike his palms. "What weapon? I don't know what you're talking about. I never even saw one."

Pike chuckled and popped the transmission into gear. As he parked in front of the hotel, he said, "So we'll leave a little later? I have to debrief with my team."

"You definitely have something to celebrate. Are any of you going to try to get in on that bounty?"

"Unfortunately it doesn't apply to sworn officers."

"That's good news for me," Slater said. "No competition. Seeing as I apprehended him, technically I'm the person who brought the guy to justice."

"You did, didn't you."

"With four federal agents as witnesses. It sounds like a solid case to me. Do you know which agency will make the payment?"

"I know who to talk to."

"So let's get the ball rolling."

"Let me think about it," Pike said.

"You don't need to be thinking about anything," Slater said intently. "You put in the paperwork, or I will—and if I have to do it, I'll bring a lawyer, and I'll have your whole damn crew subpoenaed to give depositions about it. I know how much cops love being deposed. I'll bring that horse in to make a statement if I have to."

Pike frowned and held up his palms. "OK, Slater. I get it. I'll make the call. Calm down."

"It's a lot of freaking money."

"I said I'll take care of it."

Slater pointedly looked him up and down. "You'd better, or I'll take care of you."

He climbed out, and went into his room, and drank some water. The bed looked inviting, but there was more to do. Donning his straw hat, he stepped out again and walked over to Danilo's office.

There was no vehicle in the driveway at the three houses. Slater walked up to the middle one and knocked on the door. When Danilo pulled it open, he was wearing his black uniform.

"Where's your boyfriend?" Slater said.

"Rogers?" He scoffed. "That guy is so dumb. Don't get me started. What's up?"

Slater pulled off his hat. "Can I come in for a minute?"

Danilo waved him inside and closed the door, and Slater stood facing him, relishing the cool breeze from the air-conditioning.

"I'm headed back to LA," he said. "I think you should come with me."

"I have a job here." Danilo waved at the room.

"And you absolutely love it."

Danilo looked away. "I don't really have anywhere to stay in LA."

"What about Glenda? I know she's still single."

"You talked to her?"

"We had Bloody Marys."

He chuckled. "So it was sometime before cocktail hour."

"Does she always refer to herself in the third person?"

"Isn't she adorable?"

"That's one word for it," Slater said.

Danilo took a deep breath. "What if she thinks I'm a loser?"

"You mean Rocky? Then you can move on. But it doesn't make sense to avoid her altogether just because that's a possibility. You'll always wonder what would have happened."

"This is an opportunity, isn't it. You're opening a door for me."

Slater threw up his hands. "There you go."

"Will you introduce me to her? I don't know if I can just show up on my own."

"I can do that."

Danilo nodded. "Then it's time. Let's do it."

"I can get us a ride to Albuquerque today," Slater said, "and we can fly back this evening."

"I don't really enjoy airplanes."

He frowned. "You came here yesterday in an airplane."

"Under duress."

"I suppose we can get a car in Albuquerque. It's a hell of a long drive."

"The *Southwest Chief* runs through there on the way to LA."

"That's the train?"

"The glamorous train," Danilo said. "Chicago to LA in relaxed comfort and classic style."

Slater pulled out his phone and tapped at it, studying the screen.

"Lo, the *Chief* stops in Albuquerque tonight. You'd be in LA by noon tomorrow." He eyed Danilo. "You want to take the train?"

"I love the train."

"I'll get you a ticket. Pack you stuff, and we'll walk out of here now."

Danilo didn't hesitate, and turned to step into the back of the house. That was a good sign—Slater didn't want to give him downtime to reconsider the decision, and right now it didn't seem like he would.

He sat at the conference table with his phone and bought Danilo a train ticket, then bought himself a seat on a flight a bit later. It didn't take long for Danilo to pack, and he appeared carrying a small black duffel bag.

When they stepped outside, Slater pulled on his hat.

"Where's your ride?" Danilo said.

"We'll walk."

"All the way to the hotel?"

"It takes exactly eight minutes. I saw you hiking through the brush to that downed plane. I know you can handle it."

Danilo matched his pace on the street. "So what did your federal agent friend say about that plane?"

"You can ask him yourself. He's the one driving us to Albuquerque. I wouldn't tell him you were at the crash site, though. He'll have questions."

They got to the hotel, and Slater knocked on the

door to Pike's room. When he pulled it open, Slater saw the rest of his team were inside: Weaver was sitting on the bed, and the woman was leaning on the counter. Pike stepped out, pulling the door closed behind him.

"How long is the drive to Albuquerque?" Slater said.

"Three and a half hours."

"If we leave here in an hour, that's enough time for Danilo to catch his train."

"You're not coming with me?" Danilo said.

"I'm going to fly. I'll meet you at Union Station tomorrow."

"I can be ready in an hour," Pike said. "Do you want to get us some food for the road?"

Slater opened his own room to deposit Danilo's bag, and the pair of them walked to Main Street, and the supermarket, and bought sandwiches and rice balls and fruit.

"This is road food," the clerk said as he rang them up. "Have you guys got a job out of town?"

"That's right," Slater said, and dug out his cash. "Don't tell anyone."

The clerk eyed Danilo. "Are you headed to a downed saucer?"

"We won't know until we get there," Danilo said, picking up the plastic bag. "Keep your eyes on the skies."

Once they were out on the street, Danilo stopped. "I should tell Rogers that I'm leaving."

"Will he try to talk you out of it?"

"I think he'll be happy for me."

They walked over to the next street and the trio of houses. The white SUV was in the driveway now.

"I'll wait here," Slater said, and pulled his hat down low, and found a shady spot to rest with his back against the building.

It seemed to be taking too long, but then Danilo stepped outside. He looked flushed.

"I'm free."

"You resigned?" Slater said, straightening up.

"I talked to head office in Phoenix. They're pissed, but there's not much they can do about it. The law still says we have at-will employment. For now, anyway."

Slater scooped up the bag of food, and they walked back to the hotel. He stuffed his dirty shirts into his satchel and took the room key to the front desk. Pike was there doing the same thing.

"Are you boys ready?" Pike said, and led them outside, where they loaded their bags into the old green SUV.

Slater sat in the back, and set his straw hat on the seat beside him. On the ride Pike asked Danilo lots of questions, gently interrogating him about his work on the rapid response team, probing for details on saucer crashes.

When it came to the downed plane, Danilo was smart enough to avoid implicating himself, asking Pike about it as if someone had mentioned it to him in passing. Pike related the public part of the story, explaining that it was a smuggling operation, and that they'd found the pilot, but not mentioning the plastic explosive.

Eventually Slater tuned out and watched the landscape roll by. The sun went down, and twilight set in, and by the time they were on the freeway into Albuquerque, it was dark.

Pike pulled up at the train station, in front of

a row of arches that formed an arcade. All three of them climbed out, and Pike stretched his arms.

"We got here in good time," Danilo said, lifting his duffel onto his shoulder.

"I need a minute to say good-bye," Slater told him.

"OK." Danilo stood watching him.

"Just step away, man. I'll catch up."

Danilo frowned and walked into the arcade. Pike moved close to Slater, and put his hands on his waist.

"You know, you could move out here," he said. "I know there's work in your field."

Slater grasped his arms, massaging his biceps. What was it about this guy?

"I like the desert, Pike, but I'm an Angeleno. I'd dry up and blow away."

Pike was breathing hard. "My mother would love you."

"She wouldn't," Slater said. "Not for long. Neither would you." Leaning in, he kissed Pike's neck. "You're only seeing the superficial stuff. The sex."

He chuckled. "Extremely hot sex."

"I can't do the rest of it. I'm not good for people. I'd ruin your life."

"You were going to save my life," he said quietly. "You borrowed a rod and a horse to do it. I never meet guys like you. It's kind of a problem."

Slater scoffed. "Hot people don't have problems."

Leaning closer, Pike kissed him, and they lingered in it, until Slater pulled back.

"You're giving me a stiffy."

Pike chuckled. "I get to LA sometimes. Can I call you?"

"Sure. You can check my police file for my whereabouts, or just put a tracker on my car, and sneak up behind me and tase me."

"You're not ever going to let that go, I'm thinking."

"Zap," Slater said, and squeezed his arms, and pulled away. "Bye, G-man."

Walking into the arcade, he felt a lump in his throat. That seemed stupid and sticky, having a physical reaction like that. But it wasn't real, he knew that. It was just pheromones.

"I get it now," Danilo said, stepping up beside him. "The long good-bye. He's sweet on you."

"A little, maybe."

"That guy is such a cop. Is he really your type?"

"Unfortunately he's exactly my type. It's a good thing I'm leaving town. I'd probably wind up trying to marry the fucker."

They found the ticketing counter, and Slater picked up Danilo's ticket, and handed it over.

"You got me a sleeper," he said, looking it over.

"It's an overnight ride. I assumed you'd want to sleep."

"So I guess I'll see you tomorrow in la-la land."

"Do you drink at all?" Slater said.

"Sure."

"You're not in recovery, are you?"

Danilo chuckled. "Negative."

Flipping open his satchel, Slater handed him the half-empty pint of scotch and the one of bourbon.

"I can't take it on the airplane." Slater pulled out a sample tube. "How about that DNA swab now?"

Danilo tucked the bottles into his duffel. "The people of California already have a sample of my DNA. I'm sure you can find it in a justice system file somewhere."

"I don't have access to that. This is for Rocky. So

that she can be sure of who you are before you even meet her."

"Fine," he said, and sighed. "What do I have to do?"

"Open," Slater said, and ran the cotton swab inside his cheek, then sealed it and tucked it into his bag. "I need to get to the airport." He held Danilo's gaze. "Get on that train."

He flapped his ticket. "That's the plan."

Walking back to the exit, Slater found the taxi stand, and got a ride to the airport. He was running a little late for the flight, but there were no lines at security, and he made it to the gate on time, and even found room in the overhead bin for his hat.

Stepping out to the curb at LAX, he could feel the humidity in the air, and smell the tang of ozone, so different now but instantly familiar. On the long cab ride to the Valley he dozed in the backseat, then drove the Thunderbird back over the hill, taking the 405 to South LA. It was almost midnight when he pulled up at Lenore's building.

Scrabbling in the glove box, he found a Sharpie, and dug out the sample tube, and wrote "chartreuse" and "sample 4" on it. He didn't have an envelope, but he found a rubber band, and used it to attach four C-notes to the tube, rolling them around it like a burrito. Climbing out, he dropped it into the slot in Lenore's side door.

When he finally got home, it was a relief to pull off his boots and take a long shower. He guzzled from the fifth in the cupboard, not even bothering with a glass, and then dropped onto his futon.

Pike was right: there was something satisfying about sleeping in your own bed. As he drifted toward sleep, Slater thought about him. He was such a beautiful man. Good thing he was in another time zone. He could get very distracted with that dope.

TWENTY-THREE

AYLIGHT WAS STREAMING IN the window when he woke, and sleep had helped a lot to ease his aching muscles. Checking his phone, there was a text from Lenore:

> Sample 4 is a positive match to the client sample. Paternity confirmed.

That was no surprise, but it was useful to be certain about it. He had to write a report for Della, and give her Danilo's details, but that could wait. Pushing himself out of bed, he got dressed, and went down to his garage, and drove to Cahuenga. Rocky was at the front counter when he stepped inside.

"Hey, stranger," she said, and flashed him a smile. "I was wondering how your quest was going."

"I found him."

Her expression sobered. "Is he alive?"

"So far. If everything holds together, he'll be getting off the *Southwest Chief* at noon."

"Is that the train?"

"He says he loves them. Do you want to meet me at Union Station?"

"My god." She shook her head. "You're sure he's the right person?"

"The DNA test says he's your father. I got the results this morning."

"I can't believe it."

Slater studied her for a moment. "If this is happening too fast, it's fine to meet him another day."

"I want to do it. It's just a surprise. I have so many questions."

"I'll talk you through it. But we should roll."

"I walk here from my place," Rocky said. "We can take the metro. It goes right there."

"You can take the metro back. I'll drive."

Rocky spoke to her staffer, today a woman with a puffy Afro, not the guy with the attitude, and then followed Slater out to the street. As he drove toward the freeway, he told her about how he'd tracked down Danilo, and gave her the highlights of what he knew about his life.

"He's not a saint," Slater said. "He's been in trouble, and he doesn't have a lot of money."

"But he's not a crook now, is he?" She waved a hand. "Or a drunk, or a junkie?"

"To me it looks like he's straightened himself out. When I found him he was working hard at a legitimate job. I went on a call with him. He seemed pretty focused and competent."

"You're sure he's on that train?"

"I took him to the station and bought him a ticket," Slater said. "I suppose he could have changed his mind. I can't check on him because he doesn't have a cell phone."

"Do you think he'll be there?"

"He said he wanted to be. He told me he's thought

about looking for you over the years. He's afraid you'll think he's a loser."

She sobbed and wiped at her eyes. Slater glanced at her sidelong. He hadn't expected that.

"So what do I owe you?" Rocky said, once she'd composed herself.

"The insurance company basically covered the research part. I spent two grand on DNA tests."

"Ouch. I guess it's worth it, though. You found him, and we know he's not an imposter trying to fleece your company."

Slater parked under the station, and they walked up to the concourse. The big arrivals and departures board listed the *Southwest Chief* as ARRIVING. People were streaming out from the passage where the tracks were, most of them lugging suitcases and towing wheelie bags.

"When Danilo shows," Slater said, "I'm going to bug out."

Rocky frowned. "I'm paying you to help me."

"You're not going to need my kind of help with this guy."

They watched the emerging passengers for a minute, and then he caught sight of Danilo, dressed in black, with his duffel bag on his shoulder. Slater raised his hand and caught Danilo's attention. He walked toward them, his brow furrowing as he approached. Slater heard Rocky inhale sharply.

"Rocky," Danilo said, stepping up to them.

She had her knuckle between her teeth, and her eyes were wet. She was too emotional to speak, Slater realized.

"I'm not that ugly, am I?" Danilo said.

Rocky managed a choked laugh.

"Oh, sweetheart," he said, and wrapped his arms around her.

Slater held up his palm and walked away. He wasn't sure either of them saw him go, but it didn't matter. He didn't need to watch that, all the emotional stuff. His part of it was done.

———•———

Also from Dagmar Miura

That First Heady Burn

The first book in the Slater Ibáñez series sees Slater running surveillance on an injured tech worker and tangling with blackmailers, party girls, late-night hookups with a gamut of guys, and a lot of bourbon.

slater.dagmarmiura.com

Brawl in Bardo

Slater spends the night in a dusty Mojave Desert town and finds that things look different in the liminal space between LA and Vegas, like the *bardo* between lives. Soon he's stalking a sleazy dermatologist who's in a custody battle with another croaker for a seemingly worthless statue.

slater.dagmarmiura.com

The Mason Braithwaite Paranormal Mystery Series

No one is ever quite sure whether psychic investigator Mason gets results with actual psychic power or his more mundane flatfooting, but the disheveled redhead manages to resolve some intractable mysteries.

mason.dagmarmiura.com

Penstock Canyon

While helping out a friend suffering from late-night visitations, psychic investigator Mason is confronted with aliens on the roof and mythical beings that have him questioning the very nature of reality.

mason.dagmarmiura.com

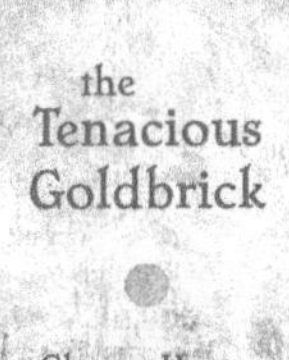

Truman and Celeste

Sometimes all a woman needs is a decent man—even if she's not sleeping with him. Join Truman and Celeste as they troll the gritty underbelly of Los Angeles, never hesitating to slam that cocktail, hit on guys, or ask the next relevant question.

truman.dagmarmiura.com

The Cape Cod Blue

The glittering, exalted world of art auctioning hides love, hate, and parricidal murder in a wealthy and socially prominent family when forgery of an anonymous Cape Cod painting is used to steal a world-famous portrait that's worth a fortune.

capecod.dagmarmiura.com

For Position Only

In the second novel in the Truth, Lies and Love in Advertising series, Craig Keller, a wealthy Los Angeles advertising magnate, is forced to face his demons or lose the woman he loves.

adeleroyce.dagmarmiura.com

The Psychic Vegan Cookbook

It has never been easier to cook vegan, and you don't even need to be psychic to do it. Whether your motivation is eating healthier or the welfare of other sentient creatures, Henrietta Flores guides you through plant-based versions of familiar dishes.

cookbook.dagmarmiura.com